DAY IN THE KNIGHT

THE LEONIDAS CORPORATION
BOOK FOUR

TARINA DEATON

For my mom.
Who always supported me, not matter what.

Editor: HEA Author Services

Proofreading: AH Levine

Cover Photo: Golden Czermak, FuriousFotog

Cover Model: Dylan Horsch

Cover Design: Lori Jackson, Lori Loves Books

AI AND 'EM' DASHES

No Artificial Intelligence was used in the creation of this novel or its cover.

Most fiction authors were using em dashes and ellipses long before AI became a mainstream thing. Emily Dickinson is rather well-known for her use of the em dash and, unless she was a time traveler, she predates AI.

Wallflower Chats has an excellent breakdown of the history and used of the em dash.

> The term "em" comes from the days of wood- and metal-set typography, delineating a space or mark that is roughly the size of the letter "m" in that particular typeface.

It is also worth remembering AI was taught on stolen, copyrighted works, including my own, without permission or remuneration to the authors. All of my previously published books are included in the 2025 Anthropic class action lawsuit.

I use em dashes and ellipses prolifically in my writing.

I don't use AI.

TRIGGER WARNINGS

Discussion and description of emotional and physical abuse, abortion, death off-page, sexual assault, and BDSM elements - discussion of further exploration includes discussion of spanking, light bondage, and anal play.

PROLOGUE

$\mathcal{A}$bby pulled the cast-iron pan out of the oven and set it on top of the stove. She stabbed the beef tenderloin with the digital thermometer and waited for the reading. 145 degrees. Perfect. By the time Tony got home, it would be done resting and be a beautiful medium rare. The salad was in the fridge, the vinaigrette blended, the couscous cooked, and the fresh green beans were ready to go into the steamer pot.

At 5:45, she threw the beans into the pot, then lit the candles on the dining room table. "Alexa, play dinner playlist."

Soft easy listening music came from the recessed speakers Tony had installed when he'd built the house. She'd always thought they were excessive, but Tony had only listened to her input about the kitchen.

She transferred the beans and couscous to covered serving dishes, grabbed the salad from the fridge, and placed everything on the table, already set with the good china.

Her stomach fluttered and she placed her hand low on her abdomen. Was it nerves about telling Tony or the little bean she'd learned about that morning? She glanced at her watch and returned to the kitchen to slice the meat. After transferring it to a serving platter, she placed it in front of Tony's place setting. All that was left to do was wait for him to come home.

Forty minutes later, the candles were dripping wax onto the crystal holders. She checked to see if there were any text messages, despite the lack of notifications or previous messages. His lack of communication had been happening more frequently over the past few months. Was it really that hard to tell her he'd be a few minutes late? Abby blinked and looked up, pressing her ring finger to the inner corner of her eye. It didn't mean anything. He'd been working to close a big account at work—he'd told her that.

The alarm panel beeped three times. *"Garage door open."*

Abby stood and plastered a smile on her face.

"Hi," she said when he entered the dining room.

"What's all this?" He pulled at his tie to loosen it.

"Dinner. Beef tenderloin, green beans, and Israeli couscous."

"I had dinner with a client."

"Oh." Would it have been so hard to send her a text?

He picked up a green bean and took a bite. "It's cold anyway." He threw the rest of the bean onto a plate.

"I had it ready for six, when you're usually home."

"I had to work. Someone has to pay for this house."

A spark of anger flashed through her, and she tamped it down. She hadn't asked for the house. It was too big. Too ostentatious. There were rooms she only went into to clean.

"It's fine. I'll pack it for your lunch tomorrow."

"Don't bother—I have a working lunch."

Gritting her teeth, she took a deep breath. "I have something else for you."

She picked up the long, thin box she'd set next to his place setting and held it out to him.

"Fuck." He took the box. "Is it our anniversary?"

She blinked. "No. That's in four months."

"Then what's this?"

"Open it."

She held her breath as he lifted the lid. He didn't speak for several heartbeats, just stared at the plastic stick with the digital display that read "Pregnant."

He finally looked at her. "Is this a joke?"

Her stomach plummeted. "No. It's real. I found out this morning."

"Did you do this on purpose?"

She flinched at his harsh tone and shook her head. "No. I was on antibiotics a couple of months ago when I had a sinus infection. The doctor said they probably counteracted my birth control pills."

Tony tossed the box and pregnancy test onto the table. "Let me know when you get rid of it."

"What?" It came out as a breath. He didn't say that.

He brushed past her. "You know how I feel about kids."

She followed him. "I know, and I was fine with that. I didn't mean to get pregnant, but you can't expect me to get an abortion now that I am."

He stopped abruptly inside their bedroom and turned. "I can and I do. I was very clear before we got married about being child-free. I told you if it was a deal breaker we'd end it. You said you were fine with it. So now, you decide—me or that." He pointed at her stomach.

"Tony—"

"End of discussion." He slammed the door closed.

FIVE YEARS LATER

Christian "Tinker" Knight stood at the back of the courtroom. Feet braced apart, arms crossed, chin slightly lifted, he stared at the girl sitting in the witness box. Her small frame and pigtails made her appear much younger than twelve.

The prosecutor stood beside the witness stand. "Melanie, is the person who hurt you in this room?"

"Yes," she whispered.

"I need you to speak louder, Melanie." The judge's voice was gentle, but firm.

The little girl hunched her shoulders and looked down but did as the judge asked. "Yes."

"Melanie," the prosecutor said. "Can you point to that person?"

Her eyes jerked up and briefly found Tinker at the rear of the room. He remained stoic.

"It was…" She faltered and looked quickly at Tinker. "It was John." She pointed to the man sitting at the defense table.

"Thank you, Melanie. No further questions, Your Honor," the prosecutor said.

The judge looked at the public defender.

"No questions, Your Honor."

The judge looked at Melanie. "Thank you, Melanie. You can go."

Melanie bolted out of the chair, passed her *guardian ad litem* as she dashed down the short aisle, and launched herself at Tinker.

He caught her in a tight hug when she wrapped her arms and legs around him, burying her face in his neck. Sobs racked her frail body, and he felt the old familiar rage begin to build. Giving in to it and breaking every bone in her mom's ex-boyfriend's body would be extremely satisfying, but it would do neither him nor Melanie any good. He squelched the urge and got Melanie the hell out of there, not waiting for her guardian ad litem to reach them.

"Melanie!" Her mom stood from her seat across from the courtroom doors and rushed to them.

Melanie reached for her mom and Tinker transferred her over.

"She did really well," Amy, the guardian ad litem, said when she caught up with them.

"She was a champ," Tinker said. "She's a brave little girl."

Melanie tilted her head to look at Tinker. "Only 'cause you were there."

"Nah. You'd have done it even if I wasn't there." He tugged the end of her pigtail.

She smiled, which was what he was hoping for.

"I can't thank you enough," her mom, Becky, said. "I don't know where we'd be without your help these last few months."

Tinker ran a hand over his short beard. "It's all part of what VACA does."

"Let me thank you with dinner. You can come over tonight." Becky looked at him with stars in her eyes.

He knew it was more than the hero worship her daughter

had. Becky had been dropping hints that she'd welcome more than the occasional drive-by he did as part of VACA—Veterans Against Child Abuse. She was sweet, but he knew her type—a woman who defined herself by her man. There was nothing wrong with it as long as the man valued her.

"It's against VACA rules," he said gently.

She knew that. And even if it wasn't against the rules, he wouldn't get involved with a woman in such a raw and emotional state. Some men might take advantage, but he did not. Plus, she had SERIOUS RELATIONSHIP written all over her. He didn't do serious, and he didn't do single moms—too big of a chance the kid would get attached. He was not fit to be a substitute father figure, and he wouldn't let a kid get emotionally involved.

"Are we ever going to see you again?" Melanie's bottom lip trembled.

"Of course. The whole club's taking you to school on Monday."

Her mouth opened in awe and her eyes sparkled. "Really?"

"Yeah. Your mom didn't tell you?" He shifted his gaze to Becky.

She looked down. "I didn't want to get her hopes up."

Tinker pressed his lips together, then gave his attention back to her daughter. "We'll be at your house at 7:45 to pick you up. I got to get back to work. Can I get a hug before I go?"

Melanie reached for his neck, and he hugged her close. She kissed his cheek and said, "Thanks for making me brave."

He swallowed hard. Twice. "Thanks for being brave."

$\sim$

THE WRENCH SLIPPED and he scraped his knuckles against the engine block. "Shit!"

Tinker dropped the wrench and shook his hand.

"You better not get any blood on Graham's floor."

He looked to his right as Paige, one of his bosses, approached from across the garage. In her four-inch heels and tight, knee-length skirt, she didn't look like she would be the chief operations officer for a security company that sometimes ran tactical operations in non-permissible environments.

But Paige was a chameleon. She was as comfortable running face-first down a wall or staring down the sights of an M4 as she was schmoozing new clients.

She was an attractive woman. He wasn't ashamed to admit he'd thought about suggesting a hot and dirty fling since she'd held a similar viewpoint on relationships. But even if she didn't sign his paychecks, he didn't shit where he ate.

And she'd recently settled into domestic bliss with her boyfriend. Come to think of it, he'd lost a few of his teammates to long-term relationships. Nash had fallen for Addison, who sometimes joined them for training and operations. Shane was ass-deep in the Guatemalan jungle protecting some pyramid his woman found. Fuck. Tinker hoped that shit wasn't catching.

"How'd it go today?"

He checked out her arm as she rested both on the frame of the truck he was working on, no indication her wound bothered her. She'd been shot a few months ago. It had been his fault. He'd waited for the shooter to spill his guts instead of taking the guy out as soon as he could.

"She did good. Prosecutor's going for max time with no chance of parole."

She nodded. "How are you?"

He glanced at her sideways before twisting the cap off the wiper fluid reservoir. He knew it was full—he'd filled it three days ago—but busy hands and all that shit.

"Do we have any jobs coming up?"

"Feeling the need to shoot something?"

"Something like that." He screwed the cap back on.

"Dani's here. I'm sure she'd be happy to get in the ring with you."

His mouth twisted. "Thanks, but I don't think getting punched in the face by my kid sister is going to help." Besides, Dani had started holding back when she realized she could beat his ass.

He hated that they all knew what had happened to him and Dani. Everyone at Leonidas had always supported them both and had helped him get his record expunged so he could work with VACA. But he didn't like it.

It wasn't even like Dani hid her past. She was open about being a survivor. She talked to survivor support groups and used her status as a champion MMA fighter to advocate for victims and raise money for programs.

For him, her openness was another reminder he'd failed her.

Paige stared at him long enough to make him uncomfortable. "What?"

"I'm worried about you, Tink," she said.

"Why?"

"This is your, what? Third case in a month?"

"Something like that. I thought you and Graham were cool with the time I give to VACA." If they weren't, he would have to reevaluate some things. He wasn't willing to stop volunteering with them.

"We are, that's not the issue," she said.

"Then what's the issue?"

"I can see the toll it's taking on you. You're not hiding it as well as you think."

He huffed out a half laugh. "Have you been taking classes with Addison?"

"No, but I'd like you to talk to her. Or someone else, but you need to talk to someone. We need you at a hundred percent and so do those kids."

"I'm good, Paige. You don't need to worry about me." He had a tight control of his emotions.

"Sorry, it's part of the job description. Talk to Addison. You can consider it part of your yearly psych eval, but I want you to talk to her."

He rubbed his head. "Okay. I'll call her this week."

"Thank you. Dani said the Knights are having a party tonight. You going?"

The irony of belonging to a club called Tarnished Knights wasn't lost on him. The last thing he wanted to do was hang around a bunch of people, but he wanted to be alone even less.

"Yeah. You?"

She shook her head. "No. Ash's parents are driving up from Savannah for dinner."

He grabbed the rag hanging on the frame and wiped his hands. "Wow. Meeting the parents already?"

She moved her arms when he waved her off to drop the hood. "Technically, I've already met them. This is the official meeting."

Tinker smirked, knowing she'd hooked up with her boyfriend at his sister's wedding. "Good luck with that."

"Yeah. Thanks." She flipped him off for good measure. "I'm here if you need to talk."

"I know."

She headed off to the exit. "Have fun. Don't get arrested."

He grunted and shoved the rag into his back pocket. He appreciated that she didn't push him to talk. She'd drop everything if he needed her to, even dinner with the new boyfriend's parents. He picked up the wrench he'd dropped earlier.

A few drinks, maybe a hot woman with no expectations, and he'd be fine.

GOING OUT WITH FRIENDS

The front of the large antebellum plantation house was lit up by spotlights. Abby peered through the windshield as Lindsey parked at the end of a line of cars on the side of the gravel drive.

"I'm so excited you came out tonight." Lindsey squeezed Abby's arm as they walked from the car and linked their elbows.

Abby twisted the corner of her mouth. She'd finally given in to Lindsey's badgering to go out with her. She'd kind of run out of excuses—she had absolutely no responsibilities that weekend and she'd even caught up on grading and lesson plans during the in-school teacher workday, so she didn't have that to fall back on.

"Come on." Lindsey must have sensed her hesitation. "You promised you'd try to have fun. You deserve a night out, Abby. Let loose. Have fun!"

"I have fun," she said indignantly.

"Going to the aquarium every weekend doesn't count."

Abby gave her a baleful look and sighed. "Fine. Who is this party for anyway?"

Lindsey shrugged. "I don't think it's for anyone—they're just having a party."

Abby stared at the row of motorcycles parked at the top of the drive. "Who's they?"

"The Knights."

"The White Knights? The Templar Knights? Gladys Knight?"

"The Tarnished Knights. They're a motorcycle club."

Abby stopped in her tracks, causing Lindsey to jerk on her arm. "Lindsey! We can't be at a…a…" She glanced around, checking for anyone nearby. "A criminal hideout," she finished with a hiss.

"Oh my god." Lindsey rolled her entire head and yanked on her arm. "First of all, it's not much of a hideout if they're throwing a party and inviting people. Second, they're not the kind of motorcycle club in your books. Most of them are military veterans and half of them are Veterans Against Child Abuse members."

Abby ignored the dig about her favorite romance genre. "Really?"

"Really. The worst any of them does is smoke weed and get drunk."

Abby chewed her lip. That didn't sound so bad. Hell, she'd smoked the occasional joint in college.

Lindsey stopped and faced her. "I've been to their parties before and it's nothing worse than any other party. Or nightclub. It's probably safer because they keep an eye on things. I promise—if you're at all uncomfortable or weirded out, we'll leave. And I know one of the members and she's a solid person."

"She?" That got Abby's attention.

"Yeah. She. I told you they weren't that kind of motorcycle club."

Abby closed her eyes and took a deep breath. She needed this. She'd promised herself she'd start getting out more often and try to remember who she was before her life went to hell and back. Old resentment and anger rose to the surface, but she pushed it down. She couldn't change the past and getting angry about it had never done her any good.

She opened her eyes. "Okay. Lead the way."

"Yay!" Lindsey did a little wiggle, then linked their arms back together. "Let's go have fun. And maybe get you laid."

Abby's jaw dropped. "What? No. That's not—"

Lindsey threw her head back and laughed.

THERE WAS a full-size suit of armor in the entryway. A literal tarnished knight. The seams and joints of the armor were patinaed and rusted. It stood with both gauntlets resting on the end of the pommel of an upright sword, point down. The breast plate and shoulder pieces were etched with delicate filigree. If it was authentic, which Abby doubted since iron and steel didn't patina the way it was on the armor, it was likely ceremonial rather than functional. The art historian part of her brain perked up and whispered, "Look at it. Touch it."

Lindsey pulled her further into the house before Abby could become *that person* at the party.

A roped-off staircase led upstairs. The downstairs was divided into four large rooms, two on either side of the center hallway.

Lindsey stopped inside the first room on the left and searched through the crowd. She waved, and a woman across the room waved back and made her way to them.

"Come on. I'll introduce you to Katherine."

"Who's Katherine?" Abby asked.

"It's her house. Her husband is the president of the club."

The older woman was a little taller than Abby, and she had her waist-length, salt-and-pepper hair pulled back into a long braid. She pulled Lindsey into a quick hug. "I'm so glad you made it."

"Thanks. Katherine, this is Abby, one of my best friends. Abby, this is Katherine, one of the coolest people I've ever met."

Katherine laughed. "I don't know about coolest, but thanks."

"Don't let her fool you," Lindsey said. "She's lived all over the world, used to fly C-17s, nursed her husband back to health when everyone said he'd probably never walk again, and wrote a book about it."

"Wow." That was impressive.

Katherine shook her head. "We all do what we have to do when there's no other choice."

She was also profound. Abby felt like she'd been doing what she had to do for a very long time.

"Anyway," Katherine said. "Welcome. Beer, wine, and other drinks are at the bar in the backroom. There's also burgers, chicken, and more sides than I want to keep as leftovers, so please help yourselves."

"Thank you," Abby said.

"Thanks," Lindsey said. "Let's get some drinks."

The bar was manned by two guys in black vests. Glancing around, Abby noticed several of the men and a few of the women, including Katherine, wore similar vests. The large patch on the back of their vests bore a depiction of the suit of armor in the foyer.

They wandered into the rooms on the other side of the house. There were probably a hundred or more people in the house, but it didn't feel crowded since they were scattered throughout the rooms. She also saw several people out on the porch through the open French doors.

"Ooh. There's someone else I want you to meet."

Lindsey led her to one of the small tables in the other room at the front of the house. The armor was visible in the foyer— they'd essentially walked in a full circle.

"Lindsey!" A dark-haired woman jumped out of her chair and hugged Lindsey, rocking from side to side. She let her go and looked at Abby. "Who are you?"

Abby was surprised at the excitedness of her question. Like a kid on the playground making a new friend. "Uh, Abby."

"Hi, Abby. I'm Angela. Or Angie. Or Ange. I'll answer to all of them. How do you know Lindsey?"

"We work together." Abby didn't know what to make of the overly friendly woman.

"You're a teacher too? That's so cool. What do you teach? Sit down. Join us. This is Dani, my best friend." Angela sat and patted the blonde woman next to her on the head.

"Don't mind Angie," Dani said, batting Angela's hand away from her head. "She gets excited when she meets new people. Like a puppy, but she doesn't pee on you—unless you pay extra."

"Shut up. It's just nice to meet new women who I don't know through work and aren't biker chicks." Angela's eyebrows pinched together, and she leaned forward. "You're not a biker chick, are you?"

Lindsey laughed, and Abby glared at her as they took seats at the table. She had a direct view of the suit of armor from her seat. "No, I'm not a biker chick."

"Oh, good."

"What's good?" A curvy brunette joined them and sat in the last vacant chair.

Abby noticed Angela side-eye Dani, who rolled her eyes.

"Hey, Julia," Angela said. "Not working this weekend?"

"No. I heard the Knights were having a party and made sure I asked for the night off." She looked at Abby. "We haven't met. I'm Julia."

"Abby." She waved in greeting.

"Did y'all come with one of the guys?"

"No," Lindsey said. "I'm friends with Katherine."

Abby caught the tone of Lindsey's voice but didn't understand the reason behind it. Julia's questions seemed innocent enough.

"I'm going to get a refill," Dani said. "Can I get anyone anything?"

"I'll take another," Abby said, holding up her beer. If she was going to let loose, she needed a little social lubrication.

"Me too," Lindsey said.

Dani took her empty glass and left.

"What do you teach, Abby?" Angela asked.

"Art and fashion design."

"Ooh, you're a teacher?" Julia asked.

"Yes. We both teach at Charleston STEAM Academy."

"That's so cute. It must be so fun to teach kids to finger paint."

Of all the condescending, fake-ass crap she'd ever heard. Now she understood Lindsey's tone from earlier. A commotion in the foyer distracted her before she could think of a snappy retort about her Master of Fine Arts and year interning as a restorationist in Prague.

A tall man with dark blonde hair and a lot of tattoos held the elbow of a woman as he pointed toward the front door. He was attractive in a bad boy from the wrong side of the tracks kind of way, even as he scowled at the woman he was talking to. Honestly, he looked like a cover model from one of her favorite MC romances, which, yes, may have influenced her opinions of motorcycle clubs and what would be going on at the party. She liked her forbidden fantasy on the page, not in real life.

The man let go of the woman and stood with his arms crossed while the woman appeared to plead with him.

"Who's he talking to?" Angela asked. They were all watching the interaction.

"No idea," Lindsey said. "I've never seen her before. Looks like a lovers' quarrel though."

Angela scoffed. "Tink doesn't do lovers' quarrels."

"Tink?" Abby asked. What kind of name was Tink?

"It's short for Tinker. It's his callsign." Dani set their beers down.

"Mmm." Julia tipped her chair back to get a better look at the man as he walked away from the woman. "Dangerous is fucking sexy, but not for long-term. I wouldn't want a convicted criminal around all the time."

Dani slammed her glass on the table. "Why don't you fuck off and shut the fuck up about something you know nothing about."

"Sor-ree." Julia stood and flounced away.

Abby stared wide-eyed at Dani as she took a long drink.

"He's Dani's brother," Angela explained. "She's a little protective."

"Oh," Abby said. "Does Julia know?"

"It doesn't matter," Dani said. "She's a gossip and a bitch and she's repeating shit she's heard people talking about without knowing the full story."

Abby almost asked what the full story was, but it wasn't her business. She didn't like to gossip, and Dani didn't seem to be in the mood to explain anyway.

Angela spread her hands on the table. "Know what we need? Shots. There's a bottle of Fireball behind the bar. I'm gonna get it."

THE KNIGHT

*A*bby wandered out of the bathroom and into the room with the bar. The bar. With the Fireball. Whew. That was some dangerous stuff. She'd been expecting Goldschlager cinnamon taste, but the whiskey had been smooth and surprisingly tasty. Angela had been able to talk her into more than a few shots.

Angela was fun. And Abby was having fun. Which kind of surprised her. She hadn't been to a party where people just had fun in so long, she'd forgotten what it was like. No one to schmooze. No one to impress, or make sure they were introduced to someone else, or get them to make a big donation to the school. Just hanging out with friends and having fun. She might be at her limit though. Of alcohol, not fun. The room was a little wonky.

Lindsey was in the front room standing really close to a tall, good-looking guy in a short-sleeved button-down. She was doing that thing with her hair where she played with the ends of it. She said it made guys think about twisting it in their hands.

Abby wrinkled her nose. The guy reminded her of Tony. So clean-cut and put together. Not a hair out of place. Not like the guy from earlier with the tight black T-shirt and tattoos and hair that looked like it'd never seen the inside of a gel bottle. She'd caught glimpses of him throughout the night, and he'd gotten more attractive each time she saw him, and it wasn't because of whiskey goggles. Even when he was scowl-y and broody. Which was every time she'd seen him. Probably brooding about his lover's quarrel.

Had a guy ever brooded over her? She sighed and made a conscious effort to swerve away from Melancholy Town. She didn't want to be that girl at the party who drunk cried. She spied the armor in the foyer and glanced around.

But she could be that girl at the party who took a closer look at the suit of armor.

Tink gritted his teeth. He still couldn't believe Becky had shown up at the house. How had she even known about the party? She must have heard someone from VACA talking about it because they didn't mingle socially with their clients, but she wouldn't say how she found out.

She'd been there to find him. He would've blown her off and ignored her, but she'd thrown him a guilt trip about how Melanie needed a strong, dependable father figure and if he'd only give Becky a chance, she knew they'd make a great couple. It was complete bullshit, and it pissed him off that she was using her daughter to troll for men.

He was antsy and couldn't stay still. Couldn't hold a decent conversation. Couldn't even finish a bottle of beer. He'd tried playing pool, but there was too much downtime between turns to brood and imagine all the shitty relationships Becky would continue to find herself in and, more importantly, continue to put Melanie in.

The party wasn't providing the distraction he wanted—he

needed to leave. Go for a ride to clear his head. He found Dani in the back room talking to a couple of the club members.

He caught her attention. "Hey, I'm gonna take off."

She frowned. "You okay?"

"Yeah. Just a lot of shit in my head. Gonna go for a ride."

"Where to?"

"Edisto."

"Be careful. Text me when you make it back."

"Yes, Mom." He kissed her on the cheek.

"You around on Sunday?" she asked.

"Should be, why?"

"I need a sparring partner."

Which meant she was probably going to kick his ass for the mom comment. "Where's Eddie?"

"Got his wisdom teeth yanked today. Doesn't want me punching him for some reason."

"Yeah, sure." Eddie was probably getting the better end of the deal.

He headed down the hall to the front door, waving to a couple of people as he passed. A woman was standing in front of Ned the Knight, staring intently at it.

"Are you okay?" he asked. "Is there something I can help you with?"

She turned her head and looked at him, her light brown eyes framed by thick dark lashes. "Do you know the origins of this?"

"Ned?"

"Who's Ned?"

She was a little unsteady on her feet, but she wasn't slurring.

"The suit of armor. Ned the Knight," he said.

She blinked at him several times. "But Ned begins with an N."

A smile broke out at that ridiculous comment.

She turned back to the armor and tucked a strand of dark, wavy hair behind her ear before hovering her fingers over the armor. "I'm wondering if it's authentic. The filigree work is fantastic, but steel wouldn't patina like this, which makes me think it's a replica. It's a decent imitation, based on mid-to late-sixteenth century probably. It would have been for ceremonial use instead of functional. They wouldn't have spent that kind of money on a suit of armor that was going to get hacked on by swords and shot up with arrow bolts."

She reminded him of Angie when she got excited about something. She was adorable. "Are you a historian?"

"Art history major." She looked down and stepped back from the armor. "Sorry. I get a little carried away sometimes."

"Don't apologize for being passionate about something."

Her smile lit up her face, and it sent a jolt of desire through him as the image of her smiling up at him, her thick dark hair spread around her face, flashed through his mind.

"What are you passionate about?" she asked.

He froze. No one had ever asked him that before. Not in a nonsexual kind of way, and he didn't think that's what she was asking about.

He almost said protecting kids, but that would lead to awkward questions about why they needed protection, and he didn't want to scare her off. His mind was oddly calm for the first time in twenty-four hours. He wanted to keep talking to this woman who gave him a small history lesson on the club mascot in the middle of a party, especially if it distracted him.

"Choppers."

"Motorcycles or helicopters?" she asked.

"Custom motorcycles. I build them." He wasn't sure why he told her that instead of security specialist. They'd always been a hobby, something he did because he loved building with his hands. "A long time ago, I wanted to be the next East Coast Choppers and have my own big-name shop."

"Why don't you?"

He crossed his arms and shrugged. "Life got in the way."

"Hate it when it does that." She leaned forward, close to his upper arm. "Who drew that?"

He looked at the tattoo she was pointing at. "Same guy who tattooed it."

"Wow. He's a really good artist."

An irrational spark of jealousy ignited in his chest.

She leaned back and looked him down and back up. She rocked back on her heels a little when she raised her head from her examination. "You *are* sexy."

He couldn't have stopped his grin if someone had offered him money. "Why do you say it like that?"

"Like what?"

"Like you're agreeing with something I said."

"What did you say?" She shook her head. "Wait. Not you. Julia said you were sexy."

Tink frowned. "You know Julia?" She didn't seem like the kind of woman Julia would be friends with.

"Nope. Just met her. Dani yelled at her."

That didn't surprise him at all. Dani did not like Julia. "You know Dani?"

"Just met her too. I like her better than Julia, though."

Tink shook his head. Who was this woman? "What's your name?"

"Abby."

"Abby." He stepped closer. "Do you want to get out of here?"

"To do what?"

"Go for a ride."

"To where?"

He unfolded his arms and placed his hands on her hips. "Your place. My place. Any place."

Abby glanced down at her hip. "Does it work?"

"Does what work?"

"Just asking women to go somewhere with you to have sex?"

"I wasn't actually thinking about sex." Weirdly, he hadn't

been. He just had an urge to have her close. Maybe go somewhere with this smart, adorable woman. "But the woman usually asks me."

She looked like she was contemplating it but then took a step back and wagged her finger at him. "Nope. No. No way. No hot, sexy, tattooed biker guys."

Tink grinned again. "So, you think I'm sexy *and* hot?"

"And tattooed."

A woman with dark blonde hair joined them and draped her arm over Abby's shoulders. "Whatcha doin', Abbs?"

"Looking at the knight."

"I can see that." She gave Tinker an appreciative up and down.

He preferred it when Abby looked at him.

"Not that knight. That knight." Abby pointed at the suit of armor.

"Uh-huh," her friend said.

"I already told that one he was too sexy." She swung her finger around to point at him.

Tink chuckled.

"Abby—are you flirting?"

"No," Abby said indignantly. She turned an unsure gaze to Tink. "Was I flirting?" She shook her head. "I don't flirt. Especially not with hot, sexy, tattooed biker guys."

"Why especially?" He braced for this kiss-off. This was the point where civilians judged him for his looks and decided he was too dangerous for their delicate sensibilities. Because having tattoos and riding a motorcycle put him in the dredges of society column before they ever had a chance to know him.

"Because it never turns out the way it does in the books?"

That was the absolute last thing he expected to hear. "What books?"

Her friend grinned. "Yeah, Abby. What books?"

Tinker could see the blush spreading across her cheeks.

"I gotta go." Abby spun out of her friend's arm and walked away.

Now he was thoroughly confused. "What books?"

Her friend winked and followed Abby.

Seriously. What was so embarrassing about a book? He ran a hand through his close-cut hair and fought the urge to chase after her. He had a feeling it would make her run faster and farther, but he could feel her slipping through his fingers. Like a dream he tried to hold on to as he woke up.

"Tink."

He turned as the club president, David "Pothole" McComb, came down the hall.

"Hey, Prez."

"Katherine said she saw you heading this way. Are you taking off already?"

"I was, but I changed my mind."

"Cool. Do you have time to take a look at my bike? It's been running rough the last few days."

Tink hesitated. He wanted to keep an eye on Abby so he could bide his time and approach her again later, but this was his club president—he couldn't exactly blow him off for a woman. Even for the first woman who had interested him in longer than he could remember.

"Yeah. Let's go take a look at it."

When they finally made it back inside, hands covered in grease, he couldn't find her or her friend. Katherine told him Angie and Dani had left right before he and Pothole came back in, so he couldn't even ask his sister about her new friend. He'd ask Dani Sunday when they met to spar. He needed to find a way to see her again.

HUNGOVER

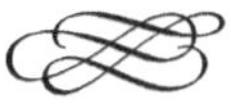

$\mathcal{A}$bby rolled over and groaned. She pulled the covers over her head to block the sunlight piercing through the gap in the curtains like a strobe light, even through her closed eyes.

Get the house with the east-facing bedroom, her mom had said. *It'll be so refreshing in the morning.* Her mom had obviously never woken up with a hangover in an east-facing bedroom.

She turned away from the window and folded the blanket off her head. Her body wouldn't let her go back to sleep now. Stupid circadian rhythm. Didn't it know she was hungover and it was the weekend? She had no reason to get up. Except to find Tylenol.

Throwing the covers off with another groan, she climbed out of bed and slid her feet into her fuzzy slippers. She shuffled down the hall to the kitchen and turned on her quick-boil electric kettle. If only her tea would steep as fast. She took her steeper and mug into the living room and curled up in her oversized chair. Fuzzbutt, her pure black cat, trotted into the room and jumped up on her lap to butt his head against her chin.

She heard the guest toilet flush. A few minutes later, Lindsey stumbled in and made a beeline for the couch, where she collapsed and pulled the folded blanket from the back of the couch over herself.

"Your asshole cat smacked me in the face."

"That's his way of saying he loves you." Abby set her steeper on top of her mug and watched the brew drain down. The fragrant scent of mango and ginger reached her.

"What does he do if he hates you?"

"Pisses in your shoes."

"Guess I'll take the love." Lindsay tossed the blanket off. "Do you have coffee or are you still contemplating your life as a serial killer?"

"There's a four-cup coffee pot and coffee on the counter just for you," Abby assured her.

"Oh my god. I'd totally marry you if I was gay." She stood with a groan and held her hands out like she was trying to steady herself.

"No, thanks. Been there. Done that. The T-shirt sucks."

"I'm not an asshole. I'd totally be worth getting married again," Lindsey said over her shoulder.

She returned about ten minutes later with a fragrant cup of coffee. "All hail java, the giver of life and consciousness."

Abby didn't have anything against coffee, but she'd gone an entire long weekend without having any and had spent two days with a severe headache dealing with caffeine withdrawals. She'd figured she'd already gone through the process, so she may as well reap the benefits and had switched to loose-leaf tea blends.

Lindsey took a sip and sighed with pleasure. "How are you feeling this morning?"

"Like there's a revival of Lord of the Dance in my head. You?"

"'Bout the same." She glanced over the top of her mug. "Do you remember much from last night?"

"I remember lots of shots."

Lindsey smiled. "Do you remember the hot biker?"

Abby groaned and slid down into her seat. Fuzzbutt meowed in protest as he was dislodged and had to resettle. "How bad was it?" She had a vague memory of talking to him. Mostly what she remembered was feeling nervous talking to such a good-looking guy.

"It wasn't bad at all. It could have been a lot better if you hadn't walked away from him."

"I think he asked for a hookup, and I don't do those. I wouldn't even know where to start."

"Usually by taking your clothes off."

If she had something to throw, she would. "You know what I mean. I've only been in long-term relationships, and the last one ended almost five years ago."

"Mmm…there's a lot to be said for no-strings sex."

Abby wouldn't know. "What about you? What happened to the guy you were talking to?"

"There was a line." Lindsey dropped her head back onto the sofa cushion.

"What do you mean a line?"

"When I came back from the toilet, there were two women fawning all over him. It wasn't worth the effort."

"Sorry," Abby said.

"Eh. You win some, you lose some." Lindsay raised her head. "If you saw that guy again, would you give him a chance?"

Abby thought about it and her honest answer was…she didn't know. She remembered rambling about the suit of armor and him being nice to her and not making fun of her. She also remembered the way his biceps had pulled at the sleeves of his shirt when he'd crossed his arms. And the way his jeans had hugged his butt.

He was the antithesis of everything she normally found attractive, and yet, she hadn't been able to keep her eyes off him.

But she'd been married to Mr. Perfect and look how that had turned out.

"You totally would," Lindsey teased.

"I don't know. It's highly doubtful he'd ever have any interest in a middle school art teacher, anyway."

"I don't know," Lindsey said. "You didn't see the way he was looking at you."

"What way?"

"Like you were the last drink of water on a desert island."

"Pfft. Unlikely."

A sly grin spread across Lindsey's face. "Do you remember telling him no hot, sexy motorcycle guys because it never turns out like it does in the books?"

Abby gaped at her. "I did not."

Lindsey laughed. "You absolutely did."

"Oh my god." Abby covered her face with her hands.

"I'll see what I can find out about him from Angela. I think they work together."

Abby dropped her hands and scratched Fuzz's ears. "That is so high school. I may as well write a note—do you like me? Check yes or no."

"Pretty sure the kids just text nowadays."

TINKER DROPPED his elbow to protect his ribs. "Oof."

He went on the offensive with a quick jab combination but failed to make contact.

"What—" He blocked the uppercut and lifted his leg to keep his knee from being dislocated. "Do you know about—" He barely blocked the hook to his face. "Abby?"

Dani backed up and shook her arms, bouncing on her toes. "Who?"

Tinker straightened his arm and popped his elbow. "Abby.

She was at the Knight's party on Friday. She said she met you. Dark, wavy hair. Green, V-neck T-shirt. A little taller than you."

He charged his sister, and she spun to avoid him, kicking him in the ass just to prove a point.

"Fuck."

She chuckled in response. "Saw that coming from a mile away."

He stretched his neck from side to side. "Abby?"

"I don't know much about her. Hey, Ange." Dani raised her voice so Angie could hear her on the other side of the Leonidas gym.

"Yeah?"

"Do you remember the woman Abby we met on Friday?"

Angie jumped onto the side boards of the treadmill before getting off and walking over to the mats where he and Dani were sparring. Although he used the term sparring loosely since Dani had surpassed his skill years ago. He was more of a human punching bag who occasionally swung back.

"Yeah. She came with Lindsey," Angie said.

"So not with a guy?" he asked.

"No. Just Lindsey. Why?"

"Just wondering." He was evading more than Dani's punches.

Angie gasped in delight. "You like her! Tinker's got a crush."

He pointed at her as he circled his sister. "You, I can take."

"Not with Dani in the room." She sat on the edge of the mat and stretched her legs out in front of her.

"Besides, I don't know her." He grabbed his water bottle from the edge of the mat.

"Then why are you asking about her?" Dani asked.

Because he hadn't been able to get her out of his head all day yesterday or that morning. Because he kept picturing the blush on her face and wondering what else he could make red. Because for the first time in longer than he could remember, he met a woman who wasn't family, a co-worker, or a buddy's old lady, and who interested him more than physically.

"Just wondering. She said she met Julia, and you yelled at her." He pointed to Dani.

"Yeah, well. Julia was talking out her ass as usual."

"She also said she liked you more than Julia."

"I hope the fuck so," Dani said.

"What *I* know is she teaches art and costume design at a local school, and Friday was the first time she'd been to a party in a long time," Angie said.

"How do you know that?" he asked.

"Because she literally said, 'I can't remember the last time I went to a party that wasn't for work,'" Dani said.

He took a drink of water. "You know her friend, though?"

"Lindsey? Yeah. We met at a professional women's symposium. She was giving a talk on women in STEM. Attended by women. Not the audience who should have attended. I think women in STEM already know about all the roadblocks ahead of them. But Lindsey was funny, so I talked to her afterward. We hit it off. Not surprising since I'm an awesome judge of character."

Tink grinned and was once again reminded of how similar Abby and Angie were. If he had to guess, Abby was probably as ridiculously smart as Angie.

"Anyway. You want me to find out more about her? I can get her number for you if you want."

"I don't need you hacking women's numbers to get a date," he said.

"That would imply you date," Dani said.

"I date."

"Uh, no. You fuck around for a few weeks and then move on."

"And?"

"That's literally the definition of not dating," Dani said. "The only one worse than you is Sleazy."

"Every woman I get involved with understands it's a benefits-only situation. I can't believe you compared me to Turner." That dude was the walking definition of man-whore.

He glanced at the large digital clock on the far wall. "I gotta go. We got a meeting about our ride to the school tomorrow."

"Can I go with you tomorrow?" Angie asked.

"Melanie's riding with me, but if you can find someone else to ride with, sure."

"I'll go," Dani said. "You can ride with me."

Ange clapped her hands. "Yay. Want me to find out about Abby?"

"I don't want you to go looking for info, but if you happen to talk to her friend and she comes up in conversation, maybe find out if she's single." He would figure out the rest from there.

Angie stood, joined Dani and leaned close. "Tinker and Abby, sitting in a tree."

He pivoted and rushed Angie, throwing her over his shoulder. She shrieked and threw her weight forward, forcing Tink to twist and grapple with her legs so she wouldn't land on her head.

"Hi-yah!" Dani tackled him and took him and Angie to the floor in a tangle of limbs—he wasn't sure what was his or theirs until one of them landed an unlucky knee to the inside of his thigh.

Fuck. He should have known better.

RIDE TO SCHOOL

"**I**'m going to drive ahead," Becky said. "I'll be waiting at the school when you arrive so I can take pictures, okay?"

"Okay," Melanie said.

Tinker watched as Becky fussed with Melanie's braid and made sure her thick hoodie was zipped all the way up. She was avoiding looking at him. He could live with her embarrassment. He didn't want to shame her, but if it kept her from making another pass at him, he'd take it.

"You ready?" he asked Melanie.

She smiled wide. "Yes!"

He grinned. He was happy to see her smiling. She was a strong kid, and he hoped being physically abused by her mom's ex wouldn't leave deep, lasting damage.

"Hang on—I forgot something." Opening his saddlebag, he pulled out a small vest and turned it so she could see the patch on the back. "I think this is yours."

The vest was a miniature version of the Tarnished Knights logo, but instead of Ned on the back, it was a gold suit of armor and read *Knight's Squire.*

Melanie's mouth opened in slow motion right before she let out a high-pitched shriek and danced from foot to foot.

"I think she likes it," Katherine said.

The other riders laughed and clapped as he helped Melanie slide into the vest. Becky adjusted the hood of her jacket. They spent another ten minutes taking pictures of Melanie with her mom and the rest of the club.

"We'll see you at the school," he told Becky. She nodded and kissed Melanie on the forehead, still not looking at him.

He settled a helmet on Melanie and adjusted the strap to make sure it was snug without choking her. "You good?"

"Yup."

"Okay, hop on up." He helped her onto the back of the seat and showed her where to put her feet, then sat in front of her and showed her where and how to hold on to him.

A thumbs-up to Sarah and Kevin, the road captains, and they were off. He fell into the middle of the column in his pre-coordinated position. They rolled out of the cul-de-sac, Melanie's neighbors waving and taking pictures as they passed.

A short ten-minute ride later, they pulled onto the school grounds. It looked like all the teachers had gathered out front to greet them. He knew Prez had cleared it with the school principal and administration. He slowed the bike to a stop and dismounted. He helped Melanie take off her helmet and held out his hand for a high-five.

"That was so awesome." Her cheeks were red from the short ride. Either that or the face-splitting grin she was sporting. He helped her off the bike and set the helmet on the seat.

She looked over at the teachers gathered around, clapping. "Ms. Abby! Ms. Abby!" She ran over to a woman with dark, wavy hair.

No. Fucking. Way.

~

ABBY FELT flames licking up her cheeks. It was like the time she'd had double spicy ramen and her entire face had been on fire.

Melanie had ridden in on the back of hot, sexy, tattooed biker guy's motorcycle. Abby didn't know what kind of karma was at work—good or bad—but she was convinced she'd done something wrong in a past life.

Principal Newton had sent out a notice about the ride on Friday afternoon and had asked teachers to gather in a show of support. Melanie was one of Abby's favorite students, and she hated that she hadn't noticed the change in her personality. Or the bruises. She couldn't imagine the pain and anger her mom had dealt with.

"Ms. Abby! Look at my vest."

The bottom dropped out of her stomach. Melanie was leading Hot Sexy Tattooed Biker guy her way—like a tiny, evil pied piper. She focused on Melanie, whose smile was as bright and beautiful as ever.

Melanie hopped to a stop in front of Abby and then hopped half a turn to show her the back of the vest.

"That's so cool," Abby said.

A woman joined them, smiling at Melanie. Abby schooled her features. She recognized the woman from the party Friday night. She glanced from him to the woman. The adoration in the woman's gaze was palpable, but he was doing his best to pretend she wasn't there.

Melanie grabbed his hand. "This is Tinker. He's my protector. He helped me be brave when I had to go to court."

Abby had no choice but to look at him. There was a twinkle in his eye like he knew a secret he was dying to share.

The woman stepped forward and held out her hand. "I'm Becky, Melanie's mom."

Abby shook her hand. "It's nice to meet you. We're so happy to have Melanie back at school."

The school bell rang and Abby glanced over her shoulder, finding Principal Newton gesturing for people to head inside.

"I know this is very exciting, but it's time to get to homeroom," she told Melanie.

Melanie hugged her mom and Tinker, then ran into the school.

Time to make a graceful and professional exit. "It was nice meeting you both."

"Actually," Tinker said. "Do you have a second?"

So much for that. "Uh, sure, but I need to get to class."

"It'll be quick."

She glanced between him and Becky.

Tinker glanced at Becky. "David or Katherine can let you know what happens next if you have any questions."

Her face fell like someone had told her there were no more free kittens. "Oh. Yeah. Okay."

Abby shifted and secondhand embarrassment rushed through her as she watched Becky walk away. The exchange was uncomfortable with awkward undercurrents she didn't really understand.

Tinker stared at her for several, even more uncomfortable, seconds before a grin spread across his face in slow motion.

She braced.

"Hi, Abby."

That was it? "Hi."

"Do you remember me?" The low timbre of his voice suggested there was more to their meeting than there had been.

"I have a vague memory of talking to you." She reached one arm across her lower back and grabbed the other arm.

His gaze dropped down to her chest, but he quickly raised it again.

She pulled her arms to her front and crossed them, but that gave her boobs a boost. She had no idea what to do with her arms. They'd only been attached to her body her whole life, but now it was like Frankenstein had given her someone else's arms and she had no control over them. She settled for uncrossing them and lacing her fingers together in front.

His mouth twitched as he watched her flail around. "What do you remember?"

More than she wanted to and not enough judging by Lindsey's teasing Saturday morning. "There was a suit of armor."

"Uh-huh. Do you remember telling me you thought I was hot and sexy?"

Her face was on fire again. "I was told I might have said something to that effect."

"You should let me take you out, since you think I'm hot and sexy."

"I don't think that's a good idea."

"Why not?"

"Because I'm sure there's really nothing about me you'd find interesting." She glanced behind him where the other bikers were getting onto their bikes to leave and sent a small prayer he'd be joining them.

He followed her gaze and nodded to an older man with his arm around Katherine. She waved at Abby and Abby waved back.

"You're an art teacher, right?" Tinker asked.

She frowned. "Yes. What does that have to do with anything?"

He winked and walked away.

"What does being an art teacher have to do with it?" she called after him.

He tilted his head back and started belting out Van Halen's Hot For Teacher.

Several voices chimed in to sing the last part. Including Katherine. Abby saw Angela on a bike riding behind Dani, both laughing. Had they just arrived or had she been so distracted by Tinker that she didn't notice them at all?

And why couldn't it be summer so a freak thunderstorm would roll in, and lightning could strike her where she stood, because that would be less painful than the embarrassment she was dying of.

She felt a presence next to her and found Lindsey and Naomi, her other best friend, laughing along with everyone else. Traitors.

"She gets out of school at four if you want to carry her books home!" Lindsey called out.

Tinker grinned and lifted his chin in their direction. What did *that* mean?

Abby glared at Lindsey. "I hate you." She spun on her heel to go into the school.

Lindsey laughed again. "You love me."

OH. My. God.

He was actually there, waiting for her to get out of school. Well, Abby wasn't interested. A tiny flutter in her belly called her out for the liar she was.

Tinker grinned when he spied her. He watched her while leaning against his bike, one leg over the other, and arms crossed over his chest. It was a total Jax Teller pose.

Okay, so she also watched Sons of Anarchy. Sometimes.

"I don't have any books for you to carry," she blurted out.

"Wanna split a milkshake at the malt shop?"

She grinned despite herself.

"How about dinner?" he asked.

"It's four o'clock."

"We can go for a ride, then get dinner." He patted the seat next to him, the one Melanie had ridden on that morning.

"I have somewhere to be in half an hour," she said.

"Boyfriend's?"

"Don't have one."

He cocked an eyebrow. "Girlfriend?"

She smiled. "Don't have one of those either."

His face fell. "Husband?"

She shook her head. "Not in years."

He nodded and seemed content to wait for her to say something. Mostly she wanted to know, "Why do they call you Tinker?"

"Because I'm good with my hands." He wiggled his eyebrows and waved his fingers like jazz hands.

A little zing tapped her nether regions at the innuendo. *Hello? Is this thing on?*

She ignored her personal mic check.

"Why are you interested?" It completely baffled her. He was objectively hot, and she was kind of average. She wasn't unattractive, but she was never going to stop traffic.

"You gave me a lecture on Ned."

She frowned. "Who's Ned?"

"The knight."

"Ned begins with an N."

He grinned and a major sense of déjà vu hit her.

"We've had this conversation before, haven't we?"

"We have. He is a replica, by the way, but purchased in Germany so he's an authentic replica."

Her brain immediately veered off into the land of questions. What part of Germany? How expensive was it? Did they ship?

She reeled her thoughts back in and cocked her head. "That was all it took? A drunk lecture on a suit of armor?"

He shrugged. "What can I say? I'm a simple guy."

She doubted that. This guy was infinitely more complex than his devil-may-care persona suggested.

He stood and pulled a wallet from his back pocket and took out a business card. "Here's the deal, Abby. I'm giving you my number. I'll give you the prescribed seventy-two hours to call me. After that, the ball will be back in my court."

She took the simple business card, and he threw a leg over his bike and started the motor.

He revved the engine once. "Call me."

She watched him drive out of the staff lot, then looked at the card. "Are you kidding me?"

His last name was literally Knight.

Christian "Tinker" Knight, Security Specialist for the Leonidas Corporation, was coming for her. Was that shiver down her spine worry or excitement?

IT'S A DATE

"You have to call him," Naomi said.

They were standing in the back of the textile room. It was a sewing room with sixteen sewing machines set up in two rows of eight, but the school administration felt "textile room" was artier and less home ec-y.

"Don't you have a class to go to?" Abby glared at her friend.

"I'm in it. I'm here to confer on the designs for the spring showcase."

Abby rolled her eyes. They'd already conferred on the costumes. "You're here to gossip."

"I am here to lend emotional support to my very good friend who, although beautiful, witty, and charming, is socially stunted. You only have one more day to call him, and then he's coming for you."

Naomi fake shivered. "Ooh, I get all tingly just thinking about it. It sounds so… so…"

"Creepy? Psychotic? Predatory?"

"Sexy," Naomi finished.

"Jesus. You're worse than I am."

"Ms. Abby?" Armando called out, his hand raised. "My needle's jammed."

Abby helped him fix his machine and adjust the tension for the fabric he was sewing and spent several minutes looking over a few more students' work. When she returned to the back of the room, Naomi looked up from her phone with a guilty expression.

No. Not *her* phone. *Abby's* phone.

"What are you doing?" she hissed.

"I'm sorry," Naomi said. "Actually, I'm not—you were never going to do it. You guys have a date Friday night."

"What?!"

The noise stopped as all the students turned to look at them.

"It's okay," Abby said. "Keep working on your projects."

She snatched her phone from Naomi. "What is wrong with you?"

"*So* many things. Which is good for my therapist's investment portfolio. Seriously, Abby, you need this. You need to get out there. Not every guy is a douchebag."

"I don't know anything about this guy. He could be a serial killer."

"I don't think Veterans Against Child Abuse would let a serial killer ride with them," Naomi said.

"Well, obviously he hasn't been caught yet."

"Abby, you have a hot guy who wants to take you out to dinner. Who cares if it's a bust and he's not *the one*?" she said with air quotes. "Whatever that means. Think of him as practice. Flirt a little, rip off the Band-Aid, break the seal."

Abby glared at her.

"Not like that. Although if you do, please tell me all the dirty details, especially if he really is good with his hands."

Would it be so bad going out one time with a guy? He was hot. And relatively amusing. And it had been a long time since she'd been on a real date.

She scrolled through the short text exchanged.

Hi. This is Abby.

Hey. I didn't think I'd hear from you.

Why did you give me your card then?

I was hopeful. 😔

You want to get drinks sometime?

I'm not much of a drinker

Are you an eater?

Of food?

😅 Yes

Yes.

How about dinner Friday?

Sounds like fun

Want to meet somewhere or you good with me
picking you up?

You can pick me up

Cool. See you at 6.

Abby stared at Naomi. "You told him to pick me up?"
"It's a date. We're doing it the old-fashioned way," Naomi said.
"What is this *we*? You're not going on a date with him."

"The colloquial *we*."

"I can't." She shook her head. "I can't."

Her phone pinged and she jumped, fumbled the phone like a hot potato, and managed to bounce it toward Naomi, who caught it.

"Jumpy?" Naomi asked.

"Just...cancel. Tell him I came down with the flu. Or small-pox. Something contagious. But not Ebola, that's too contagious."

Naomi held the screen toward her.

Need your address.

Are you allergic to anything?

"Serial killers don't ask if you're allergic to anything," Naomi said.

"Unless they want to make sure the drug they slip you doesn't kill you before they can."

"Stop watching *Dateline*." Naomi glanced at the students and said in a low voice, "Melanie thinks the world of him, and if anyone should be wary of men, it's her. Kids are good judges of character. You are doing this."

Abby had to concede her point about Melanie. "Fine. But if he kills me, I'm haunting you until *you* die."

"DOES anyone know what's wrong with Tink?"

Tinker glanced across the room to the bar where Harrison and Angie sat. From an outsider's perspective, they looked like any other couple on a date, but their vantage point gave them a clear view of the front entrance of the restaurant and the hall to the restrooms.

Tink sat at a table for one on the far side, where he had a clear view of the dining room and the kitchen entrance.

"He looks fine. Why do you think something's wrong with him?" Nash asked. He and Addison were on the other side of the restaurant.

Their earpiece communications link let them talk to each other without making it obvious.

"He keeps smiling," Harrison said.

"So?" Addison asked.

"So, it's not his usual shit-eating smirk. It's an actual, honest to god, smile," Harrison said.

Angela gasped. "Did you ask her out?"

"Ask who out?" Nash asked.

"Y'all can stop talking about me like I'm not here anytime now," Tink said.

"Oh my god! You did!" Angela squealed in his ear, and he grimaced. From across the room, she looked incredibly happy.

"While I'm enjoying the potential deep dive into Tink's dating life, target number one walked in," Paige said. She and Graham were sitting outside the restaurant since they'd met their target previously.

"Angie, can you adjust camera three down slightly?" Graham asked.

Angie fiddled with her phone on top of the bar. "Good?"

"Yup."

Tinker stared over the top of the menu and watched their target follow the maître d' through the dining room to a table close to his own.

"Remember, he has to pass the packet before we can grab him," Paige instructed. "Our client wants hard proof and wants this done quietly."

"I still don't understand why he didn't go to the police," Nash said.

"It's hard to believe your own son would steal from you and

sell secrets to the competition," Addison said. "He wants to see it with his own eyes. He's probably hoping he's wrong and this will all be for nothing."

"The gambling debt didn't sell it for him?" Tink asked.

They'd started investigating Arthur Nathan Clark IV about two months ago, when his father had noticed money being siphoned out of smaller companies' business accounts.

"Guess not," Paige said. "Target two is at the entrance."

A slightly overweight older man walked through the dining room and joined Arty IV. He waved off the waiter when offered a menu.

Tink couldn't hear what he said to Dani. "Paige, you got comms on them?"

"Yeah, it's recording."

The team remained quiet, waiting for the handoff.

"He's reaching into his jacket." Angie had the benefit of watching the feed from the cameras they'd installed earlier in the day, thanks to a few hundred slipped to the manager.

Sure enough, Arty pulled a long manila envelope, folded in half lengthwise, from his suit jacket pocket and laid it on the table.

"Wait until Lewis takes it," Graham said.

As soon as Lewis, their second target, put his hand on the envelope and pulled it across the table, Tink was up. He made it to the table and grabbed the envelope from Lewis's hand before he could tuck it away.

"Excuse me," Lewis said with a thick Southern accent. "Who the hell do you think you are?"

"The guy hired to stop you from buying your competitor's intellectual property." Tink looked at the other man. "Arty, your father and the Board of Directors would like a word with you."

Tink knew the minute the wide-eyed man decided to bolt. He sighed. "Runner."

Arty dodged between tables. Angie hopped down from her

barstool and appeared to stumble right before she body-checked good ol' Arty to the ground.

"Good job, Angie," Addison said.

Angie flipped her hair over her shoulder. "Thanks. I've been practicing."

Lewis, still in his chair, sputtered, "You can't prove anything."

Tink slapped him hard on the shoulder and squeezed. "Sure thing. Mr. Clark III's lawyers will be in touch."

He tucked the envelope into the inner pocket of his suit jacket and buttoned it at his waist. Ignoring the stares from the other diners, he joined Harrison and Angie while Nash and Addison spoke with the manager.

"You know you didn't have to body check him, we can't arrest him," he said.

Angie shrugged. "I know, but it was fun."

Arty looked up from the chair Harrison had helped him into. "You mean…you're not cops?"

Tink scowled. "Do I look like a cop?"

"Then you're not taking me somewhere?"

"Why would you think that?" Harrison asked.

Arthur pointed at Tink. "Because he said—"

"I said your daddy and BOD wanted a word with you."

"Then I can…I can go?"

Angie waved him away like an annoying fly. Arthur bolted from his seat and sprinted for the door.

"Why are there so many of us here? This was an easy job," Angie said.

"Tink was here as muscle. You were here to control the video and audio. Harrison was here to keep you from getting hit on," Paige said through comms. "Addison sweet-talked Graham into including her and Nash so they could get their dinner paid for."

"Ooh, putting that psych degree to work by manipulating the boss. Nice," Angie said.

"I heard that," Graham said.

"Someone had to be here to smooth things over with the manager. Besides, we're expensing it to the client." Addison raised a glass of wine in their direction before taking out her earpiece.

"Tink, Graham will meet you in the lobby to get the packet," Paige said. "Y'all are clear for the night. We'll debrief tomorrow —nine a.m."

Harrison held out his hand and slapped Tink on the back. "I'm hanging around. I made reservations for me and my girl. I'll catch y'all tomorrow."

Angie joined Tink and slid her arm through his. "So…where are you taking her?"

Tink glanced down at her. He wanted to be annoyed at her meddling, but she was as much a sister to him as Dani was. Not that they weren't both annoying most of the time.

"I don't know yet."

Angie tugged on his arm. "What do you mean you don't know? You have to know. And you have to tell her where you're taking her."

"Why? I asked if she had any allergies."

Angie stared at him like he'd said the moon was a giant helium balloon. "Because she has to plan what to wear."

"What does it matter what she wears?" He was thoroughly confused. This was the book thing all over again—which he still didn't understand.

"What does it—? Graham, tell him."

Graham sauntered up to them. "You gotta tell her where you're taking her. At the very least, you need to tell her to dress nice or casual."

Tink pulled the packet from his jacket and handed it over. "How do you even know what we're talking about?"

Graham took the envelope and tapped a finger in front of his ear. He saluted with the envelope and left.

Tink scowled and yanked the device out and handed it to Angie. Stupid earpieces.

Angie released his arm and faced him. "If she dresses up and you show up in jeans and one of your black tees, it's going to be awkward and embarrassing, especially for her. Same goes if you show up in this and she's in jeans and a tee." She gestured to his suit.

"This is why I don't date—too many fucking rules."

"The rules are easy. Number one." She held up her pointer finger. "Pick the restaurant, unless she invites you out. Don't ask her what she feels like or where she wants to go. Number two, tell her where or tell her how to dress: black tie, dressy, casual, or plan on getting dirty. Three." She continued to tick off fingers. "Be gentlemanly but take her lead on opening doors. Number four, don't get smashed. No one likes a sloppy date. Number five, be yourself, be honest, but don't tell her your whole life story."

He stiffened at that last rule.

Angie placed her hands on his shoulders. "That's not what I meant. No one wants to hear their date's baggage on the first date, regardless of what it is. Guarantee there are going to be things she doesn't share with you right away. Some things take trust, and that takes time."

This was getting complicated. He'd asked Abby out on a whim. Hell, he couldn't even explain why he'd ridden to the school to see her again. Some compulsion had him checking his watch and pointing his bike toward West Ashley instead of home.

He hadn't actually thought she'd get in touch with him, and he'd already decided he wouldn't try to track down her info. She was a SERIOUS RELATIONSHIP, and he was not. He should cancel and save them both the hassle.

"Don't," Angie said.

"Don't what?"

"Cancel. Don't try to deny it, either. I can see it on your face. Something told you to ask this woman out on an actual date. And Harrison was right, you've been smiling to yourself all night." Her gaze softened. "Give yourself a chance, Christian— you deserve it."

He disagreed with her on that part but decided to go with it. "Fine. Any suggestions on where I should take her?"

Angie grinned and slipped her arm back through his. "So many! Does she like seafood? What about shrimp and grits? Or you could go for soul food—but you don't like collard greens."

Tink sighed. He may not regret the date, but he would definitely regret asking Angie for advice.

GETTING READY

*A*bby's phone pinged. She wiped her hands on the dish towel and grabbed the phone from the counter, briefly seeing Tinker's name before the notification disappeared.

She stared at the blank screen. Their date was that night. She hadn't heard from him since Naomi had agreed to go out with him on her behalf.

Was he confirming or canceling? Why didn't she know which one she was more nervous about? Her thumbs hovered over the screen.

Mmmm...I don't have time for this. She set the phone face down on the counter.

All through finishing breakfast and getting ready for work, she ignored the heavy presence of her phone. Just there, within easy reach, his text waiting to be read. It was ridiculous, but it was like she'd been handed Pandora's box. As soon as she opened it, she wouldn't be able to close it.

She had first period free—she'd read it then. Decision made, she tossed the phone into her purse and tried to forget about it. Easier said than done. As soon as the last student filed out of homeroom, she closed the door and rushed to her desk, fingers itching to open the text.

> I was told to let you know we're going to
> Lavender and Sage for dinner.

That was it. That's what she'd spent all morning stressing over.

"You are such a dork," she whispered.

Her thumbs wiggled over the screen while she tried to figure out how to respond.

Okay was too impersonal.

Can't wait was…just no.

She settled for:

> Thank you. I like that restaurant.

Simple, polite, agreeable. In no way, shape, or form, easy.

This was so stressful. She was not cut out for this. Tony had pursued and wooed her. At the time, she'd described it as a whirlwind romance and she'd been swept off her feet. Many years of therapy later, she knew it by a different name: love bombing.

Maybe this way wasn't easier, but it was smarter.

Her phoned pinged and this time she checked immediately.

> You've been there before?

> Once for a friend's birthday. You?

> No. Dani & Angie recommended it.

> Are you in class?

> No. I have this period free.

Her phone rang almost immediately. She bit her lip and answered. "Hello?"

"Hey." His voice was low and deep.

She sank into her chair and spun so her back was to the door. "Hi."

"You don't mind me calling, do you?" he asked.

"No. I wouldn't have answered if I couldn't talk."

"Good."

She didn't know how to respond to that. "Why did you call?"

"We haven't actually talked. I was surprised you messaged me."

She cringed. "I, um, have a confession. That wasn't me. My friend Naomi messaged you, pretending to be me."

There was a moment of silence. "But you didn't cancel."

"No," she said softly.

"I get it if you feel pressured by your friends. Do you want to go to dinner?"

"I do," she said. "I would have explained and canceled if I didn't."

"If you're sure," he said.

"I am. I would like to have dinner with you."

"A'ight. I'll see you at six."

A thought occurred to her. "Wait! Are we riding your bike?"

"Do you want to ride on my bike?"

Her mind flitted through the MC books she'd read and the implications of being on the back of a guy's bike. She didn't know if it was true or his mindset or if she even wanted it to be his mindset. Or true.

"I need to know if I should wear pants." What a lame excuse.

"Nah. I have a car. I'll see you tonight." He didn't give her a chance to say goodbye.

It was oddly disappointing he had a car. The thought of pressing close to his back, wrapping her arms around him, feeling the heat of his body and the vibration of the bike under her was…was…damn it. It was arousing.

She was too busy banging her head on her desk to scrub her dirty, dirty mind to hear the door open.

"What are you doing?"

Abby looked up to find Lindsey staring at her with concern.

"Trying to knock some naughty images out of my brain." She rubbed the middle of her forehead.

Lindsey grinned. "Naughty images of a hot, sexy biker guy you're going on a date with tonight?"

Abby glared at her. "Is there a reason you're here?"

"Yes. I know this is your only free period today. Naomi and I will be at your house right after school to help you get ready."

Abby returned her phone to her purse and closed the bottom desk drawer it was in. "I don't need help getting ready. You're coming over to ooh, ahh, and giggle when he picks me up."

"Well, duh." Lindsey left as the bell rang, indicating the end of first period.

Abby rolled her eyes. Goddess save her from well-meaning, interfering friends.

～

"I THINK she should wear the blue one."

"That's too dowdy. She should wear the red one."

"That is one-hundred and eighty degrees from dowdy. She should not wear it on a first date."

"She should absolutely wear it for a first date. It screams available."

"It screams *fuck me*."

"Exactly."

"Oh yeah. I see your point. You should wear the red one, Abby," Naomi said.

Abby stood in the door of her ensuite bathroom and shook

her head at her friends arguing like the fairies from Sleeping Beauty. "No."

"Oh, come on," Lindsey said.

"A, the red dress is too much for Lavender and Sage. B, the only time I wore it, I was so uncomfortable the entire night I couldn't enjoy myself."

Naomi looked at the dress in question, hanging on the back of Abby's bedroom door. "Why do you still have it if you're not going to wear it?"

"It's an expensive freaking dress. I don't want to throw it in the donation bin," Abby said.

"You should take it to Second Chances. They do consignments," Lindsey said.

Abby went back to the mirror to finish her makeup. "I keep meaning to." If she had a dollar for all the things she kept meaning to do, she could retire.

"What are you wearing?" Lindsey asked.

"Classic little black dress." She swiped on a coat of mascara and stepped back for a critical review. The shades of shimmery gray made her light brown eyes pop. She always felt they were her best feature and kept her from being too Plain Jane.

Average height. Average boob to hip ratio. Average brown hair. But depending on how she wore her makeup, her eyes could be the color of caramel or as dark as whiskey.

"You're not wearing the dress you wore for last year's showcase, are you?" Lindsey asked.

Abby left her bathroom and made a sharp turn into her small walk-in closet. She shut the door and pulled the garment bag from the far corner. Reverently pulling the dress from the bag, she prayed it still fit, because despite Naomi and Lindsey's argument about what she should wear, the blue dress was too dowdy.

For one moment, the zipper stuck but then kept going as far

as she could get it. She let out a sigh of relief. It was a little tighter in the bust than she remembered, though.

She slipped into her strappy heels and opened the door for the big reveal. "I need one of you to finish zipping me up."

"Sure." Naomi hopped off the bed while Abby turned her back. "This is Dior."

"Yes," Abby said over her shoulder.

"This is vintage Dior. Did your ex get this for you too?"

"God, no. It was my grandmother's. Mom is too tall for it, so she gave it to me when Gran passed."

She turned to face her friends. "So? Too much? Too little?"

"Just right," Naomi said. "You look like Audrey Hepburn."

"You are so getting laid tonight," Lindsey said.

"Not the point of this date." Abby grabbed the clutch from the end of the bed and checked the time. Tinker should be there soon.

"Then what is the point?" Naomi asked.

"To rip off the Band-Aid. To get out there and start living life again."

"That's sweet," Lindsey said. "But you should add getting laid to the list."

"For the love of—" Abby threw up her hands and left her bedroom.

"All I'm saying is orgasms release endorphins and endorphins make you happy."

"Well, if that's all it takes, I'm releasing plenty of endorphins on my own," Abby said.

The doorbell rang.

"Ooh, he's here!" Naomi clapped her hands. "Are you going to bring him in and introduce us?"

"Hell no."

*A*bby stepped out of the house and pulled the door shut behind her. "Hi."

Fuck. Tinker was so fucked.

Her hair fell in soft waves around her face, and whatever she'd done to her eyes made them almost glow. He'd wondered if he'd remembered them wrong from the first time they'd met, but no. Her dress was simple but accentuated the dip of her waist and curve of her hips. The skirt ended slightly above her knees, showing off toned calves.

He'd always been a leg man.

Hell, who was he kidding? He was a leg, ass, tits, dimples in the small of a woman's back, man.

"Hi. Are you going to invite me in?"

She gripped her purse in front of her. "No. Lindsey and Naomi came over to harass me while I got ready, and they're still here. Inviting you in would be awkward for everyone, and by everyone, I mean me."

He grinned. He bet it would be fun to rile her up. He glanced toward the window and sure enough, two sets of hands had separated the blinds, and her friends were peeking out from between the slats.

"Then you're ready?" he asked.

She nodded and walked down the short path to his car. Keeping Angie's advice in mind, he helped her with the door, closing it after she was in, and she rewarded him with a smile.

Maybe there was something to this gentlemanly thing after all.

She was glancing around the interior of the car when he joined her. "What?"

"It's not what I expected, but it fits."

He started the ignition. "What were you expecting?"

"Something more beat up. Toolbox in the back seat with grease-covered engine parts."

He grinned again. He liked that she was honest. "I have a couple of those, although the toolbox and engine parts are in the truck."

"This is the same kind of car they used for the General Lee, right?" she asked.

"You know cars?"

"No. I used to watch Dukes of Hazard with my dad. He always said he wanted a Charger. Every single episode. It's pretty much the only car besides a Mustang I can recognize."

"My dad got this from a junk auction. We started working on it when I was in the eighth grade."

"I'm glad the doors work," she said. "I don't think I could have slid in through the window in this dress."

"I definitely would have enjoyed watching you try." He winked. "Why'd you say it fit me?"

What did she think of him? How had she judged him from the few times they talked?

"You don't seem like a sensible mid-sized SUV kind of person," she said.

"Why not?" He put on the blinker to turn into the parking lot of the restaurant.

"Too…what's the word I'm looking for? New?" She lifted her hands and rubbed her fingers against her thumbs. "Automated maybe. Newer cars are mostly computer. They're probably hard to tinker with."

He pulled into an empty spot, shifted into neutral, and stared at her.

Damn.

She looked down. "Sorry if that was presumptuous."

"No. Very accurate actually." He set the parking brake and shut off the car. By the time he got out and rounded the hood, she had one leg out. He held out his hand to help her the rest of the way out of the car.

He closed the door and took a step closer. "Abby?"

"Yes?"

"I forgot to tell you, you look beautiful."

Her gaze dropped and she cleared her throat. "Thank you. You look very nice as well."

"I know. I clean up good."

She laughed. "Well, there's nothing wrong with your ego."

He grinned and changed his grip on her hand, holding it in his, and led her toward the restaurant.

They were seated at a small table along the far wall, the large windows giving them a clear view of the deck around the building and the marsh beyond. He pulled out Abby's chair facing the windows, then took the chair on the side next to her so he could see the rest of the restaurant.

Their waiter handed them menus, filled their water glasses, and asked if they wanted anything else to drink—both passed.

"You can have wine or something since I'm driving," he said.

Abby shook her head. "I don't drink often. Last week was the first time I had more than a glass of wine in a very long time." She cocked her head. "Do you drink?"

"The occasional beer, but that's all."

She nodded and looked over the menu quickly, then set it aside.

The waiter returned to take their order. Tinker wasn't ashamed to admit he was overwhelmed by the menu. He was used to much simpler food. "What are you having?"

"The salmon with mango chutney and asparagus."

"Sounds good. I'll have the same." The waiter took their menus and left. "Do you like teaching?"

"I do. I like working with kids and watching them discover their talent. Even kids with no natural artistic ability can create. Do you like being a security specialist?"

He smiled as the waiter set down their waters. "Yeah. It's always something different."

"What does a security specialist do?"

"A little of this. A little of that," he said.

"That's vague. Is this one of those 'if I tell you, I'll have to kill you' kind of things?"

"No. We do everything from contract military operations, to corporate security, to personal security. A few months ago, I was assigned to provide personal security for a well-known actor. His regular guy had to have last-minute surgery, so they called us up. It's not that I can't talk about it, except for whatever non-disclosure agreement we sign, there's just so much we do."

"What's your last name?" he asked.

Abby smiled like she knew an inside joke. "Day."

"Wait. Really?"

She chuckled and nodded. "We are literally Knight and Day. Why do they call you Tinker?"

He liked that she didn't let him off the hook with his stupid answer from the first time she'd asked. "Classic case of a little boy who liked to take things apart to see how they worked. My mom called me her little tinker. It stuck."

"She doesn't call you that anymore?"

Tinker shifted and adjusted his jacket. "My parents died in a car crash when I was seventeen. Drunk driver."

Abby rested her hand over his fist. "I'm so sorry. That must have been incredibly difficult for you and Dani."

She might be the most genuine person he'd ever met. "Thank you. It was a long time ago."

"You never get over the loss of a parent," she said.

"Yours?" He flipped his hand palm up and held hers.

"My dad. Six years ago. Aggressive colon cancer. By the time my mom talked his stubborn ass into going to the doctor, it was too late. They gave him six months. He made it nine."

"I'm sorry," he said softly.

"Thank you."

He inhaled deeply. "Well, this took a maudlin turn."

Abby cocked her head and looked at him with a puzzled expression.

"What?"

"You're not at all what I expected," she said.

"Why? Because I used a word like maudlin?" He was used to people having preconceived ideas of who he should be. He usually didn't care, but he didn't want Abby to think he was who he projected to the outside world.

"Yes." She shook her head. "No. Well…yes."

He leaned closer and played with the tips of her fingers. "You expected me to be like the bikers in Sons of Anarchy, didn't you?"

She blushed and looked at their hands. "Maybe."

"I kind of hate that show for how it romanticized outlaw MCs. Every time someone sees me on my bike with my cut, they either look like they're afraid I'm going to attack them, or they look at me like I'm a snack."

The corners of her mouth tilted up. "I don't think you mind either of those scenarios."

He grinned. "Both situations can be useful."

Her golden eyes stared into his. "I'm sorry I stereotyped you."

So. Fucked.

He hooked a finger under her chin and slowly pulled her face closer. Barely brushing his lips over hers, he felt the quick intake of breath. "Thank you."

He brushed his thumb across her bottom lip and was rewarded with her tongue darting out and licking the spot.

Throat clearing broke them apart. The waiter set their plates in front of them, and Tinker took the opportunity to give his dick, pressing painfully against his zipper, a chance to simmer down.

TINKER HELPED Abby out of the car and walked her to her door. She turned to face him. "Thank you for dinner. I had a good time."

He stepped closer. "I'm not sure if I should be insulted or flattered that you sound surprised."

She smiled. "Definitely flattered. I haven't been on a date in a long time. I was nervous and thought I'd do something awkward, and you'd never want to see me again."

"I definitely want to see you again." He slid his hand behind her neck and pulled her forward. Any resistance from her and he'd let her go, but she glided forward, gaze on his mouth.

One small touch of their lips and it was like a dam burst, releasing a flood of desire and sweeping them both away. Abby hit the wall next to her door with a small grunt.

He shifted his mouth to her neck, scraping his teeth along the soft skin. "You okay?"

"Yes," she gasped. She slid her hands under his jacket, fingers digging into the muscles of his back.

He moved back to her mouth. Hot, open tongues sliding together. He might drown in her.

He slid his hand under her skirt and behind her knee. She responded to the slight pressure and lifted her leg, hooking her heel-clad foot behind his. He nestled into her center and skimmed his hand up her thigh to the lace edge of her panties. Fisting his other hand in her hair at the base of her neck, he angled her head for deeper access.

"Mommy?"

A bucket of ice water wouldn't have cooled his desire, but that one word sure as hell did.

He stared at Abby while she searched his face. He caught the slight tightening of her lips as she pushed at his chest and lowered her leg. He stepped back and ran a hand through his hair. His fingers still tingled from the heat of her skin, and his thoughts were scattered.

He focused on the little boy in dinosaur pajamas staring up at them. An older version of Abby stood behind him.

Abby went to the little boy and brushed her fingers through his hair, smoothing it down. She rested her hand on his shoulder and looked at Tink.

"This is my son, Will."

"Hi, Will," he said lamely.

The little boy tucked his face into her skirt.

"I need to get him into bed," she said. "Thank you again for dinner."

"You're welcome." He backed away down the path. "I'll call you."

Her smile was slight and quick. "Goodnight, Christian."

She didn't believe him. In that moment, he knew she was right. Because no matter how much he liked her, how much she set his blood on fire, a kid changed everything.

~

ABBY SHUT the door gently and threw the bolt. The deep rumble of his car, so like his bike, growled, then faded as he left.

"I'm so sorry, sweetie," her mom said. "I didn't know he was still awake. I didn't even realize he'd gotten out of bed until I heard the lock turn—I thought you were coming in."

Abby rubbed her mom's arm. "It's okay."

"Did you have fun at least?"

Abby smiled. "I did."

"Good. Are you going to see him again?"

"I'm not sure. We'll see." That was as big a lie as the one Christian had told her. She wasn't sure at what point during the night she'd started thinking of him as Christian instead of Tinker, but it didn't matter. She would never see him again.

"Let's get you to bed." She picked up Will and took him to his bedroom. Fifteen minutes of snuggles later, he was asleep, his fuzzy blanket clutched against his cheek.

She eased her arm out from under his head and went to her mom's room. Technically, it was now the guest room, but she always thought of it as her mom's room.

She knocked softly and pushed the door open. "Can you unzip me?"

Her mom set down her book and crossed to her. "You think he won't call because of Will."

"Yes." She turned once the zipper was down.

"He might surprise you," her mom said.

"I don't think so. It's okay. It was just a date."

"You wore your grandmother's dress. You wanted it to be more than just a date."

"What I wanted and what it was are two different things. Good night, Mom."

"I love you, sweetie."

"Love you too."

Abby hung the dress on the padded hanger and carefully

zipped up the back. She ran her hands down the garment and flared the skirt.

She had wanted more. For the first time in a long time, she'd done something for herself. Something selfish.

His taste lingered on her tongue. The skin of her thigh branded from his touch. She had never felt such intense desire or need for a man. It had been consuming. He would have consumed her.

And she would have let him if they hadn't been interrupted.

The look on Christian's face when she said *my son* was probably the same face he'd make if a dismembered hand had perched on her shoulder and snapped twice.

For one moment, fire had burned through her. She remembered what it was to *feel* alive, to be desired, to be wanted.

She wouldn't let go of the feeling now that she had it. It might not be with Christian, but it would be with someone who saw her and made her feel.

Better to have her heart bruised now than broken later.

SURPRISE GUEST

"**Y**ou should call him."

Abby sighed and shifted the phone to her other ear. "It's been an entire week. I'm not calling him."

"Maybe he's had a crazy week at work."

"Naomi, I love you, but please let this go." She'd accepted that Christian wasn't going to call. "He doesn't want to be involved with a single mother, and that's fine. It's a lot to take on. I get it."

"I know. I'm just disappointed for you."

She set the basket full of dirty laundry on top of the dryer and switched the phone to speaker so both her hands were free. "Well, don't be. I have a coffee date this afternoon. If nothing else, he showed me I am ready to get back out there. But I'm being upfront about having a son, and hopefully any prospects will weed themselves out."

"Your mom taking Will?" Naomi asked.

"Yes. They're going to the aquarium."

Naomi laughed. Will always wanted to go to the aquarium. If he could live there, he would.

"Want me to call during your date so you have a reason to leave if it sucks?"

"No, I'll be fine." She finished loading the washer and set the basket in front of the dryer.

"Okay. On another note, are you sure you don't want to go to Colorado with me and Lizzie next week?"

She took her phone off speaker. "I would love to go spend a week in Colorado with you, but not in April. It still snows in April. I am not prepared for that."

"Believe me, I'm right there with you, but her grandparents want more than a long weekend with her. They asked to take her to Alaska with them this summer, but she's not on board with six full weeks in a camper with them."

"Can't say I blame her. That wouldn't have been my idea of fun as a ten-year-old either."

She checked the clock on the wall. "I need to get Will up and to my mom's. I'm taking Lindsey to the airport before my coffee date."

"Do you think we should put a tracker on her? If anyone was going to end up the basis for a CSI episode, it would be her," Naomi said.

"She'll be fine. It's a week in Vegas for her cousin's wedding —her whole family will be there. How much trouble can she get in?"

There was a moment of silence.

"Maybe slip it in her purse," Naomi said.

"I'll see if it will fit in her phone case," Abby said.

ABBY SIGHED and walked into the aquarium. Her mom and Will would either be at the touch tank or the ocean tank. They could spend all day in the aquarium, and they'd go back and forth between those two exhibits. She waved to Frank, one of the employees, and he pointed in the direction of the touch tank.

Yeah, they were regulars. Sure enough, Will was bent over the short wall, elbow deep in the water.

She kissed her mom on the cheek. "Been here the whole time?"

"Pretty much. They have a new starfish."

Abby squatted next to Will. "Hey, Buddy."

He popped his head up and grinned. "Look. A new sta' fish."

"Maw Maw told me. Does it have a name yet?"

He shook his head.

"Maybe we can think of one tonight. About fifteen minutes and then home, okay?"

She kissed him on the head and stood, joining her mom at the bench around the pool.

"How was your coffee date?" her mom asked.

"It was good."

Alan, her date, had been perfectly lovely. Attractive, polite, humorous, asked her questions about herself, her family, and her job. He was also a single parent, divorced, and spoke kindly about his ex.

"Are you going out with him again?"

"He invited me to dinner next week. I said I'd check with you to see when you're available to watch Will, if you don't mind."

She'd accepted, willing to give it another chance, but she knew it wouldn't lead to anything. He was too nice of a guy to cross off after a single coffee date.

"I never mind," her mom said. "Tuesday or Thursday work best. I have wine night on Wednesday and Mahjong on Friday."

"Book club, Mom. It's book club, not wine night."

She waved a hand. "Whatever. We never talk about the book we're supposed to have read. Half of us have given up the pretense and don't even bother. We're there for wine and to gossip about our kids. I'm excited to finally have something to contribute."

Abby rolled her eyes. Her mom had been a major proponent of the *Abby should get out and date* movement. "What about Monday?"

"You can't go out with him on Monday."

She frowned. "Why not?"

"Because it's only two days from now. Going to dinner with him on Monday denotes an eagerness you don't feel," her mom said.

"I'm not uneager," Abby said defensively.

"You're ambivalent at best."

Abby groaned and rubbed her fingers across her forehead. She hated when her mom was insightful and *right*. "He's a genuinely nice guy. Smart, attractive, talked well about his ex. Why wasn't there a spark?"

Alan had everything that should have attracted her to him, but there was no tingle. No whoosh. No flight of butterflies in her stomach.

Her mom patted her arm. "You're not a spark plug, sweetie— it's not going to happen with everyone. No matter how perfect they seem."

ABBY PUT the car in park and shut off the engine. In the rearview mirror, she could see Will had fallen asleep. Naps were hit or miss recently, but an afternoon at the aquarium usually tired him out. The trick now was to get him out of the car, into the house, and into his bed without waking him up.

She managed the first part and was attempting the second, trying to isolate the house key without dropping the entire ring.

"Excuse me."

Abby turned and found a young girl standing behind her.

She looked familiar—probably one of the neighbor kids selling something for a school fundraiser.

"Hi. Can you come back later this afternoon?" she asked in a hushed tone.

The girl stepped closer. "Are you Abigail Day?"

That got her attention. "Why are you asking?"

"I'm Anthony Messina's daughter."

Abby's mind blanked. "Tony doesn't have a daughter."

"He does." She shrugged her shoulders and toed a pebble. "He just doesn't admit it to anyone."

Abby struggled for breath. Will was getting heavy and sweat beaded at the base of her spine. She couldn't come up with a single reason why a girl claiming to be her ex's daughter would be on her doorstep.

"Why are you here?"

"I need your help."

ABBY PULLED Will's door closed but left it cracked. She'd managed the third part of getting him out of the car, despite her pounding heart.

Tony had a daughter she knew nothing about. They'd been together three years, and he'd never breathed a word about her existence. He'd gone out of his way to make sure Abby understood they would be child-free, and the whole time he had a living, breathing child he'd never even mentioned.

She clenched her fists. That. Asshole.

Taking a steady breath, she shook her hands and went back to the living room.

The girl sat on the edge of the couch with a glass of water. She raised it. "I hope you don't mind."

"No." Abby sat on the love seat perpendicular to the couch. "What's your name?"

"Olivia. Livie."

"Olivia Messina?"

She shook her head. "Holder. My mom changed my name when her and Tony divorced."

"How old are you?

"Twelve."

She would have been six when Abby married Tony. "How —?" Abby rubbed her palms on her jeans. "How did I not know about you?"

Olivia nodded. "I guess that answers that."

"Answers what?"

"When I was little, I thought he left because of you."

Abby shook her head. "Olivia, I didn't—"

"I know. My mom always said it was all him. She said we should feel bad for you since you were married to him."

Abby wanted to defend herself, but she felt a level of sympathy for the next woman Tony married, so she understood.

"Does your mom know you're here?"

Olivia looked down at the glass in her hand. "She died. Six months ago." A tear dripped down her cheek, and she wiped it away.

"I'm so sorry," Abby said.

Olivia nodded.

"Are you living with Tony?"

She shook her head. "I was staying with my mom's half-sister and her husband, but I can't live there anymore."

Abby was at a loss. "Olivia, why are you here?"

Tears streamed down her face. "I want to live with you."

DAMSEL IN DISTRESS

inker zoomed in on the floor plan of the venue he was assessing. A local businessman was holding a party for his daughter's eighteenth birthday and had hired Leonidas to provide the security. Paige had tasked him as lead. On one hand, he appreciated the vote of confidence. On the other, it was a fucking birthday party.

The party was in six weeks, and he had plenty of time to coordinate the security plan, but there he was on a fucking Saturday afternoon trying to distract himself. Working on a custom build in his shop hadn't gone so well—he'd laid a shitty weld twice. He'd finally given up and come to the office hoping mundane office work would distract him.

Something smacked him on the shoulder. He flinched and turned as Angie continued to smack him on the shoulder.

"What the fuck, Ange?"

"You—" *Smack.* "Didn't—" *Smack.* "Call—" *Smack.* "Her—" *Smack. Smack. Smack.*

He rolled his chair out of striking range. "What the hell are you talking about?"

"Abby. You never called her after your date. You fucking ghosted her."

He caught the sticky notepad she threw at him. "How the hell do you know that?"

"Because her number isn't in your call logs."

"You hacked my phone?"

She braced her hands on her hips. "I pull call logs every month."

"Do Paige and Graham know?"

"Uh. Yeah. I give them to Paige."

"Why?"

She shrugged. "I don't know. She asked me to pull them, I pull them. Not the point! Why the hell did you ghost Abby?"

Tink rolled back to his desk. "Not really any of your business, Ange."

"Bullshit. She's nice, Tink. And pretty. And smart."

"And a single mom."

"So?"

"So, I don't get involved with single moms."

"Wow." She dropped her hands from her hips. "You are the last person I expected to hear such a judgmental and misogynistic comment from. Turner? Sure. Jayne? Maybe. You?" She shook her head. "I'm really disappointed in you, Christian."

She turned and walked away. Unfortunately, she didn't take the shit ton of guilt she'd dumped on him with her.

Trying to focus on the security plan was useless—he couldn't concentrate for shit. He kept picturing Abby's face the last time he'd seen her, but now Angie added a voiceover in his head saying *I'm so disappointed in you.*

It wasn't that he didn't like kids. He'd seen the heartbreak on too many little faces when they'd realized an adult they'd trusted had betrayed them. Too many little hearts hardened too soon.

As much as the disappointment from Angie and Abby stung,

seeing that look on the face of a little kid would destroy him. He never wanted to be in another position where he let someone down and ruined their life.

It was useless. He flung the pen he was holding onto his desk and leaned back. The security plan could wait till Monday. Going home was useless, and he had no interest in going for a ride. He'd go down to the gym and blow off some steam.

His phone rang and Abby's name appeared on the screen.

"Angela," he hollered. "Is this you?"

"Is what me?"

"Are you calling me pretending to be Abby?"

"Why would I do that?" Her voice was getting closer.

"Because you're a busybody."

"But I'm not a sadist," she said as she rounded the corner of his cubicle.

She didn't say she couldn't do something like that. He answered the call. "Abby?"

"Oh. Hi. I was getting ready to hang up."

He motioned for Angie to go away. She crossed her arms and gave him her most mulish look.

He rolled his eyes. "Hi. I'm sorry I haven't called, it's been busy at work."

It was a lame excuse, and he knew it. So did Angie, judging by the look on her face.

"Sure. Of course." Abby didn't sound like she believed him either. "I'm calling to see if you have Katherine's number."

"Katherine McComb?" he asked.

"I don't know her last name. Lindsey introduced us at the party. She said Katherine is on the board of VACA. I need to ask her for advice. Lindsey's out of town and not answering her phone, and Naomi doesn't know her."

Meaning the only reason she called him was because she had no choice. It shouldn't have felt like a gut punch, but it did.

"Or if you can give me Angie's number, I'll call her and see if she has it," Abby said.

Angie wagged her fingers for his phone. He shook his head. No way. Angie huffed and stomped off, probably going back to her desk to interfere.

"What kind of advice?" he asked.

"It's difficult to explain over the phone, but I have a situation and I'm not sure what to do. I'm hoping she can give me some resources."

"What kind of situation? With your son's dad?" Why was she being so evasive?

"It's complicated and I'd rather not get into it over the phone. Do you have Katherine's number?"

He made a split-second decision. "I'm on my way."

"That's really not necessary—"

He ended the call, not giving her another chance to tell him it wasn't necessary, and grabbed his jacket from the back of his chair. He also ignored Angie when she called, "I sent her Katherine's number."

His phone buzzed in his back pocket the entire twenty-minute ride to Abby's house. Her car was the only one in the driveway, so either she hadn't been able to get a hold of Katherine, or she hadn't arrived yet.

He checked his phone on the way to her door. Several missed calls from Abby, as well as a few texts from her and Angie. Angie's last text was blunt. *Don't get involved if you're just going to walk away again.*

That stopped him in his tracks. Fuck. He didn't know what he was going to do. Abby had mentioned a situation and he'd reacted purely on instinct. Damn it. He was standing in front of her door. He wouldn't walk away until he knew she was safe and there wasn't a threat against her or her son.

She answered the door almost immediately. "You didn't need to come."

He drank her in, telling himself it was to check for marks or bruises, but the rush of blood to his cock might as well have set his pants on fire. He was an idiot for thinking he could walk away with no regrets. Now that she was in front of him again, he didn't know how he'd done it before, but knew he wouldn't be able to do it again. Not easily. And not until he knew she was safe.

"Are you okay?" He stepped across the threshold, forcing her to take a step back.

She sighed and closed the door. "I'm fine. Katherine's on her way. She should be here in about ten minutes."

He nodded and took off his jacket, throwing it on the bench behind the door. "You want to give me a rundown of your situation?"

She crossed her arms. "I really don't."

His eyebrows rose. "Why?"

"A few reasons."

He took a step closer. "What are they?"

Her chin went up. "I don't want to have to repeat myself when Katherine gets here."

"And?" He knew there was more than that.

"And I'm not sure why you're here."

"You said you were in trouble."

"No. I said I had a situation, and I needed advice. From Katherine. The only thing I needed from you was her number. We both know you wouldn't be here if I hadn't had to call you. So why are you here?"

Her backbone was fucking sexy. He found it entirely too hot that she wasn't giving him a pass. Wasn't afraid to call him on his shit and wasn't telling him it was fine and acting like he hadn't fucked up to save face.

"I screwed up. I'm sorry. I should have called."

"Why?" she asked.

"Why what?"

"Why should you have called?"

His lips tilted up at the corners, and his dick pulsed against his zipper. Jesus, her attitude was like his own Pavlov's bell.

"I should have called to tell you I was an idiot and to ask you out again."

She pressed her lips together. "I won't play games. I don't have the time or energy to deal with bullshit. If that's what you're into, you can fuck all the way off, right now."

Ding. "It's not and I won't. I fucked up once—I won't do it again."

A knock on the door interrupted them, and he had to settle for her noncommittal "Mmm hmm" when she pulled it open.

"Tinker. I thought that was your bike outside. I didn't know you knew Abby," Katherine said.

"We met when we did the school ride for Melanie," he said.

She looked between him and Abby. Katherine was one of the most perceptive people he knew, so he knew she picked up on the tension between them. Especially when she asked, "Everything okay?"

"Yes." Abby stepped aside. "Please come in. Can I get you something to drink?"

"No, thank you," Katherine said.

He shook his head. Her glare said she hadn't meant to include him in her offer.

"Okay. Let's sit." Abby gestured to the living room.

The main area was open with the dining room to the right of the front door and the living room directly in front of them. He saw a kitchen and a short hallway on the other side of the dining room with a hall leading to another part of the house. Large windows made the space feel bright and airy.

Abby sat on the love seat and gestured for him and Katherine to sit on the couch. He took the spot on the far end.

Abby laced her fingers together and took a breath. "I'm not

sure how to explain the situation or even what help I need, so I'll start at the beginning.

"I was married to a man I believed was child-free. Meaning he had no children and he didn't want to have any children. We divorced about four years ago, shortly after I accidentally got pregnant. He didn't want a baby, and I wasn't willing to have an abortion. His name isn't on the birth certificate, and he has no role in my son's life."

Tinker clenched his fists. Motherfucker.

Abby took another breath. "I recently learned my ex was not only married before we were, but that he also had a daughter."

"How long were you together?" Katherine asked.

"Three years. Married for two," Abby said. "He was adamant about not having children, so it never occurred to me to ask if he had any."

"How did you find out about his daughter?" Katherine asked.

"She showed up on my doorstep this afternoon, asking for help."

"What kind of help?" he asked.

She turned her attention to him for the first time since they'd sat down. She was barely holding it together. He recognized panic and fear creeping in.

"She wants to live with me. I don't even know if that's something I can legally do," she said.

Katherine reached over and took Abby's hand. "Okay, back up. What about her mother?"

"She died about six months ago. Olivia went to live with her mom's half-sister and her husband. She didn't share all the details, but I got the sense there was some neglect, maybe even abuse. That's what made me think of calling you. I don't know if this is something you can help with, but I didn't know where else to start."

"Do you have some paper and a pen?" Katherine asked.

"Of course." Abby stood and went down the hall, returning quickly with a notebook and pen.

"Let's move to the dining room," Katherine said. "Tinker, make yourself useful and get us some water."

He frowned at Katherine, but did as she directed, finding glasses in the cabinet next to the sink and filtered water in the fridge.

Abby gave him a small smile when he set the glass in front of her.

"Okay. Let's start at the beginning," Katherine said. "What's the daughter's name?"

"Olivia Holder," Abby said.

"Her mother's name?"

"Gayle Holder. G-A-Y-L-E," a voice said from the hallway Abby had gone down.

A young girl with shoulder-length brown hair stood at the edge of the room, holding a blue folder.

"Olivia, do you want to join us?" Abby asked. "This is Katherine, the woman I told you about. This is Tinker, he works with Katherine."

A pang hit deep in his chest, like someone had shoved a knife under his rib cage. It cut deep that she didn't acknowledge their relationship—however new and tenuous it was.

Olivia nodded and sat next to Abby. "My name is Olivia. I'm twelve. I'll be thirteen in September. My mom was Gayle Holder. She died October twentieth. I haven't seen my father since I was four and he gave up his parental rights."

She sounded like she was reciting a speech. He had no doubt she'd rehearsed what to say, either to Abby, the cops, or anyone else that asked.

"I have my birth certificate and social security card. My mom made sure I had copies before she died. I know sometimes kids have a say in where they want to live. I don't want to go back to that house." Her voice rose in panic.

He knew that tone. Had heard it from too many kids. The panic was based on fear. The fear based on something that had already happened or something they knew would happen. That deep well of anger creaked open, and he swiftly slammed the lid back down on it.

Abby covered Olivia's hand with hers. "It's okay. We're going to figure this out."

"Olivia, can I ask why you came to Abby? Do you have any other family? Grandparents or other aunts or uncles?" Katherine asked.

"There's no one else. My mom told me to find Abby if I needed to," Olivia said.

"What?" Abby asked. "When?"

Olivia opened the folder and pulled out a sheet of paper, handing it to Abby.

She took it and glanced at it. "Can I read it out loud?"

Olivia nodded and looked down at her lap.

"Dear Livie,

I'm so sorry I'm not there anymore and that you have no one to count on. I wish things could have been different, that I had made different choices, but if I had, I wouldn't have you, my beautiful girl.

I don't know how things will be with Edith. We weren't close growing up, but I hope she will take care of you and protect you. If things get bad, call Abigail Day. She was your father's second wife. Everything I've found out about her makes me believe she is a good person and will help you.

I hope it doesn't come to that. I hope you live a happy, wonderful life.

Always remember I love you.

Mom."

Olivia sniffed and wiped her nose with the back of her hand as Abby set the letter back down.

He had to know. "Olivia? What did your mom think your aunt had to protect you from?"

Her shoulders hunched in and her hair fell forward over her face, making her appear smaller. He wasn't sure she would answer and looked to Katherine for help.

"He started coming into my room," Olivia whispered.

"Who did, sweetie?" Abby asked. "Your uncle?"

Olivia nodded.

"Did he hurt you, Olivia?" Katherine asked.

She shook her head. "He would stand next to my bed. He touched himself...there. A few nights ago, he tried to lift my T-shirt, but I pretended to be asleep and rolled over. I ran away the next day."

"Where does your aunt live?" Abby asked.

"Kentucky."

"How did you get here?" Katherine asked.

"Greyhound part of the way, train the rest."

He caught the stark look of terror on Abby's face when she glanced at Katherine.

"You said you have your birth certificate?" Katherine asked.

Olivia nodded and pulled it from the folder.

"Okay. I'm going to take pictures of these and reach out to some of my contacts. I'll wait until Monday when all the offices are open, okay? Abby, how does your schedule look next week?"

"It's spring break. I have the entire week off."

"Okay. I'll make some calls and set up appointments for next week."

Abby looked at Olivia. "Okay?"

Olivia nodded and Abby looked back at Katherine. "Okay."

That was the signal for them to stand.

"I'll be right back," Abby told Olivia.

Tink grabbed his jacket and followed Katherine outside. Abby closed the door behind them.

"Jesus." She covered her face with her hands before scraping her hands over her scalp and grabbing the back of her neck. "Anything could have happened to her."

"She's safe," Katherine said. "The important thing now is to make sure she stays that way."

Abby nodded and blew out a breath.

"Is her father an option?" Katherine asked.

"I doubt it," Abby said. "I wouldn't know how to get a hold of him anyway."

"We'll keep that option as a last resort," Katherine said.

"You good with me bringing Angie in on this?" he asked Abby.

"Why?"

"Need to check for any police reports or Amber alerts."

"Oh, shit. Will they come for her?"

"They won't know about her until we report it through the courts," Katherine said. "But first, I'm going to consult with a lawyer and a social worker friend of mine."

Tinker gathered Abby in his arms, grateful she didn't fight or pull away. "We'll take care of her, Abby."

He wasn't going anywhere.

CPS

*A*bby paced back and forth in the small reception area of the Department of Family Services. She ran her finger over the cuticle of her thumb, raw and chapped from being chewed on. She eyed the office door of Erin Readman, the social worker Katherine had made the appointment with.

"Hey." Katherine touched her shoulder gently. "How's it going?"

"I'm not sure. She spoke with both of us and then asked me to step out so she could speak to Olivia alone."

"That's normal," Katherine said. "She needs to get an unbiased account from Olivia. A lot of times, the parents or guardians answer for the kid or give unspoken direction—or threats. Erin is one of the best. She really cares about the kids."

Katherine pulled Abby over to the chairs and got her to sit. "How did it go this weekend?"

"Kind of surreal. I took her shopping for clothes Saturday after you left. She would only let me get her a few things. I took her and Will to the Isle of Palms on Sunday."

"How has she been with Will?"

"She's been great," Abby said. "She's played with him and read with him. She's been like a big sister."

"How has she been with you?" Katherine asked.

"Reserved and polite is probably the best way to describe it."

"That's to be expected," Katherine said. "She's been through some major emotional trauma in the last six months. It's going to take some time for her to get a sense of you. I know one of the recommendations from Erin will be for a therapist."

Abby nodded. She'd already planned to ask hers for a recommendation.

"Have you given any thought to long-term arrangements?" Katherine asked.

"A little. In a vague kind of way," Abby said. "I feel like everything happened so fast. I've been so focused on what's happening in the moment, figuring out what help and resources I need that I haven't let myself really think about it."

"If the court grants you guardianship, would you take her in? Permanently?" Katherine asked.

Abby inhaled and tried to envision all the ways life would change with the addition of a twelve-year-old girl, and she couldn't. Everything she pictured felt like a cheesy fairytale story or a tragic Lifetime documentary. But...

"Yes. I...don't know how to explain it, or describe it, but I feel about Olivia the same way I feel about Will. She's a piece of me, even though she's not mine."

She laughed and heard the edge of panic. "I have no idea how it's going to work or any illusion that it's going to be easy, but...yes. She belongs with me and Will."

"It's good that you're scared," Katherine said.

Abby laughed disbelievingly. "How is it good?"

"It means you care and that's the most important thing."

Abby wasn't scared—she was terrified. She had no idea what to do with a traumatized preteen.

Katherine reached into her small tote bag and pulled out a

business card. "Here. My friend Magda is a family law attorney. She can help you navigate this whole process. I told her to expect your call."

Abby might be edging into heroine worship territory. "Thank you so much for all your help. I can't tell you how much I appreciate everything you've done. I don't know what I would have done without you."

"I think you would have figured it out. You don't seem like the kind of woman to back down from a challenge."

The office door opened, and Erin stepped out. "Hi, Katherine. Abby, could you join us?"

Abby and Katherine stood.

Katherine pulled Abby in for a quick, tight hug. "You have my number. Call if you need anything."

Abby nodded and went into the small, yet comfortable office. The office had surprised her. She'd expected sterile government-issue decor, but the room was surprisingly warm and welcoming. Next to a small seating area there was a child-sized table and chairs and bins with dolls and toys.

Erin welcomed her with a smile, which Abby returned nervously as she sat next to Olivia in the chairs across from Erin's desk.

"Olivia shared the events and circumstances that brought her here to you. Under usual circumstances, a runaway would be placed with a foster family," Erin said.

Abby's heart thudded against her chest and her stomach twisted. "But—"

"*But…*" Erin held up her hand. "Given the familial connection, tenuous as it is, I agree it's in Olivia's best interest she stay with you while we get the permanent placement settled with the court."

Abby sighed and her shoulders relaxed. "What does that involve? Getting it settled with the courts?"

"You need to go through the approval process to become a foster parent," Erin said.

"Even though we have a family connection?" Abby asked.

"Yes, it's standard procedure when a guardian isn't legally designated by a parent," Erin explained. "Even if the guardian is a close relative."

"Okay. What else?" Abby asked.

"With what Olivia told me, I'm going to file for temporary emergency custody. She'll be assigned a guardian ad litem—someone who will represent Olivia, and only Olivia, in court. I will reach out to the Social Security office to have her mother's death benefits sent to you."

Abby looked at Olivia. "Do you already have an account that money goes to?"

Olivia shrugged. "I didn't even know I was supposed to be getting money."

Abby rubbed Olivia's shoulder. "We'll get it taken care of this week."

Erin beamed at her, then looked at her notes. "I'll have to confirm the biological father, Anthony Messina, terminated his parental rights."

Abby inhaled sharply. Please, god, don't say he needs to be involved in this.

"I understand he is also your son's biological father," Erin said.

"Technically, yes. But he's not on the birth certificate," Abby said. "Does it matter?"

"It shouldn't. But your son and Olivia being half-siblings helps your case," Erin said.

Erin went through the application process, scheduled a home visit, and discussed the process to obtain legal guardianship of Olivia. It was so much information. So much paperwork. Why was it so hard to give a child a home?

Abby's phone pinged and she pulled it from her purse. It was a reminder to pick up Will from the sitter. She looked at the time on her phone, then glanced at the wall clock to confirm it was correct.

"I need to pick up my son," she told Erin. "Is there much more we need to go over?"

"I think I have everything I need. If there's anything else, I'll give you a call," Erin said.

Abby stood, shook Erin's hand, and thanked her. Olivia was quiet while they left the office. She'd been quiet for most of the meeting, only answering questions when asked directly.

Abby buckled in but didn't start the car. "Olivia, are you okay with all this? I know this is a lot and it's happening fast. If you're uncomfortable or want to slow down the process, we will. If there's someone else you'd rather live with, I'll contact them and explain the situation."

"There isn't anyone else." Her voice was so soft and small Abby could barely hear her.

"I don't want you to feel like you have no choice or no voice in this process. This is *your* life. If you *want* to live with me, I will do everything in my power to make it happen. No matter what."

Olivia looked at her, brown eyes shiny with tears. "I want to live with you," she said firmly.

Abby nodded. "Then let's make it happen."

By the time they picked up Will and made it home, Abby had a list of twenty-thousand and one things to do, the most pressing of which was to make dinner since they ate early, around five-thirty, to give her time to play with Will before his bedtime at seven.

Abby stood in front of the open fridge waiting for a package of chicken breast to magically appear. She sighed and closed the door. She'd completely forgotten to go to the store yesterday for the weekly shopping. Sunday was her usual shopping day, but with everything that had happened with Olivia, she'd forgotten all about it.

There were three possible options. Pack the kids back up and go to the store, which was never ideal because Will always asked for extra snacks and she always ended up getting more things than she needed. Ask Olivia to watch Will while she ran to the store—not ideal at all to relegate Olivia to the role of babysitter three days after she joined their family. Or pizza, which was a once in a while treat, but seemed like the best option.

Midway through ordering online, the doorbell rang.

"I get it!" Will called.

Abby chased after him. "Will! Do not open the door by yourself." She got to the door as Will turned the deadlock and opened the door. The little escape artist. She reminded herself again to install a lock higher up out of his reach.

She picked him up and set him on her hip. Her eyes widened at the sight of Tinker standing on the threshold holding two paper bags from her favorite barbecue place.

"Piggy!" Will said.

"Tinker." He pointed at himself.

Abby internally shook herself and tried to scoop up what remaining wits she had. "Hi. What are you doing here?"

"I ran into Katherine and asked how today went. She said it seemed to go well, but you might be a little overwhelmed with all the information you got. I figured I'd take a chance you weren't up for making dinner."

He held up the bags from Porky's Pit Stop, the fat cartoon pig chowing down on a rib. That always struck her as wrong.

"If you've already got it covered, it'll keep in the fridge till tomorrow," he added.

She shook her head and opened the door wider, sweeping her arm out in invitation. "I was in the middle of ordering pizza, so this is a lot better. Thank you."

She shut the door, slid the deadbolt, and set Will down. "Go wash your hands for dinner."

He ran off yelling "piggy" at the top of his lungs. She shook her head and led the way into the kitchen. Every nerve ending in her body seemed to be tuned to his presence at her back. It felt electric, like a current running between them. Which was ridiculous. He was just a guy who happened to make her clit pulse *one* time.

He set the bags down on the counter and started unpacking them.

"This is a lot of food," she said.

"I wasn't sure what you'd like, so I got one of everything."

Her mouth fell open. There were at least half a dozen options on the menu, and that didn't include the sandwiches. "You're staying to help eat this, right? We'll never be able to get through all this."

He stopped, arm still in a bag, and looked at her. "You good with that?"

Oh. She'd just invited him to dinner. On one hand, it seemed mean not to invite him when he'd gone out of the way to bring her food, and good food at that. On the other, she wasn't sure why he'd done it or what he hoped to get out of it. Was there an ulterior motive? Was it an apology for ghosting her before?

"I won't stay," he said.

Abby shook her head. "No, stay. It's fine."

"You're thinking about it too hard for it to be fine," he said.

"I just—" She took a deep breath. "I'm not sure why you're doing this."

He stepped closer, crowding her against the counter. "I like you."

She cocked her head. "Yeah. And? Now I have two kids instead of only one."

Tinker brushed a strand of hair over her shoulder. The tip of his nail grazed the side of her neck, and all she wanted to do was lean into it. To ask for more. But she had more to think about than just what she wanted.

"I fucked up. I'm sorry. I don't have an excuse. I don't get involved with women who have kids. It hasn't been a great experience. The women want a father figure for the kid, and the kid gets attached. Everyone's heart gets broken, but especially the kid's. It's not fair to the kid."

"What makes this so different?" She understood what he was saying. It was one reason she'd been so anti-dating, especially since Will was still so young. She didn't want Will to get attached to someone who would leave.

"You."

"Me? That's it?"

One corner of his mouth tilted up. "That's all I got." He brushed his thumb against her cheekbone and stepped back, putting some space between them. "For tonight, we'll keep it simple. Tell them I'm a friend you invited over for dinner. You've had friends over for dinner before, right?"

Abby crossed her arms. "Yeah, but not friends who are men."

"You don't have any friends who are guys?" He went back to unloading to-go containers.

"Work friends, but not personal friends."

"Why not?"

"Because inevitably being friends isn't enough and they want to sleep with me, then get mad when they're 'friend zoned.'" She emphasized with air quotes. "So, I don't bother."

His grin grew. "I want to sleep with you. But I won't pretend to be your friend to get in your bed. You'll let me in when you're ready."

Her mouth worked to make words, but no sound came out.

"You should let the kids know dinner's ready." He swatted her on the butt and started opening cabinets. "Where do you keep your plates?"

POST DINNER

inker plunged the scrub brush into the soapy water, then ran it over the plate to remove the stuck-on bits of barbecue. He glanced to his right where Olivia rinsed and placed the clean dishes on the drain board.

She hadn't said much at dinner to anyone other than Will. He'd caught her glaring in his direction a few times with assessing eyes that had seen too much in her short twelve years.

"You have some questions for me?" he asked.

"How long have you known Abby?" There was an accusing edge to her voice.

"About a month, I think." He shut off the water and dried his hands on a dish towel.

"Are you dating?"

"Not yet, but I'd like to."

She crossed her arms and leaned against the far counter of the galley-style kitchen. "Does Abby want to date you?"

He suppressed a smile. "I hope so, but that's up to her."

"Why were you here on Friday?"

He leaned against the opposite counter and slid his hands

into his pockets. "I'm friends with Katherine and we work together in the same organization."

"What organization?" she asked.

"Veterans Against Child Abuse. We help kids feel safe again, especially when they have to testify in court. We go with them so they know they have someone there to protect them. That's how Katherine knew who to call—she's helped other kids and families."

"And that's your job?" she asked.

"No. I work for a company as a security specialist. I volunteer with VACA."

"Are there other guys like you who volunteer?"

He nodded. "Lots."

She chewed on that bit of information—literally biting at her lip. Finally, she asked, "Are they all as scary looking as you?"

He grinned. "Scarier."

A shriek split the air, and Will came running into the kitchen in only his underwear.

"William, get your nekkid butt back in here!" Abby chased after him, holding what appeared to be his pajamas.

Will shriek-laughed and ran through the kitchen, around the living room, and back to the kitchen. Tinker caught him around the middle and tossed him into the air, eliciting another high-pitched laugh.

He settled him in his arm. "I think your mama wants you to put some clothes on, Little Man."

"Again! Throw me again!" Will kicked his feet and Tink shifted him to the side, so his pointy little feet didn't take out his manhood.

"How about you put on your pj's, and I'll throw you..." He glanced at Abby, who held up two fingers. "Two more times."

"Okay." Will wiggled and kicked to be put down. Tink handed him over to Abby, who held him like a sack of grain under her arm.

"Come on, Monster. We'll fly back to your room and put some clothes on. Then Mr. Tinker can toss you."

Will stuck his arms straight out in front of him as Abby rushed back down the hall. Shit, what did she lift? He could only imagine the strength it took to wrestle a wriggling little boy every day.

A short time later, Will ran back down the hall in dinosaur pj's and demanded Tink throw him. He kept his word and threw him an extra time for good measure.

Olivia offered to read to Will before bed, giving Tink a steady look before taking Will upstairs.

Abby collapsed on the couch and rested her head on the back cushion, eyes closed.

Tinker sat next to her, facing her. "Is he always that energetic?"

"Yes. He always gets a huge burst of energy right before bed."

A large black, shorthaired cat jumped on the back of the couch and meowed, rubbing its head against Abby's.

"Who's this?" he asked.

"This is Fuzzbutt Noodlehead."

That was unexpected. "Fuzz what?"

She smiled and opened her eyes, shifting so she could scratch the cat under its chin. "Fuzzbutt Noodlehead. I don't even remember where the name came from. I think my mom suggested it as a joke, and Will loved it and wouldn't agree to anything else. So now he's Fuzzbutt."

"What about Will's dad?"

Abby shifted her gaze from the cat to him. He could see the wheels turning in her head, trying to decide how much to share. Finally, she blew out a breath and twisted her body to face him, tucking her legs under her.

"I divorced his biological father before Will was born." She rested her arm on the back of the couch and propped her head in her hand.

He knew there was more to the story. Her tone was challenging, likely to see if she could scare him off again. "You don't seem like the kind of woman to deny a good dad access to his kid. What happened?"

Her mouth twisted. "It was an accidental pregnancy. He wanted me to terminate—said it was him or the baby. I chose Will."

"Motherfucker." He never planned to have kids, but if it happened, he sure as fuck would take care of his child.

"Pretty much." She lowered her hand and scratched Fuzzbutt again. "I moved here. Went back to school for my teaching degree while I was pregnant."

"Why Charleston?" he asked.

"My mom retired here after my dad passed away. She had a couple of friends who lived here at the time. She offered to move in with me to help with rent and Will after he was born."

"And Olivia and Will have the same father."

She nodded. "I still can't believe I didn't know about her. Who does that? Who abandons their child?"

"You'd be surprised at the number of assholes who do," he said bitterly.

Her eyes, a deep whiskey color, searched his face. It felt like she was searching for his soul, cataloging every flaw and chink he had.

She smiled softly. "What about you? Why Charleston?"

The vat of rage he kept a tight lid on bubbled and hissed. He worked to keep his voice even and steady. "We moved for Dani when I was in high school. There was a dance coach here she wanted to train with."

"Dance?" she asked. "I thought she was an MMA fighter."

"She is, but when she was younger, she was an internationally ranked ballroom dancer." He was still so proud of her accomplishments, but the anger and disappointment swirled and mixed with pride until he couldn't tell where one ended and the other began.

"How did she go from dancing to fighting?"

That he wouldn't get into. Couldn't. "It's a long and complicated story for some other time."

She searched his face again. "Okay. Thank you again for dinner."

"You're welcome." He picked up a strand of hair on her shoulder, rubbing the silky strand between his fingers. "I'd like a do-over. I know I messed up the first time. I want to make it up to you."

Abby leaned back slightly and straightened her spine. "Why now? Nothing about my situation has changed. In fact, the situation is significantly more complicated than before."

Tinker ran a hand over his short hair. "I...don't have a good reason. Not one that won't make me sound like a complete and total asshole, anyway." He took a breath. "I've made it a point not to get involved with women with kids. Not because of baggage or exes or baby daddies."

While he thought about how to say what he needed to say, Abby asked, "Then why?"

"Because kids get attached and then they get hurt. Adults go into things knowing there's a risk. Kids? All they know is one day you're gone. I'm not going to put a kid through that if I can avoid it."

"But you're willing to put Will through it?"

"I'm willing to take the risk."

Olivia cleared her throat as she stood at the end of the hall. "Will is asleep."

"Thank you, sweetie. Do you want to watch a movie?" Abby asked.

"I'm going to read in my room, if that's okay," Olivia said.

"Of course."

Olivia turned, paused, and turned back. "I'll have my earbuds in listening to music. Loud."

Abby stared at her retreating form. He grinned as a deep blush spread across her cheeks as she realized what Olivia had implied.

She looked at him, wide-eyed. "Did she just tell us she wouldn't be able to hear us making out?"

"I think she did."

She lowered her gaze and the blush spread higher on her cheeks. "That's not… We don't…" She cleared her throat.

He was so far out of his depth. In any other situation, he'd drag her across his lap and kiss her until she forgot to be nervous or embarrassed. But implied permission or not, he wasn't going to get X-rated on her couch with two kids in the house.

"And it's not only Will anymore, it's Olivia too. So why are you willing to risk hurting them?"

Her words doused every single iota of arousal building.

Tinker looked down the hall Olivia had disappeared down. "Because that girl showed up at your door and you didn't hesitate for even a minute."

"I hesitated plenty," Abby said.

Tinker picked up a strand of her hair again, twirling the end around his finger, the silky strand smooth against the rough pad. "Not in a way that mattered. You're rearranging your whole life to protect her. That makes *you* someone worth taking a risk for."

Abby gaped at him. "I…I don't know what to say to that."

"Say you'll go on another date with me."

She took a deep breath. "I can't."

Tinker pressed his lips together and let the strand of hair fall from his fingers. It had been a long shot. He'd blown it the first time, walking away when he'd learned about Will. She had no reason to trust him. No reason to think he'd do anything different.

He nodded. "I understand. I'll still help, through VACA or Katherine. Whatever you need."

"I can't for at least the next two weeks."

"What?"

"We're working on the Spring Showcase as soon as we go back to school on Monday, and it's going to have all my attention for the next two weeks," she said.

"What's the Spring Showcase?"

"The art and drama departments have an evening where there are short drama performances, with costumes created by the fashion students and scenery from the art students. There's also an art and fashion exhibition in the main foyer and theater foyer."

"It sounds like a lot of work," he said.

"It is. It's a big deal for the seniors because we invite recruiters from some of the top colleges and institutes in the country, even some from overseas. It's not unusual for several students to receive scholarships from the portfolios they present."

"All this happens after school, right?"

"Most of it," she said. "Some of it happens during the day."

That damn strand of hair beckoned again. "Who watches Will?"

"My mom."

He nodded absentmindedly. He could work with two weeks. It would give him time to rebuild her trust. A hint of a plan formulated in his mind. One that would convince her he was serious and he meant what he'd said.

"Abby." He tugged on the strand of hair again.

"Mm hmm?"

"Why don't you walk me out?"

Her eyes widened slightly. "Oh. Okay. Sure."

He stood and took her hand to pull her up. He kept her hand in his until they were outside and he'd pulled the door shut behind them.

"You really are amazing, you know that, right?"

She scoffed. "No, I'm not."

It killed him she couldn't see it. That her fuckwad ex-husband had walked away from her and his kid. "Yes. You are. For one, you're raising a son, by yourself."

She shrugged. "Lots of women do that."

"You took in a kid that isn't even yours. That you have no ties or loyalty to," he said, as if she hadn't spoken.

"What was I supposed to do? Hand her back to her aunt and abusive uncle? Put her in the foster care system?"

He couldn't help grinning. She was seriously sexy when she got fired up. "A lot of people would have, yeah."

"Well, I'm not a lot of people," she said.

"Exactly."

Her lips moved and he knew he had her, even if she didn't see anything extraordinary in what she'd done. "What's the second one?"

"Second what?" he asked.

"Second reason. You said, 'for one.'"

"Oh, yeah. That kiss."

Her gaze dropped to his lips, and he caught her short intake of breath.

"That kiss I haven't been able to get out of my head." He wrapped his hands around her hips and pulled her closer. "That kiss lives rent free in my mind on repeat. Every now and then I imagine where things would have gone if we hadn't been interrupted. Would you have let me slide my fingers under the edge of your panties? Would you have let me kneel between your legs and flick your clit with my tongue?"

"Christian," she said on a gasp, her breath warm on his lips.

"Would you have said my name like that while you ground your wet pussy against my face?"

"Holy fudge. It's lust," she whispered.

"Maybe." His mouth was so close to hers that his lips brushed against hers when he spoke. "But I've been in lust, and this is way more than simple lust. You know it too, even if you're not ready to admit it."

"And if it is only lust?"

"Then I'll have the memory of you riding my face to keep me happy well into my old age." He sealed their lips together. He slid his hand down over her jeans into the crease of her ass, and he swallowed her groan. He wasn't blowing smoke just to get her to agree. He knew lust and whatever this was, it was a fuck ton more than that.

She hiked her leg up over his hip and wrapped her arms around his neck. She felt it too.

He wanted to strip her naked, wrap her legs around his waist, and bury hilt deep in her waiting heat. He couldn't even fool himself into thinking one time would get her out of his system. Abby wasn't a scratch to itch.

Tearing his mouth away, he pressed his forehead to hers and tried to get his breathing under control. He panted like he'd run a five-miler and all they'd done was kiss.

"I didn't plan for that to get out of hand," he said.

"What was your plan?" She sounded just as winded.

"Sweet, chaste kiss. Tell you I'll call you tomorrow and to sleep tight."

"Jesus. If this is your idea of sweet and chaste, I'm not sure I can handle dirty and raunchy."

He lifted his head and smirked. "I think you'll do just fine."

She blushed and licked her lips. His gaze followed the track of her tongue as it slipped back into her mouth. Fuck, he needed to leave before he did exactly what he told her he wanted to.

"We'll pick this back up in two weeks." He gave her a quick, hard kiss, refusing to linger like he wanted to. "I'll call you tomorrow. Sleep tight."

She laughed and pushed him away. "Goodnight."

THE NEXT DAY

Abby inhaled deeply and stretched. She felt the warm, heavy press of a body next to hers and glanced over.

Will's dark head peaked out from beneath the covers. She sighed. She loved that he still crawled into bed with her, but at the same time, it would be nice if he stayed in his own bed occasionally. Especially if, at some point in the future, there might be another person in bed with her.

Whoa. She pumped the breaks on that thought, even as she remembered their kiss last night. And his words. Sweet merciful Mary, he had a dirty mouth. But if he lived up to his promises… A delicious shiver traveled down her back.

She glanced at Will. The logistics of finding time for Tinker to do any of the things he said was hard to imagine. It was hard enough figuring out her day-to-day life, never mind adding another adult with their own needs, schedule, and priorities. She'd tried dating after Will had turned one, but it had been too hard to find the time to date anyone seriously.

The most she'd managed was four dates with a guy who managed one of the tour companies downtown. She'd fallen asleep on their last date, which was supposed to have been the

Netflix and chill date. He'd called her the next day and told her he didn't think it would work out. She'd agreed and that had been the last time she'd seriously considered another romantic relationship.

She kissed the top of Will's head and threw back the covers. Tea first. *Then* existential crisis.

Padding down the hall, she peeked into Olivia's room but found it empty—the bed neatly made. In the kitchen, Olivia was putting the clean silverware away.

"Good morning," Abby said.

Olivia glanced over her shoulder and closed the drawer. "Morning."

"Thank you for emptying the dishwasher." Abby flipped the button on the kettle and pulled her steeper from the cabinet. "You didn't have to."

Olivia shrugged. "It was one of my chores at home with my mom. She ran it at night, and I'd empty it in the morning."

"What other chores did you have?"

"I had to put away my clothes when they were clean, set the table for dinner, and keep my room clean."

"Did she pay you an allowance?"

"Five dollars a week." Olivia sat at the counter and picked at her cuticles.

"That seems fair." Abby measured tea into the steeper. "What do you usually eat for breakfast?"

"Cereal mostly, but Mom would make pancakes on Saturday."

She didn't mention what her aunt and uncle would do. She was probably left to her own devices, but Abby didn't want to press. It was the first time Olivia had given her any answer other than "whatever" or "it doesn't matter."

"We do waffles on Saturday—is that okay? Will likes to put the syrup in all the little squares."

Olivia smiled. "I like to do that too."

Abby smiled back. "We can alternate between pancakes and waffles, but I'm warning you now: Will won't eat pancakes unless they have a whipped cream face, and then he pretends he's a dinosaur devouring his poor pancake people."

And that got a small laugh.

"What kind of cereal do you like? I don't keep sugary cereals but if there's something that's your absolute favorite, we can get it."

"The most sugary cereal my mom would let me have was honey-nut O's."

"I think your mom and I had a lot in common."

Olivia's gaze fell back to her hands. It was probably too soon to be talking about how she and her mom were similar.

Abby cleared her throat. "You're in luck. We have honey-nut." She pulled the box from the pantry and set it on the counter, then got two bowls, spoons, and the milk jug.

"Thank you." Olivia poured cereal into one of the bowls and added milk.

Abby took a pen and notepad from the junk drawer. "What kind of food do you like for dinner? It'll be nice cooking for someone else who will eat more than five bites before they're full." She mock glared at Olivia. "Or are you one of those people?"

Olivia shook her head. "I like a lot of foods. Mom had a rule that I had to try a little bit of everything she made."

"That's good. Anything you're allergic to?"

"No."

Abby nodded and drafted out a menu for the rest of the week and the grocery list for it.

Olivia finished her cereal, rinsed her bowl and spoon, and put them in the dishwasher.

Abby bit her lip. Hopefully Olivia wasn't doing all these things to be on her best behavior or because she thought Abby would kick her out if she did anything wrong.

"I'm going to take a quick shower before Will wakes up," Abby said.

"Okay. Can I watch TV?"

"Of course."

They were going to have to have a conversation about Olivia asking permission for everything. Rules were important, but so were expectations. Olivia was still so nervous and defensive. It was going to take time for her to feel completely comfortable. She was feeling Abby out as much as Abby was feeling her out, but having some ground rules would help.

She showered, forgoing washing her hair for one more day. Will wasn't in her bed when she left the bathroom. She dressed quickly and grabbed her cell from the nightstand, knowing he'd probably sweet-talked his way into eating in the living room in front of the TV. Sure enough, he was at the coffee table, eating and watching a kids' show.

"Will. What is the rule?"

His eyes widened as he tried for a look of innocence. "Olivia said I could."

"But you know better. The rules don't change just because there's someone else here. At the counter or the dining room table." She tilted her head in that direction.

"But Mommy—"

"William. Now, please."

"Yes, ma'am." He picked up his bowl and carefully carried it into the kitchen.

"He's—"

Olivia was paper white, curled up in a ball in the corner of the couch, tears streaming down her cheeks and a look of stark terror on her face.

"I'm sorry," she whispered. "He said he was allowed. I thought it was okay."

"Olivia." Abby took a step toward the couch. Olivia curled in on herself even more.

Abby stopped. "Livie, honey, I'm not mad. I didn't think to tell you he needed to eat in the kitchen. I should have told you."

Olivia's gaze darted from Abby to the hall. Shit in a handbasket—what had those people done to her? She wanted nothing more than to pull her in a tight hug and tell her it would all be okay. But she knew Olivia wouldn't—couldn't—take the comfort in her current state.

"I'm going to go into the kitchen with Will," she said softly. "When you're ready, why don't you join us and we'll talk about our plans for the day, okay?"

Abby didn't wait for a response. Olivia needed space and time. Lots of time.

Will was slurping the last of his milk from the bowl and several drips slid down his chin onto his pj top.

He lowered the bowl and smacked his lips. "Ah." And burped.

"What do you say?" she asked.

"Dee-licious."

Her lips twitched. "Excuse you. I think you've been spending too much time at Timmy's." His best friend was the fourth of five boys. Saying their house was hectic was putting it mildly.

"Go wash your face and get dressed, Bubs. Pj's in the laundry."

"Okay." He hopped down from the stool and looked at her. "Did I get Livie in trouble?"

Jeez, this kid. She squatted so they were eye level. "No, Baby. She isn't in trouble. But you know the rules. It's not nice to trick Livie, okay? She doesn't know all the rules yet, and it scared her when she thought she was in trouble. You have to help her until she knows what's allowed and what's not. That's a really big job —do you think you can do that?"

He nodded enthusiastically. "I want Livie to stay with us."

"I do too, Bubs. We're going to work really hard to make that happen. Now, go change. Maw Maw will be here soon."

He skipped out of the kitchen.

Abby sighed and stood. Her cell phone pinged. She glanced at the screen and smiled when she saw Tinker's name.

Morning beautiful. How's your day going
so far?

Should she be honest or gloss over Olivia's mini meltdown? What the hell? He already knew how crazy her life was, and it wasn't like any of it had run him off yet. Plus, he might have some advice.

Great. Until it wasn't.

Her phone rang almost immediately. She clicked the green dot.

"Hey," she said.

"Hey. What's going on?"

She laid out the events of the short morning. "She just needs time."

"And therapy. Have you been able to get her an appointment? We have a psychologist we use frequently. She may be able to help until you can get her in somewhere."

"We have an appointment on Thursday. I hope we'll be okay until then."

"You've got this."

She appreciated the vote of confidence. "Thanks for calling."

"You're welcome." His deep voice rumbled through her head, soothing the rough edges of the morning. "Let me know if you need anything today."

"I will," she said. Olivia appeared in the kitchen and hovered as if afraid to come closer. "I need to go."

"Later," he said.

"Bye." She ended the call and lowered the phone. "You okay?"

"I'm sorry," Olivia said. "For how I reacted and for letting Will eat in the living room. I should have known better."

Abby set her phone on the counter. "Olivia, I'm not angry—not even at Will. I'm annoyed because he took advantage of you, but I'm not angry. You've only been here a few days, and I don't expect you to know all the rules. We'll sit down tonight and have a family meeting. We can go over my expectations, your expectations, and the schedule for next week when school starts back and I'm at work. Okay?"

Olivia nodded. "Okay."

"Okay. My mom should be here in a little bit. Do you have any questions before she gets here?"

"What should I call her?"

"Will calls her Maw Maw, but let's start with Ms. Sue for now. That's what all her kids called her."

"Her kids?" Olivia asked.

"She was an elementary teacher. First through third."

"Is that why you became a teacher?"

"Partly. Mostly it was because no one was paying for private art lessons or hiring docents. As an art teacher, I still get to create things, but I also get kids excited about art and help them realize it's more than just portraits of fruit bowls."

Olivia smiled. "Will I go to the school where you teach?"

"I hope so. It would make things infinitely easier. Usually, kids have to apply and send in a portfolio if their focus is art or take a placement test if it's for math or science."

"I'm really good at math," Olivia said. "I took pre-algebra at my school in Kentucky."

"Really?"

"Yeah. The guidance counselor was good. She had the school test me and put me in the advanced class."

"I'll send her an email later today to get your records."

"You hoo! Anyone home?" Abby's mom called from the front door.

"We're in the kitchen, Mom."

Her mom came in and kissed her on the cheek. "Hey, Hon."

"Hey, Mom."

Her mom turned to Olivia. "You must be Olivia."

"Yes, ma'am." Olivia wrung her hands. "It's nice to meet you."

"None of that ma'am stuff. You call me Maw Maw, just like Will. Come here." She pulled Olivia into the tight hug Abby had wanted to give her and kissed her head.

Olivia froze for a moment, then wrapped her arms tight around Sue's waist. And cried.

"Jesus. I can't imagine what that poor girl has gone through," her mom said softly.

They trailed behind Olivia and Will as Will dragged Olivia to his favorite aquarium exhibits.

"She doesn't have any other family?"

Abby shook her head. "Just Tony."

Her mom glanced at her. "And there's no chance...?"

She inhaled and stared blankly at the tank in front of them. It was something she and the social worker had talked about. "Tony signed away his rights. The social worker is going to try reaching out on the off chance he'll change his mind. But I don't think he will. If forced, I think he'd turn her over to the State."

"What did the lawyer...Margaret...say?

"Magda. She said say nothing to no one," Abby said.

"But?" her mom prompted.

"But, Erin, the social worker, thinks I should try to reach out to him. That I might be able to talk him into taking Olivia."

"And?" her mom prompted.

"Can I admit something ugly?" Abby asked.

"About Olivia?"

"Kind of. I'm worried he's going to say yes. And if he says yes to Olivia, he's going to want access to Will."

"That would not be great," her mom said.

"I don't want him in our lives. Even if he doesn't want anything to do with Will, I'm not going to wash my hands of Olivia and send her off with him. But should I try talking to him?" She looked at her mom. "Am I being selfish by not reaching out to him? For Olivia's sake?"

"Do you think it will make a difference?"

Abby shook her head. "No. If anything, I think it would drive him to be vindictive in some way."

"If the roles were reversed, would you want me or Naomi or Lindsey to reach out to him about Will if anything happened to you?"

"Hell, no." There was no doubt in her mind. Naomi was her secondary guardian if anything happened to her or her mom. Tony had never even been a consideration in her guardianship plan. "I wouldn't want to subject Will to that kind of rejection or emotional damage."

"Then go with the lawyer's advice. Don't say nothing to no one," her mom said. "It's not selfish to want to protect yourself and Will. Or Olivia. But I wouldn't be your mother if I didn't ask: are you sure you're up for this? It's a lot—taking on a preteen girl."

Abby smiled sardonically. "I'm not sure at all. But I know I can't hand her back over to her aunt or put her in foster care. We're the closest thing she has to family. Will *is* her family by blood. I don't have any illusions this will be easy. Or quick. But I can't turn my back on her."

Her mom stopped and rubbed Abby's arms. "I'd be very disappointed if you did. I'm here when you need me. However you need me. It'll be nice to have a granddaughter."

Abby smiled and tears pricked her eyes as relief washed through her. She'd been worried. She shouldn't have been, her mother was one of the most giving and accepting people she knew, but there was always the small chance she'd tell Abby she was making a mistake.

"Thank you," she whispered.

"You're welcome," her mom said.

They turned and trailed after the kids again.

"I do have a favor to ask. A small one."

"What's that?"

"I might need you to babysit in a couple of weeks. After the showcase."

"Of course. Is this the man from the coffee date?" her mother asked.

"Uh…it's someone else," Abby said.

"Ooh. Look at you. Dates with two different men so close together."

"Don't get excited. It's Christian."

"Christian, the man who didn't call you after I caught you on the porch kissing, Christian? The man you were so disappointed about because you knew he wasn't going to call you back? That Christian?"

"Could you please stop saying Christian?"

"Well, that's his name, isn't it? What else should I call him? Tinker? That's a ridiculous name for a grown man." Her mom could be like a dog with its favorite chew toy when she sank her teeth into something.

"Yes, that's him. He helped me when Olivia showed up."

"Helped how?"

"He gave me Katherine's number, who set me up with the social worker and helped get the ball rolling to get legal guardianship of Olivia."

"Did he?"

"Yes, Mom. He did. Can you watch the kids?"

"I suppose. But he has to come in the house and introduce himself properly," her mom said.

"Please don't embarrass me," Abby begged.

"When have I ever embarrassed you?"

"Oh, I don't know…Homecoming, Junior Prom, Senior

Prom. That time I brought Phil home from college for Thanksgiving break."

"How did I embarrass you with Phil?" Her mom looked offended.

"Mom, you asked him if he was gay."

"Well, wasn't he?"

"That's not the point. It was embarrassing," Abby said.

"You were embarrassed because you didn't know and thought he was there as a love interest."

It was a moment she relived occasionally, like the ghost of mortifications past snuck into her room late at night to laugh at her.

"Again, not the point. Just please promise you won't do anything embarrassing."

"I'm sorry, dear. I love you, but it's my job as your mother to embarrass you as often as possible."

"Ugh." Abby dropped her head back and stared up at the life-size blue whale model hanging from the ceiling. "I'm putting you in a home the first chance I get."

"Just make sure it's a nice one." Her mom patted her shoulder and caught up with the kids.

GOOD NIGHT

How was your day?

*A*bby smiled. She'd been waiting for his nightly text. He'd messaged her every night since he'd brought them dinner.

Pretty good. Lindsey came over for dinner and we were able to catch up.

Did she go somewhere during your break?

Vegas for a cousin's wedding.

Sounds fun.

It's not really my scene.

What have you got going on next week?

I have to call around for a handyman and electrician and hope someone has availability in the next two weeks.

Why?

For the school showcase.

You don't have people at the school to do that?

Not really. Our design teacher usually directs them, but she had to take emergency medical leave and we're kind of in a lurch.

The students came up with some complicated sets and exhibits this year and it's outside the scope of anyone else's expertise.

So I'm calling around at the last minute.

Can you talk?

Uh...sure.

Her phone rang immediately. "Hey."

"Hey. Why kind of stuff do you need done?" he asked, by way of greeting.

"Help building the sets and running the electric for the displays."

"It doesn't sound too difficult. How long is the other teacher out?" he asked.

"Well, she's about eight months pregnant and was put on bedrest over spring break, so at least until the end of the school year."

"And you don't think any of the other teachers can help? What about custodial staff?"

"They're great, don't get me wrong, but they are 'the AC or

heating isn't working' type of custodial staff. We have an IT department, but they're limited to audio-visual support, making sure the Wi-Fi works, and kids can log in to their devices."

"Don't parents usually help with that sort of thing? Isn't there an overachieving PTA president or something? Or do they run bake sales and ban books?"

Abby laughed. "No book bans, thankfully. We've got progressive families. And the PTA pretty much just runs bake sales and teacher appreciation day. We have parents who volunteer their time, but it's a lot of lift and the parents who have volunteered don't have the expertise we need and the parents who have the expertise don't have the time to volunteer. Thus, calling around tomorrow."

"I know some people. Give me a day – I'll make some calls and see who owes me a favor," he said.

"That's really not necessary. Gloria, the Design teacher, gave me some numbers to call. I didn't mean to unload on you."

"Abby. I wouldn't offer to help if I didn't want to. What time do you need someone there?"

Abby picked at the comforter. It would save her a lot of time and headache if he knew people already. She hated relying on him, or really anyone, for things like this. It always felt like taking advantage.

"Abby? You there?"

"Yes, sorry. Ideally, tomorrow around three. We have a meeting to review the plans we made before the break and to discuss our objectives, do a walk through, and figure out what's manageable," she said.

"Alright. I'll get you some help tomorrow," he said.

"Thank you." She didn't want the conversation to end. It was the first time she'd heard his voice since he'd brought them dinner. "How was your day?"

"Kind of boring. I'm lead for an event, so I've been focusing on the security plan for that."

She snuggled down into her pillow. "What does that involve? I don't know anything about your job."

"It's not anything exciting. Making sure we have enough people to cover the entrance and keep an eye on things."

"What kind of event is it? Or can you tell me?"

His long, deep sigh came through the phone. "It's a sweet sixteen."

"Like a birthday party, sweet sixteen?"

His voice was thick with his disgruntlement. "That's the one."

"Who hires security for a birthday party? I mean, other than Beyonce?"

"Rich people who want to show off."

"That's ridiculous," she said.

"No argument from me, but it's still a job. Sometimes it's planning security for a birthday party, sometimes it's storming a castle in Crimea."

"Storming a what, where?" she asked.

"One of our jobs last year involved infiltrating a castle in Crimea. That is a job I can't say much about. It's one of those things that never really happened."

"So, super-secret."

"More along the lines of not wanting to pay the legal fees for violating the NDA," he said.

"Got it. What about VACA. How are you involved with them?" It was a question she'd been wondering for a while.

"Katherine organizes all that. She's never shared the details, but I get the sense she didn't have the greatest childhood. It was her and Pothole at the beginning. They started as foster parents, saw a need, and filled it."

"Pothole?"

He chuckled. "Katherine's husband, David."

"Why is he called Pothole?"

"It was before my time, but the story goes he was rolling

down the street and saw Katherine. Turned his head to check her out and hit a pothole. Laid his bike down hard and that's how they met."

"Was he in the military, too?"

"Yeah," he said.

"Did you serve together?"

"No, he was Army. I did a short stint in the Marines," he said.

"What was that like?" She didn't know anyone personally who had served in the military. All she knew was what she saw in films and on TV, which was probably only fifty percent accurate, if she had to guess.

"It was what I needed to do at the time. I was seventeen and needed a way to support Dani. Military was the best option for a kid fresh out of high school with a chip on his shoulder, no marketable skills, and pissed off at the world. The Marine recruiter was the first one to greet me when I walked into the recruiting office."

"That must have been hard. Dani's very lucky to have a brother like you." She couldn't imagine being responsible for another human being at seventeen. Hell, half the time she was surprised they'd let her go home from the hospital with Will.

Tinker cleared his throat. "Yeah. How's Olivia settling in? Did she start school?"

She sensed he didn't want to talk about the situation anymore, whether from being uncomfortable with the subject or embarrassed by her praise, but she let him change the topic.

"She's good. She starts tomorrow. We were able to get her into most of the classes she was interested in," she said.

"What classes wasn't she able to get in?"

"Design, for obvious reasons. She has to take theater instead. She hasn't said anything, but I don't think she's too keen about performing in front of people."

"Don't blame her. I hated getting up in front of people in school."

"I find that surprising. You strike me as the class clown type," she said.

"You're not wrong, but there's a difference between being a cut up and having to perform on command for people."

"True. We're far enough into the school year where she won't have to do anything big. They're changing units in a week or so and they'll be doing video production for the rest of the year."

"That's more my speed," he said.

"Made a few movies have you?"

Tinker chuckled low. "I may have made a few private home movies."

A flush ran through her body and her comforter felt heavy and warm against her bare legs.

"What about you?" he asked. "Any fantasy roles you've starred in?"

"I—. It's not—. Not—."

Tinker laughed. "I'm kidding. I've never made any home movies. Too much shit on the internet as it is. Don't need someone getting pissed off and posting my ass for the world to see."

Her body still felt unusually warm. "I don't even know what to say to that."

"I might be willing to make an exception for you though." His voice was deep and low. Intimate.

An image flashed through her mind—her and Tinker in a bed, a camera on a tripod pointed at them. She didn't think it was possible to feel even hotter, but a bead of sweat formed at her temple. "I—. I'm—."

Tinker laughed again. "Good night, Abby."

"Good night." Her voice came out high pitched and squeaky as the phone went dead. She stared at the blank screen for several seconds before tossing it on the bedside table.

He was diabolical. He put that image in her head and then

just said goodnight. Like she was supposed to get any sleep with thoughts of his bare ass moving up and down. Clenching as he thrust.

Oh god. She flipped the lamp off and flopped down on her side, punching the pillow for good measure. It was a long while before her brain shut off and she was able to fall asleep.

HERE TO HELP

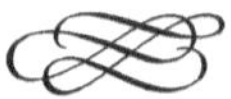

*T*inker watched as the man behind the reception desk punched a few numbers on the phone, messed up, hung up, and started the whole process over again.

He glanced up at Tinker before turning his chair slightly and cupping his hand around the mouthpiece of the receiver. It didn't help.

"Can you come to the front office, please? There are some..." He glanced at Tinker from the corner of his eye. "Some people here to see you.

"I don't care! Just get here now!" He replaced the receiver in the cradle and turned back to the front, now with the fakest smile Tinker had ever seen plastered on his face.

"She'll be a moment." He folded his hands primly on the desk.

"Uh-huh. Thanks." Tinker knocked on the counter and the guy jumped. Tinker rejoined James and Ben at the front of the reception office.

They'd both agreed to meet Abby to discuss helping with her showcase. He'd sent her a couple of messages earlier in the afternoon to let her know but hadn't heard back. She probably wouldn't be comfortable with two strange guys showing up, saying *we're here to help*, so he'd come to help with introductions.

"Jumpy little fella," James said.

"Think it's the vests?" Nick asked in a low voice.

"Could be," James said. "Could be he's just twitchy."

Tinker grunted as movement at the door caught his attention. Abby and another woman pushed through the glass door. Abby's hair was twisted up and held with a clip, a pencil sticking out of the knot.

She glanced between the twitchy guy behind the counter and Tinker. "Hi...what are you doing here?"

"You said you needed help with your showcase," he said.

"Uh, I did. Who are they?"

He pointed at the man next to him. "This is Nick, he's an electrician, and this is James, he's a wood working genius. I sent you a couple of messages earlier about them coming, but I guess you didn't get them."

She shook her head. "I've had my phone on silent all day."

A door with a placard that read "Principal" opened, and a man in a suit and tie exited with a couple who stared at the group of men with startled expressions.

"Uh...Phillip, can you please escort Mr. and Mrs. Garcia out?" the suit asked the guy at the reception desk.

"Of course," Phillip said, standing quickly and gesturing for the couple to follow.

Tinker and his friends stepped back so the couple could pass. Abby's mouth twisted as they walked by, but he wasn't sure why.

"Abby," the suit said. "Who are your guests?"

Abby squared her shoulders. "Oh, right. They're here to help with the showcase. Since Penny is out on maternity leave, we need outside help this year. They've kindly cleared their schedules to help. This is Christian, and Nick, and James." She pointed at each man in turn. "Gentlemen, this is the principal of the school, Isaac Newton."

James, the oldest of them, held out his hand. "Your parents were physicists?"

Newton smiled wryly and shook James's hand. "No, but they had high hopes for me. Unfortunately, theoretical physics didn't interest me, and I went into mechanical engineering before switching to teaching. We really appreciate your help, gentlemen. This showcase is a big deal for a lot of our students and the highlight of our school year. The school doesn't have a football team, but if we did, this would be our homecoming game.

"Abby and Naomi can take you to the conference room for the planning meeting. We can get your information after to get you into our system so you can just sign in next time you're here." He looked at Abby and Naomi. "Abby, you have lead on the showcase this year, right?"

She nodded. "Uh-huh."

"Great. If you want to escort our guests to the conference room, you can catch me up later. I need to wrap up a few administrative things, so I won't be at the meeting."

"Okay." She shared a look with the other woman, Naomi, as Newton walked away.

Naomi leaned close and said in a low voice, "Maybe he's getting laid."

Abby smiled and smacked her on the shoulder. "Stop."

"Do you have a better explanation?" she asked.

"Stop," she repeated, laughing.

Phillip returned to the office and nervously walked through the group.

Abby looked at them. "Are you comfortable leaving your driver's licenses here so Phillip can put you in the system?"

Tinker shrugged and looked at James and Nick. They both shrugged and pulled out their wallets and licenses to hand over to Phillip.

"What am I doing with these?" Phillip asked as he took them.

"Principal Newton wants them added to the system so they can sign in when they're here," Naomi explained. "They're helping with the showcase."

"Oh," he said weakly. "Okay."

Abby's lips twitched and she turned to Tinker, James, and Nick. "Shall we?"

"Sure."

"Sounds good."

"Lead the way."

Tinker held the door open as they all filed out.

"This way." Naomi pointed down the main hallway.

Tinker fell in step next to Abby, shortening his strides to match hers. "What was all that?"

"All what?"

"You looked like you didn't expect that Newton guy to agree to let us help," he said.

"I was expecting more pushback," she admitted.

"Because we're bikers?" James asked.

"Because Newton is a stickler for the rules," Naomi said over her shoulder. "Usually, non-parent or guardian visitors must be cleared ahead of time. The sponsor needs to submit a written request, explain the purpose of the visit, and provide a copy of the visitor's ID."

"Makes sense," Nick said. "Especially with all the school shootings and stuff. Never know who's walking in."

"Oh, we understand the why, we just don't understand why he didn't kick up a fuss about none of it happening." Naomi pointed to one of the halls leading off the large atrium they entered.

"He has been much more flexible about things lately," Abby added.

"Maybe he's gettin' laid more," James said.

Naomi laughed as Abby shook her head as they walked into

the conference room. The noise stopped almost immediately as everyone caught sight of them. Naomi introduced them and then went around the conference table and introduced the department representatives, which included Lindsey, and three student council members. Their group sat at the empty end of the table, closest to the door.

"You guys do the toy drive for the children's hospital, right?" A Hispanic woman with short, curly hair asked. Thea, the science teacher, if he remembered correctly.

"We do," James said.

She nodded. "I recognize your vests. My son was hospitalized for two months at the end of last year."

"He okay?" Nick asked.

"Yes. He broke his femur in two places, dislocated his elbow, and had a concussion." Thea's voice was tight as she recounted his injuries.

"Damn," Nick said. James smacked him in the chest with the back of his hand. "I mean…dang. How'd he do that?"

"Motocross. He got run off the track by a competitor and crashed hard." Her lips formed a thin line.

"He still competing?" James asked.

"Not yet," she said. "He still has six months of physical therapy to get through, and to be honest, I don't know that I'm okay with him riding again."

"I get it," Tinker said. "It can be a dangerous sport. No parent wants to see their kid hurt."

She nodded and a few of the other teachers chimed in with agreement. The tension he'd felt when they'd first walked in seemed to leave the room. He wasn't sure if it was her intention or not, but he appreciated her helping put people at ease.

He hadn't thought about their vests when they'd shown up at the school and how people would take it. They'd worn their vests when they did Melanie's ride, but that had been in a kind of official capacity—not rolling up into the front office.

"Let's go ahead and get started," Abby said. "As most of us know, the theme for this year's showcase is *Fusion*. The student council came up with the tagline "Where Creativity Meets Curiosity." I'd like to go around and have each department highlight their needs outside what they can provide themselves or have already completed. Nick, James, and Christian are here to help with anything we can't handle ourselves since Penny is on bed rest."

The math department rep started, and each teacher chimed in.

Abby slid her notepad over and tapped it. He leaned forward. In tight script she'd written, *Do you need something to take notes?*

He slid her pen from her hand and replied, *I wasn't supposed to be part of the meeting. I'm just here to introduce James and Nick.*

She nodded once and pulled the notepad back to her.

A twinge of something hit him quick. Yearning, maybe? He wanted her to write something else. He'd never been the guy in school girls wrote notes to. She'd taken the time to check on him, even if it had been to ask if he needed to take notes, and he liked it.

"What kind of budget are you looking at?" James asked.

Tinker realized he'd missed the last few minutes of the conversation, so it was probably a good thing he couldn't get time off to help.

"Five thousand dollars," Abby said. "I know it's not a lot, so if we need to adjust designs, we can do that."

"You got drawings? Measurements? That kind of thing?" Ben asked.

Lindsey, he remembered her, placed a large tube of paper on the table and unrolled it. "Grades four and five are doing a medley of *Alice in Wonderland*. Grade six is doing a scene from *Willy Wonka*, and seven and eight are doing two ensemble scenes from *Into the Woods*. Each performance is fifteen to twenty minutes. We want to be able to have an interchangeable set for the performances so we can turn them around or move them from one side to the other to cut down on the time between performances."

She continued to explain the set designs for the upper elementary and middle school before moving on to the high school.

Tinker leaned close and whispered, "What kind of art do you teach?"

Abby tucked her chin into her shoulder. "Fashion design, sculpture, and visual arts," she said softly.

A sly grin formed. "Visual arts like video?"

Her blush was instantaneous. "Painting."

"I like the way you blush." He did. He imagined that blush at inappropriate moments of the day. Like right now, in the middle of a meeting about school plays, but he couldn't help himself. She popped into his mind whether he wanted her to or not.

"Right, Abby?"

SHE JUMPED at the sound of her name. "Yes! What? No." She took a calming breath. "What?"

Walter, Matt, and Thea weren't even trying to hide their amusement while the students were snickering behind their hands. Lindsey had a shit-eating grin on her face.

Not that she could blame them. She'd been embarrassingly close to kissing Tinker. When his tongue had peeked out of his mouth and touched the center of his upper lip... Whoo, she needed to get control of herself.

"The showcase is in two weeks, Friday beginning at five p.m. Right?" Lindsey asked

Abby narrowed her eyes at her soon to be ex-friend before

turning to James and Nick. "Yes. The doors open to the parents and public at five. The fashion show is at six and will run about forty-five minutes. The theater performances start at seven and should be over shortly after eight."

"When can we start working on production?" James asked.

She appreciated that he, at least, wasn't cracking a smile. "We have a student production crew for the theater performances. The next meeting is tomorrow at three."

"The deadline for completion is the day before the showcase?" Nick asked.

"Ideally everything will be done on Wednesday," Naomi said. "Although there are always last-minute issues that pop up, we have a final dress rehearsal Thursday."

"All right," James said, closing the cover of his small notebook. "I'll be here at three tomorrow. I'll assess what the students are capable of and figure out if I need to bring in any outside help."

"You're really going to help us?" Lucas, one of the students, asked.

"Sure. Why not?" Nick asked.

"Don't you have like, work or something?" Chloe, another student, asked.

"That's one of the great things about being retired, young lady. I get to decide when I work and when I don't." James pushed his chair back and stood. "Miss Lindsey, if you have time to escort me to the theater, I'll take some measurements and figure out how much material you're going to need."

"I would be honored, Mr. James." She rolled up her drawings and tucked them under her arm. She rounded the table and hooked her arm through his elbow as they left.

Tinker chuckled.

"What?" Abby asked.

"The old man still has some game."

"Ew," Taylor, the other student council member, said, not quite under her breath.

Naomi laughed. "You'll get it one day."

The girl didn't say anything but judging by her wrinkled nose, she didn't agree.

Tinker leaned close. "Walk us out?"

Abby nodded. Why was she suddenly nervous? She had to walk them out anyway since they couldn't be in the school unescorted. Maybe it was the low rumble of his voice, or the intimate way he'd asked, or the gleam in his eyes. Such a simple question and yet she couldn't help but wonder if there was an underlying meaning.

The presence next to her was almost physical as they walked to the office to retrieve their IDs and then to the front door. Once outside, Nick said goodbye and headed to a beat-up pickup truck parked in the visitor lot. The kind of truck she'd expected Tinker to drive on their first date.

She turned and faced Tinker. "Thank you for coming today."

"Sorry to spring it on you with no notice," he said. "I hope it doesn't cause too many issues."

"It shouldn't. Will you be coming to help?"

There was something about his grin that bordered on mischievous. "Eager to see me?"

"Just…curious about whether you'll be helping or not." She was not going to admit her heart skipped a beat at the thought of seeing him every day.

"I'll pop in a couple afternoons, but I have that event I'm lead for as well as a few other jobs I'm helping out on."

"Okay." She didn't know what else to say.

They stood there for an eternity, staring at each other, not saying anything. It was probably only a few seconds.

"Sooo…I'll see you later?" she said.

"I'll text you tonight." He leaned forward and kissed her

quickly before she could react. He lifted his eyebrows quickly. "Bye, Ab."

"Bye." She reflexively waved a hand as he turned and strutted away from her. He really did have a nice ass.

"Bye, Ms. Day," a singsong voice said.

Abby looked to her left and saw two of the seniors from the student council walking toward the student parking lot. "Bye, girls. Drive carefully."

The girls watched as Tinker's bike roared to life and giggled at each other. Abby rolled her eyes and headed to her car. Who was she kidding—if Naomi or Lindsey had been there, she'd probably have squealed and giggled too.

NEED AN ERASER ROOM

Tinker couldn't stop by the school until Thursday afternoon. He was due back at Leonidas to update Graham on the birthday party event but decided to stop by the school to invite Abby to a barbecue on Sunday. Who was he kidding? Even without an excuse, he'd started heading to the school after his meeting.

Messaging and talking to Abby on the phone every night wasn't cutting it. He wanted to see her. He was more restless than usual, twitchy. It didn't help that Angie kept giving him sly glances and muttering "mmm hmm" when she passed him.

Phillip, the front office assistant, grimaced when Tinker traded his license for the visitor's pass. So Phillip hadn't warmed up since their last meeting. Tinker made his way down the hall and spotted James in the atrium, holding up a sheet of plywood and patting his tool belt.

"Need a hand?" Tinker asked.

"Hey. Grab that tape measure over there on the toolbox." James pointed to his right, holding the sheet vertical with his left.

Tinker snagged the tape measure and placed it in James's hand.

"Hold this." James wobbled the plywood and Tinker grabbed the edges.

Movement in a hallway drew his attention, and he smiled as Abby entered the atrium with a student. She was holding a sheaf of papers and pulled a pencil out of her bun to scribble a note as she walked.

"Hold it still, dingus. I can't make clean measurements if you're jerking the wood all over the place," James said.

Tinker realized the sheet was leaning and moved it back into position.

James made several marks along the edge and released the tape measure, letting it retract with a snap. "Quit mooning and go talk to her. I know that's why you're here anyway."

"I came to see if you needed any help. And I'm not mooning."

"See those girls?" James pointed to the far side of the atrium. "Giggling over the floppy-haired kid over there? You might as well join them for all the help you're giving me right now. Mooning." He harrumphed to drive his point home.

"I'll show you mooning," Tinker said. Not that James was wrong. He felt more than a little ridiculous showing up at the school just to catch a glimpse of Abby.

"Better not. Showing your ass in a school will get you put on all sorts of lists."

"Anyone tell you you're a pain in the ass?" Tinker asked.

"The missus. All the time. Why do you think I'm here? She saw you."

"What?" Tinker looked and found Abby waving at him with a look of surprise. "You got this?"

"I've had it, dunderhead. Go."

"Cool. Later." He let go of the wood and left James muttering to himself.

"Hey," Abby said. "What are you doing here? I didn't think you were able to help."

Tinker shoved his hands into the pockets of his jeans. "I had some time and figured I'd stop by."

"I wish I'd known—I'd have asked you to grab me a coffee on the way. Although, if you're on your bike, I guess you don't have cup holders."

"I'm in one of the TLC cars," he said. "Next time, I'll message you first."

She smiled softly. "Okay."

He glanced at the clock on the wall over her head. Damn, he needed to go back to the office, but he didn't want to leave without kissing her. "I need to head back. Do you have a minute before I leave?"

"Yeah, sure."

"Uh, somewhere private?" He tried to make his voice somber.

It must have worked because two frown lines appeared between her brows. "My classroom is close; it should be empty."

Tinker kept his hands in his pockets as he walked with her down the hall. They entered a large room full of art and fabric. The front half of the room held large easels and shelves full of what he assumed were art supplies. The back half had sewing machines, dummies, and fabric tucked into every nook and cranny.

Abby stopped at her desk and set the papers down. "Is every-thing okay?"

Tinker stepped close and grabbed the sides of her face before kissing her. He meant it to be somewhat chaste, lips closed. But Abby gasped and her lips parted. Not a lot, but enough for him to take advantage and slide his tongue along her bottom lip. Hers touched his lightly, but that was all it took for him to launch a full-on assault of her mouth.

Before he even knew what he was doing, her ass was on her desk and his hard-on was nestled in the juncture of her thighs.

"Where's the eraser room?" He nipped along her jaw as her head fell back.

"We don't have one. Smartboards. No chalk." Her voice was raspy.

"Where do all the kids go to make out then?"

"No idea. I'll ask." Abby wrapped her arms around his head and pulled his mouth back to hers.

Just as he braced a hand on the desk to ease her back, a tone came over the announcement system. They jumped apart as if they'd been caught by a teacher.

"As a reminder, all student clubs and activities need to be supervised by a teacher."

"Shit." He ran his hand over his head, flattening his short hair. "I'm sorry."

"Are you though?" she asked.

He grinned. Busted. "Not really, but that wasn't what I intended to do."

Abby straightened her shirt and smoothed it over the waistband of her jeans. "What did you intend?"

"Ask if you wanted to barbecue on Sunday." He rushed on before she could protest. "I know you said no dates, but it'd be a family thing."

"I don't have a grill," she said slowly.

"While that is a travesty, Graham is having one at Leonidas on Sunday."

She frowned. "Wouldn't that make it a work thing?"

"Not with Leonidas. We don't have a lot of boundaries."

"Doesn't that get awkward?"

He nodded. "More than you'd think. Especially with Angie. The woman has zero boundaries."

Abby grabbed one of her elbows and leaned against the edge

of her desk. "I'm not sure I'm comfortable leaving Olivia and Will with my mom yet."

Tinker shrugged. "Bring 'em."

"Really?"

"Family barbecue. Graham has his daughter this weekend—she's around Olivia's age. I'm sure she'll appreciate having someone her own age to hang out with. She usually plays on her phone and rolls her eyes at us. You'd be doing Graham a favor."

Abby stood and took a step closer. "So...he'd owe me a favor in return?"

"He'd owe me one since I invited you." He snagged her hips and pulled her forward again. "But I'd owe you one."

She ran her hands up his biceps. "Hmm...what kind of favor?"

He grinned and leaned forward so their faces were only a breath apart. "I have some ideas."

A throat cleared from behind them.

Abby jumped again and Tinker reluctantly stepped away from her.

Lindsey stood in the doorway, grinning like she held a winning lottery ticket. "Hey guys. Whatcha doin'?"

"Talking," Abby replied.

"Uh-huh. A couple of your students are looking for you. I'd told them I'd get you to avoid them interrupting your... conversation."

Abby looked at him. "I need to get back to work."

"Same. You on for Sunday?" he asked.

He could see the excuse forming as she opened her mouth.

"Bring Lindsey if it makes you more comfortable."

"Bring me where?" Lindsey asked.

Tinker looked at her. "Barbecue at Leonidas on Sunday. Low-key. Family's invited."

Lindsey turned an excited and pleading look to Abby, and he knew he had an ally.

Abby sighed. "Okay. What time?"

"Two o'clock. I'll send you the address." He kissed her quickly before turning toward the door, giving a grinning Lindsey a conspiratorial wink on his way out of the room.

LINDSEY SQUEED and clapped her hands.

Abby grabbed them to stop her. The last thing she wanted was for Tinker to hear Lindsey clapping and squealing like a schoolgirl. "Don't get too excited. It's a work barbecue."

"That's good! He's introducing you to his friends and coworkers. That means he wants them to know who you are."

Abby picked up her clipboard and led Lindsey to the door. "I'm not sure… It wasn't too long ago he was running scared because I have a kid. Now I have two and he's introducing me *and* my kids to the people who are essentially his family."

"He's been good the last couple of weeks, right? He's not running anymore. I think it's great he wants to introduce you to his people. He knows all of yours."

"He hasn't met my mom yet," Abby said.

"Ask if she can go too. Really make it a family affair."

"What?" Abby looked at her askance.

"What, what? Your mom's cool as shit. Plus, she can help keep an eye on Will in case you want to *talk* to Tinker again."

Abby shot her a baleful look as they entered the atrium. Lindsey just grinned back.

"I'll ask tonight when he texts me. Right now, I need to focus on this. Who was looking for me?"

"What?" Lindsey asked.

"You said a student was looking for me," she reminded her.

"Oh. I made that up. I saw you sneaking off and figured I'd interrupt before you both got naked."

Abby shook her head. "Thanks. I guess."

"That's what friends are for," Lindsey said.

"Are they though?"

That night she didn't wait for Tinker to initiate their nightly text exchange.

～

Hey. Is it okay if I bring my mom on Sunday?

Sure. The more the merrier.

Thank you. She can help keep an eye on Will and she wants to meet you officially.

HER PHONE RANG a few seconds later, Tinker's name flashing across the screen. "Hey," she answered.

"Meeting the parental unit already. That's a big step. That means things are getting serious."

She didn't know how to respond to that. He sounded like he was joking, but meeting the parents was a big step in a relationship, unless they already knew the parents. Then it wasn't a big deal. Was she taking things too far, too soon? Maybe she shouldn't go on Sunday. Meeting his friends, meeting hers, and her mom. It suddenly felt overwhelming.

"Abby. I can hear you overthinking it. I'm kidding. Of course your mom can come."

"Thank you," she said quietly. "It was just…I—"

Tinker chuckled. "I'm sorry I gave you a hard time. It's all good."

"Okay."

"Hey. You can always tell me what you're thinking. I'd rather you tell me straight up than beat around the bush because you think I might not like what you have to say."

"It's just, sometimes I overthink things, then I don't know

how to say what I want to say." It was something she'd struggled with her entire adult life. The only time she hadn't struggled was when Tony had given her the ultimatum.

"Just blurt it out. I promise it won't hurt my feelings."

Abby pressed her lips together and took a deep breath. "I really like you, Christian, and I want to see where this goes, but I'm also afraid of where it will end up."

The line was quiet for several seconds, prompting her to look at the screen of her phone to see if they were still connected.

"I like you too, Abby." His voice was low and earnest. "I don't have any guarantees, but I want to see where this goes as well. All I can promise is I will never purposely hurt you."

Wasn't that all anyone could ask for? "Okay."

"Okay."

"I'll see you Sunday," she said.

"I'll talk to you tomorrow."

BBQ

Tinker checked his phone for the umpteenth time. Abby was supposed to call him when they arrived so he could meet them in the lobby. He'd been too impatient to wait once they'd finished setting up the platform for the barbecue. Harrison and Graham were on grill duty. The sides and drinks were all in the coolers and the plates and stuff had been carried up. All that was left was to wait.

"What are you all fidgety for?" Graham Senior asked.

Tink glanced at him. "I'm not fidgety."

"Hmm. You're dancing around like you got ants in your pants."

Tink assessed Graham Senior, who'd become a semi-permanent fixture at the reception desk. He'd only meant to fill in temporarily when the last receptionist had quit after having a short-lived fling with Turner. Paige had been so mad about it, she'd threatened to fire Turner. If he wasn't the only one that could pilot their helicopter, she might have. Graham talked her down and convinced his dad to answer the phones since he was always hanging around the building anyway.

The arrangement had worked for the last five or six months,

136

and no one seemed in a hurry to hire an actual receptionist. So everyone who came to Leonidas was greeted by Graham Senior.

"How old are you, Senior?"

"What's that got to do with anything?"

"Graham's in his early forties, so that would make you early-to-mid-60s? I don't think you're old enough to say things like 'ants in your pants.'"

"Wisdom has nothing to do with age," Senior said.

Tink's phone pinged. Abby and the kids had arrived. He shoved off the reception counter and through both sets of double glass doors to the parking lot. Abby's mom, who he hadn't officially met, and Lindsey were with them.

"Hey, you made it." Jesus, he sounded like an idiot. Of course they made it, they were standing right there.

Abby smiled. "We did. Tinker, this is my mom, Susan."

He shook her mom's hand. "It's nice to meet you, ma'am. Officially, that is."

"Well, at least he found his manners," Susan said.

"Mother!"

Susan cocked an eyebrow and shrugged a shoulder. He twitched his mouth, trying not to smile. "Yes, ma'am. I'd forgotten them at work that day. Picked them up as soon as I got in on Monday."

He took a large bowl from Olivia. "Here, let me take that. I'll give you guys a tour of the office, then we'll go out back where we're set up for the barbecue."

He held the doors for them and was the last one into the foyer. "This is Graham Senior. He kind of works here."

"I'm holding down the fort for a while." Senior stood from his desk and held his hand out to Susan. "You can call me Aiden."

"You're actually Aiden Graham, Senior?" He hadn't realized Senior was actually a senior.

"Why do you think everyone calls me Senior?"

Tink shrugged. "'Cause you're old. I didn't think you had a first name. I thought you were like Madonna or Cher."

"Well, it's Aiden," he said gruffly.

"I'll start calling you Aiden then." Tink didn't think Senior would like that, and he was right.

"Not you," Senior said. "Just Ms. Susan."

Susan blushed and tucked a stray strand of salt-and-pepper hair behind her ear. "You can call me Sue."

Tink looked between the older man and woman flirting with each other and still shaking hands, although at that point there was more clasping than shaking. Damn, if Senior didn't still have some game in his wise, old bones.

"Senior, you gonna let go of Ms. Susan so we can go out back?" Tink asked.

Senior glared, but slowly released Susan's hand, then gazed back at her. "I'll lock up the front and join y'all out back in a few minutes."

"No rush, Aiden," Tink said. "We'll be at the tower."

He laughed when Senior flipped him off behind the women's backs. Abby gave him a questioning look, and he shook his head. "Just giving Senior crap."

They walked into the main office area. "This is where we do all our office work. Paige and Graham Junior are the owners, and they have offices here. Angie has a setup in the corner where she does all her computer voodoo, and the rest of us are spread out at the desks."

"This is a lot of space. How many work here?" Abby asked.

"About a dozen or so. There's a few that are on jobs overseas. I know Graham bought the building with intentions of expanding. There's an entire lower level with a garage, storage, and a gym."

"Wow," Lindsey said. "What is it you do?"

"Security, mostly." Tink turned left down the hall that took them to the back lot.

"What kind of security?" Lindsey asked.

"Personal protection, event security, corporate espionage, military contract, rescue—if it falls under the definition of security, we probably do it."

He pushed through the door at the end of the hall and stood aside for them to exit.

"Look, Mama, a helicopter!" Will jumped up and down next to Abby.

"I see that," Abby said.

Tink scanned the Back 40, what they sarcastically called the training lot behind their building, trying to imagine how it would look to a civilian. Or a four-year-old boy in this case.

The observation tower, where they were going to barbecue, stood in the near right corner. A large, paved area, about forty yards by sixty yards, acted as the landing pad for the company's UH-60 helicopter and separated the office building from the training village.

He looked at Will's wide eyes and back at the TLC operations zone. Yeah, he'd have been excited when he was a little boy too if he'd been taken to a place like this.

"Can we go for a helicopter ride?" Olivia asked.

She stood beside Susan, one leg crossed over the other, the sleeves of her zip-up hoodie pulled over her hands, and her long hair partially obscuring her face.

He hated to disappoint her, especially since it was the first thing she'd said since she'd gotten out of the car. "Not today, but I'll talk to Graham about arranging something. His daughter, Sierra, has probably already asked."

Olivia nodded but didn't say anything else. He looked at Abby, who gave him a quick smile.

"Who's ready to climb some stairs?" He led the way to the observation tower and up the external stairs.

"You made it!" Angie threw up her hands and cheered when they reached the top.

Tink looked around the platform and looked at Will. "Is he going to be okay up here? I didn't even think about that."

The space was big enough for the barbecue, several tables and chairs, plus folding camp chairs. It was bordered on all sides by a four-foot-high slatted railing except for the stairs. The space between the slats were too small for Will to climb through. But what did he know? Who knew what a four-year-old could fit in?

Abby glanced around, then knelt in front of Will. "No climbing on the railings and no going near the stairs, okay?"

"Okay, Mama."

"Promise me."

"I promise," he said.

"I'll keep an eye on him," Susan said.

"We'll all keep an eye on him," Angie said as she joined them. She squatted down in front of him. "Hey. You must be Will. I'm Angie."

Will leaned toward Abby.

"I heard you like dinosaurs," Angie said. "Is that true?"

Will nodded.

"Well, I happen to have my favorite dinosaur next to my seat. Do you want to see it?"

Will glanced up at Abby.

"You can see," Abby said.

Will looked at Angie and nodded.

"Cool." Angie stood and held out her hand. Will took it and she led him toward one of the camp chairs under the large canvas sail.

Paige broke off from the small group she'd been talking to and approached. "Tink, are you going to introduce everyone?"

"Uh, yeah. Paige, this is Abby, her mom Susan, her friend Lindsey, and her stepdaughter Olivia. And the little boy Angie is playing dinosaurs with is her son, Will. Everyone, this is Paige, Mi—"

"Don't." Paige pointed a threatening finger at him.

He smirked. "My boss."

Paige gave him a side-eye and held out her hand to Abby. "It's nice to finally meet you."

Abby glanced at him as she shook Paige's hand. "Finally?"

Paige grinned. "We may have all given Tink dating advice when we found out he was taking you to dinner."

He cleared his throat. "Just which restaurant I should take you to."

"Oh," Abby said.

An awkward silence descended for several moments until Graham's daughter joined them.

"Hey, I'm Sierra. You're Olivia, right?"

Olivia nodded.

"That's a cool name. Very classic. I'm named after a mountain range. Ugh. Can you even? Do you want a soda?"

Olivia glanced at Abby.

"Go for it." Abby waved at Sierra.

"Sure," Olivia said as she followed Sierra over to the cooler.

"She's a good kid," Paige said. "Current dissatisfaction with her name, notwithstanding."

"Let me introduce you to the rest of the team," Tink said. He guided Abby over to the table and set down the bowl.

He tapped Graham on the shoulder. "This is my other boss, Graham—Sierra's dad. Devon and his wife, Addison. Ash, Paige's significant other. Samara, our finance officer. Harrison, Turner, and Jeremy. And I believe you've met my sister Dani and, of course, Angie."

Abby shook hands with those closest and waved to everyone else. "This is my mom, Susan, and my friend, Lindsey. Thank you so much for inviting us."

"The more, the merrier." Graham glanced over to where Sierra and Olivia had their heads together looking at a phone. "I know Sierra appreciates having someone her own age to talk to, so I'm pretty sure I need to thank you for coming. All I got this morning were eye rolls and preteen huffiness because she was being forced to hang out with a bunch of old people."

Abby laughed. "Glad I could help out."

"Food's ready!" Harrison called. "Come get it while it's hot."

Tink rested his hand on Abby's lower back. "What do you want to drink? Beer, wine, soda, water? Something stronger?"

"Diet soda, if there is any," she said.

"Sure. Susan? Lindsey?" He took their drink orders and went over to the cooler while they gathered around the food table. He returned with their drinks, then fixed his plate. Lindsey sat next to Turner, who had his charm turned all the way on, and Abby's mom stood at the food table next to Senior.

"Should I tell you to warn Lindsey about Turner?" he asked as he slid in next to Abby.

She glanced at the other end of the table. "What about him?"

"He's kind of a playboy."

Abby grinned at him. "Like you?"

Tink snorted. "I look like a monk compared to Turner."

"I think she knows. They've met before."

"They have?"

She nodded. "Mmm hmm. The night we met. At Katherine's."

"Oh yeah. I forgot he was there."

"Abby, what do you do?" Addison asked.

"I teach art and fashion design at Charleston STEAM Academy," she said. "What about you?"

They fell into easy conversation. Tink ate and watched Abby fit seamlessly with his friends and family. They had these barbecues every other month or so, and Tink usually had a couple of beers, ate, and left. An hour later, they were still talking and laughing. Abby and Lindsey shared funny stories about the kids they taught while Harrison and Jeremy tried to outdo themselves with the most embarrassing Tink story they could remember.

He shook his head each time and took their ribbing good-naturedly. "Just remember I've got as many stories about you as you do about me. Payback's a bi—" He glanced at Will on the other side of Abby. "Biscuit."

"Well, now I want to hear stories about them," Samara said. "I feel like I don't have enough dirt on anyone."

"Ohh!" Angie raised her hand. "I've got some."

"No!" Harrison and Jeremy shouted, sending everyone into peals of laughter.

Tinker leaned close to Abby and whispered, "Angie has dirt on everyone."

"Even you?" she whispered back.

"She's known me for almost fifteen years, so especially me."

A slow smile spread across her face. "I'll have to get her to share some of those stories with me."

He zeroed in on her mouth and her full bottom lip. He hadn't tasted her in days, but the memory lingered like the last notes of coffee after the final sip.

"Mommy, I'm bored," a little voice said beside him.

Reality crashed into him, and he remembered their audience. Judging by Abby's shuddering breath, so did she.

"Dad, can we play hide-and-seek in the village?" Sierra asked.

"Yeah, if it's okay with Abby," Graham said.

"What's the village?" Abby asked.

"It's the training village across the tarmac," Paige explained. "We use it for our tactical training."

"Is it really houses?" Susan asked.

Paige shook her head. "No, just plywood facades. Some of them have rooms, but there isn't any electrical or anything like that."

Abby shrugged. "Sure."

"Yes!" Sierra pumped her arm. "Can we do camouflage?"

"Ange, do you mind taking them down?" Graham asked.

"On it, boss. Come on, girls, let's get gussied up. Will, you want to come too?"

Will nodded and Angie took his hand. "Let's go."

HIDE-AND-SEEK

$\mathcal{A}$bby grinned when Olivia, Sierra, and Will returned from the building with Angie. The girls were dressed in dark green coveralls, rolled at the hems and sleeves, while Will wore a large black T-shirt over his clothes that hung past his knees. Their faces were covered in streaks of tan, brown, and black.

"We didn't have any coveralls small enough to fit him," Angie said. "But he wanted a 'uniform' to wear too."

Will raised his hands like claws and roared.

Her mom pretended to clutch her chest. "Oh my goodness, you're terrifying."

"Ms. A, can you give me your number so I can send you the pics we took? Liv said she doesn't have a phone," Sierra said. "What's up with that?"

"Sierra, that was rude," Graham said.

"Sorry." Sierra looked down and slid her phone into the pocket of her coveralls.

The gruffness of Graham's voice made her want to apologize as well. "It's okay. I'd planned on getting her a phone this weekend. We haven't had a chance to get to the store yet. I'll give you my number before we leave."

"Okay." Sierra still seemed subdued when Olivia slid her arm through hers and whispered something. Sierra grinned and they strolled off toward the village.

Warmth spread through Abby's chest that had nothing to do with the late spring day. She wasn't sure where Sierra lived most of the time since both Tinker and Graham had mentioned it was her week with Graham, but she hoped it was close enough that she and Olivia could continue their friendship. This was the first time she'd seen an honest smile on Olivia's face. Having her own friends was what she needed to settle in. Abby made a note to ask Tinker about it later.

"Hide-and-seek! Hide-and-seek!" Will jumped up and down in front of them.

"Okay, little man." Tinker bent so they were close to eye level. "You see that village over there?"

Will looked in the direction Tinker nodded. "Yeah."

"Do you think you can beat me there if we race?"

"Race!" Will took off, pumping his little legs for all he was worth.

Tink looked at Abby. "That little cheat."

She couldn't help but laugh at his look of shock. "He's faster than you'd think."

"Gotta go." He gave her a quick kiss and took off after Will.

Heat suffused her cheeks. She wasn't sure if he'd given any thought to kissing her in front of his coworkers, and she felt them all staring at her. But when she looked around, it was only Angie and the tall woman, Samara, and they weren't looking at her. The women hugged and Samara headed toward the building while Angie headed toward her.

"Samara isn't playing hide-and-seek?" she asked.

Angie laughed. "No. And I quote: 'Oh, honey, no. I don't do dirt.' You ready for hide-and-seek? I can't remember the last time I played. The village is perfect for it, but they only ever use it for tactical training as far as I know. At least, no one has ever invited me to play hide-and-seek."

Abby smiled as Angie kept up a steady stream of conversation while they walked across the tarmac toward the village and the rest of the group. It looked like almost everyone else had decided to play as well.

"Is my mom here?" Abby asked.

Olivia shook her head. "She said she was going to watch."

"Who's it?" Paige asked.

"I'll be it," Graham said.

"No," Paige said. "You'll take it too seriously."

"How can you take hide-and-seek too seriously?" Graham demanded.

"I agree with Paige on this one, Boss," Harrison said. "You're too competitive."

"I'll be it," Jeremy said. "I'll go behind the tower and count to two hundred."

As soon as he rounded the corner, he shouted, "Go" and started counting.

Angie grabbed Will's hand and exchanged a look with Tinker. "Come on, Will. I know the best hiding spot. They'll never find us," she said.

"What was that?" Abby asked.

Tinker raised his eyebrows. "What was what?"

"The look Angie gave you."

"What look?"

His picture of innocence wasn't fooling her. "The 'hubba hubba' look."

He grinned. "Hubba hubba?"

Abby frowned. She hadn't imagined the look. "You know what I mean."

"Yeah, I know what you mean." He grabbed her hand. "Come on. He's at fifty."

She jogged along behind as Tinker power walked to one of the buildings. He entered the open doorway and glanced left and right before leading her further into the makeshift building. It was laid out like a small house with room names spray painted on the plywood walls. They passed through the living room, kitchen, and dining room before reaching a bedroom. He pulled her to the side of the door and pressed her against the wall.

He ran his mouth up the side of her neck and nipped her earlobe. "I've been dying to do this all day."

She grabbed his upper arms and tilted her head. "Someone is literally trying to find us."

"We have a few minutes, so we should make the most of them."

He took her mouth, hot, wet, and hard. He buried his hand into the hair at the nape of her neck, and he tilted her head. Abby gave herself over to the sensation of his mouth and hands, wrapping her arms around his neck. Lifting onto her toes so she could align their bodies better.

Tinker moved back to her neck. "I want to touch you, Abby. Please let me touch you."

His voice was deep and growly and full of need, vibrating against her skin. How could she turn down a request like that? "Yes," she panted.

He spun her and put her hands on the wall. One hand went under her shirt and cupped her breast, pinching and rolling her nipple through the thin material of her bra. His other hand popped the button on her jeans and pulled down the zipper before sliding in and unerringly finding her clit.

Abby whimpered when his finger slid through her slick folds. How? How was it like this every time? How did she forget all her inhibitions once his hands were on her? His friends and coworkers, *her kids*, were only a few thin sheets of plywood away, but every nerve ending in her body was consumed by the feel of his hands. His calluses dragging roughly across her skin sent sharp sparks of desire coursing through her.

Her orgasm was already building—had started the minute he'd asked to touch her. He dragged his finger through her slick juices and around her sensitive nub. She shifted her weight to one arm and grasped his hard thigh to pull him closer while pushing back against him, the thick, full length of him rubbing against her ass.

"God. Christian."

"Shh," he whispered. "You have to be quiet, or they'll find us."

She grabbed the back of his head and strained her neck, searching for his mouth. He gripped the side of her face and kissed her—deep, rough, and hot. His rough finger tracing steady circles around her clit. She moaned and bucked against him.

He cupped her mound and slid two thick fingers into her. He pumped in and out, grinding the palm of his hand against her clit.

She felt like a plasma ball. Her muscles quivered as the sparks continued to course inside her, seeking a point of discharge. She bucked against his hand when it hit, ripping through her like a cannonball. It exploded outward before collapsing in on itself and bursting outward again. She dropped her head to his shoulder and arched her back, riding the wave of bliss coursing through her.

Slowly, she became aware of the world around her. Laughter in the distance. His hand gently caressing her through her underwear while he rubbed his lips back and forth on her neck.

"You good?" he asked.

"Define good." Because good didn't even begin to describe it.

She felt his smile against her neck. "Can you stand on your own?"

"I have legs?"

His deep chuckle vibrated against her skin. "Yeah. You have legs. Think you can use them?"

"I can try." She blinked her eyes several times and lowered her arms while he zipped and buttoned her jeans.

She bit her lip and shyly turned to face him, unease worming its way through her. "I feel guilty."

He tilted her chin up to look at him. "Because Will's hiding? Angie's with him."

"Yes, but also because I always seem to…you know. And you don't."

He grinned. "Oh, I do. As soon as I get home while I replay you coming on my hand."

"Oh." Now she had the image of him sliding his hand up and down his length while he thought of her. And her cheeks were on fire.

He chuckled and lowered his mouth to hers, languidly tangling their tongues together.

She jumped when a throat cleared close to them.

They looked toward the doorway. Jeremy stood there, looking up at the ceiling with a wide grin. "You're it."

"I DON'T WANNA GO, Mama. I wanna play again." Will sat abruptly and kicked his feet back and forth, tears streaming down his face as he cried to stay and play more hide-and-seek.

Abby set her hands on her hips and stared down at her son. He was beyond tired and would fall asleep as soon as they reached the car. Which would make it difficult to get him to sleep that night. They should have left an hour ago, but selfishly she'd been having fun. And not just with Tinker. All his friends had welcomed them with open arms.

"I know, Bubs, but it's time to go. Mr. Tinker and his friends need to lock up so they can go home." She bent and scooped up her son, hugging his upper body and legs so he couldn't squirm out of her grasp and hurt himself or both.

He screamed and kicked his lower legs back and forth. Abby pressed her lips together.

"Abby, we can—"

She pressed her lips together and shook her head at Paige.

"Okay."

"Sierra, can you help Olivia get their stuff together?" Graham asked his daughter.

"Sure, Dad." Sierra and Olivia jogged off toward the tower where Abby had left their things.

"I'll walk you out," Tinker said. "Do you want me to take him?"

She shook her head. "It's okay. He's difficult when he gets like this. He wouldn't go with you anyway."

"Abby, I've got your keys," Lindsey said. "I'll start loading up the van."

"Thank you." She called her goodbyes over Will's continued cries and fell in step with Tinker as they walked across the wide paved area toward the building. She knew the moment Will fell asleep. His cries turned to deep snuffles and his breath puffed out against her arm.

"Wow. That was fast," Tinker said as they walked through the open office area.

"Yeah. When he gets like this, the easiest thing to do is bear hug him until he passes out." She looked down at his relaxed face—so angelic compared to the demon possession of a few minutes ago.

"I'm sorry if I kept you for too long," Tinker said as he unlocked the outside doors and pushed through them.

"I wanted to stay. We were all having fun." The side door of her minivan was opened on Will's side, and she eased him into his booster seat and buckled him in. She turned to Tinker.

"Thank you for inviting us. Everyone was wonderful and I had a really good time."

He grinned and stepped closer. "I had a good time too."

She could feel the blush rushing across her face. "Not just that," she whispered.

"Abby, I can't find Maw Maw," Olivia said.

Abby started and looked over at Olivia and Sierra.

"Come to think of it, I haven't seen her since we started playing hide-and-seek," Lindsey said. "Did she go home?"

"I don't think so. She told Olivia she was going to watch. I assumed from the tower," Abby said.

"I saw her and Grandpa go into the building during one of the games," Sierra said.

"She went in with Senior?" Tinker asked.

Sierra nodded. "Yeah."

Tinker tilted his head back. "Ah. Yeah. Follow me."

"Lindsey, will you stay with Olivia and Will?" Abby asked.

"Sure, we'll be here."

"Thanks." Abby followed Tinker back into the building. Instead of turning to the right to where the offices were located, they went left to an elevator and pressed the button.

"What's downstairs?" Abby asked as they entered the elevator.

"Garage, firing range, gym, supply room, and…"

"And what?"

"We call them crew rooms. It's where we sleep if we stay overnight for some reason." He looked down at her. "There're beds in the rooms. For us to sleep in."

"Oh." She realized what he hinted at. "Ooohhhh."

He led her down the industrial gray hallway and knocked on a door, waited, then pushed it open. Empty. He did the same for the next room with the same result. The third room was locked and he knocked louder. "Senior! Abby and the kids are leaving."

The door opened and the older Graham filled the doorway.

Abby peeked around him and caught her mom straightening her blouse.

Abby gasped, even knowing what she'd been likely to find. "Mother!"

"Oh, hi, honey. Aiden was giving me a tour of the building. It's really quite impressive." She pushed past Aiden. "Did you grab my purse? This way, right?" She pointed down the hall toward the elevators. "Are you coming?"

Abby shook her head and looked at Aiden, who folded his arms and grinned. Grinned! She and Tinker caught up with her mother as she entered the elevator. His shoulders were shaking, and his face was red from holding in his laughter. She looked away from him and pressed her lips together so she wouldn't be tempted to join him.

Lindsey was leaning against the hood of the van when they got back to it. "Hey. You found her. Where was she?"

"She was getting a tour of the building from Graham Senior," Abby said.

Lindsey glanced at her mom and raised an eyebrow. "She was getting something, but I don't think it was a tour."

"Eww," Abby said.

Tinker lost the fight and doubled over, laughing.

Lindsey held up her fist as Sue passed her. Sue fist-bumped her and got into the back row of the van. Lindsey grinned and got in the passenger side.

Tinker was still chuckling when he opened the driver's door for her. "Text me when you get home so I know you got there okay. Don't give your mom too much grief."

"I'm not talking about it."

She backed out of the parking spot and waved at Tinker through the windshield.

"Well. That was fun," her mom said from the back. "We should do that more often."

Thankfully, they had stopped at a red light, because Abby started laughing so hard her eyes watered.

SHOWCASE

*T*inker stood inside the entrance of the gymnasium and watched what could only be described as controlled chaos. He didn't know if James had built it or they had rented it, but a raised T-shaped platform bisected the back half of the space. Students were walking from one end to the other, striking a pose, turning, and going back the way they came.

One kid did a full three-sixty, posed, and took a selfie, causing the other students to stop and wait. The kid behind him said something the first kid didn't appreciate, and it looked like they were going to get physical before they both stopped, looked in the same direction, and glared at each other before walking back down the runway. He expected one of them to shove the other, but they made it to the end before going their separate ways. If he hadn't seen the argument, he would've thought it was choreographed. Maybe it was—what did he know?

Abby stood at the end of the catwalk, watching the two walk away. He saw her shoulders rise with a deep inhalation, like she was breathing in patience instead of air.

He hadn't had a chance to see her since the barbecue. They'd texted and spoken on the phone a couple of times, but she'd been tied up with the showcase, and he'd worked a couple of jobs for Leonidas in addition to finalizing the plan for the birthday party.

It'd been torture.

Her friend Lindsey power walked up to her, said something, then jogged back the way she came.

He was impressed. He'd never given much thought to what teachers did outside the classroom. He'd assumed they went home and graded papers.

"Isn't stalking a crime?"

Tinker glanced at Olivia and smiled. "I'm watching, not stalking."

"What's the difference?" she asked.

"They don't give stalkers cool visitor's passes." He tapped the badge clipped to his shirt.

She rolled her eyes. "Why are you here?"

"Moral support. Why are you here? Helping out?"

She shook her head. "I got here too late to do anything for the showcase. I said I'd help backstage for the theater part, but there was never anything for me to do."

The way she said it and shrugged made him think there was more to it. "If theater kids are anything like they were when I was in high school, I wouldn't take it personally. They're more cliquey than any other social group."

"They had theater when you were in school?"

She didn't have to sound so surprised. "Yup. We even had color TV and cable."

If eye-rolling was an Olympic sport, she'd be medaling.

"I'm not saying you're old. I'm just surprised. This is the first school I've been to with an actual theater. The school in Kentucky didn't even have a stage in the cafeteria."

"Good save," he said.

"Thanks."

Three boys walked by them and the one closest said, "Hi, Olive Oil." The boys laughed and kept walking.

Tinker stared after them. Probably not a good idea to beat the shit out of a bunch of middle schoolers. "Who was that?"

There went the eye roll. Definitely called for it that time. "Ugh. A kid from my math class and his gooner friends. They're so cringe. Like calling me Olive Oil is original. I'm gonna sit over on the side and do my homework."

He watched Olivia walk to the far side of the gym and sit against the wall. She didn't talk to any of the kids she passed, and no one paid her any attention. Except the kid who'd called her Olive Oil. He was trying to play it cool, but he was definitely watching her.

Tinker remembered what it was like being twelve and liking a girl, thinking the way to get her to notice him while not being the laughingstock of his friend group was to be a complete jackass.

The kid's friends left, leaving him alone, and Tinker took his chance.

"Hey. Kid."

The kid was wide-eyed and glanced around, checking to see if Tinker was talking to him. Or looking for an escape. Maybe both.

"I'm going to give you the benefit of the doubt and impart some wisdom. If you like Olivia, quit being a fuckwit—it's not impressing her or anyone else. Figure out a way to tell her you like her without being an asshole.

"But if you are just a fuckwit." He dropped his voice to barely a whisper. "Cut that shit out. You won't like what happens if I find out you're picking on the new kid to score cool points with your friends. Got it?"

"Ye—yes, sir."

Tinker stared at the kid for several seconds to drive his point across. He nodded once and left him to think whatever he wanted about what Tinker might do to him. Not that Tinker would. He'd never hurt a kid. But he looked scary enough to make the kid wonder, and he could teach Olivia a few things that would hurt the kid if it came down to it. He spotted Abby at the edge of the stage.

She was alone, flipping through a sheaf of papers. "Hey."

She glanced up, a look of surprise and, he hoped, pleasure on her face. "Hey. What are you doing here?"

From far away, she'd looked like the calm in the storm. Up close? She looked like one of those motivational posters that said "hang in there" with a picture of a cat dangling from a branch.

She was the cat.

"Came to see if you need help with anything," he said.

She looked at her watch. "About a thousand things."

"Start with one."

It looked like she was about to say she didn't know or there wasn't anything he could do, but then asked, "Can you take Olivia home? She usually goes home with me, but I'm stuck here. I feel bad she has to hang out with nothing to do. I'd have my mom pick her up, but she has Will, and her car is in the shop. She has a loaner, but she forgot to get his booster seat out of her car, and I didn't leave my booster at his daycare this morning, so she can't pick up Olivia because he can't ride without a booster seat. She didn't tell me until after she'd already picked him up. The daycare is only a few miles from her house, but I'm not comfortable with them driving across town—"

"I need your keys," he said.

"What?" She stared at him blankly.

"Your car keys. I'm on my bike and I don't have a spare

helmet, so I need to borrow your car to drive Olivia home."

She blinked several times. "Really?"

"You need her home, right?" he asked.

"I don't *need* her home…"

He cocked a brow at her, and she trailed off. "Yes, that would be very helpful. Let me go get my keys."

She hurried off and he shook his head. She'd learn when he offered, he meant it.

He headed over to where Olivia was sitting against the wall, knees drawn up, a book resting on them. "Hey, kid. You wanna get out of here?"

Olivia looked up. "I have to wait for Abby. Ms. Sue doesn't have a seat for Will, so she can't pick me up."

"I got all that from Abby. She's going to give me her keys so I can drive you home."

"Oh. Then, yeah." She shoved the book into her bag and stood, slinging it over her shoulder.

"Um, excuse me. Olivia?" The kid from earlier stood next to them.

"Yeah?" Suspicion was heavy in her voice. Tinker didn't blame her—he wasn't sure where this was going either.

"Um." He glanced nervously at Tinker, then Olivia. "I was wondering if you'd be my partner for the Mathletics competition next month."

Olivia frowned. "What's the joke?"

"No joke. I'm serious. You're really good at math and I think we could win."

"How do you know I'm good at math?" she asked.

"I mean. You killed that quiz last week and you weren't even here for most of it."

"Why are you asking me now?"

"Uh, someone told me I should quit being a fu—fart head." The kid cut a quick glance at Tinker again.

Olivia still looked skeptical, but said, "Sure…I guess."

The kid's face relaxed. "Oh. Cool. I'll tell Ms. Stein on Monday."

"Okay," Olivia said.

They stood there for several uncomfortable seconds.

"Okay. Uh, bye. I'll see you Monday. Bye." He waved and walked away.

"Bye." She watched him walk away. "That was weird." She looked at Tinker. "Did you say something to him?"

"Just to stop being a fu—fart head."

"Do you think he was serious?" she asked.

"He asked in front of me, so yeah."

"Huh. Weird."

Abby joined them and handed Tinker her keys.

"What time will you be done here?" he asked.

She looked at her watch. "Hopefully not later than nine. We're going to do a basic cleanup and then break everything down tomorrow."

"All right. I'll bring your car back after I make sure Olivia is inside."

"Okay. Thank you, again."

"Ms. Day!!"

Abby glanced toward the voice. "I'm sorry, I need to go." She touched his arm and rushed off to help a student who looked they were on the verge of tears.

He might owe all his teachers an apology.

TINKER MARVELED at the transformation that had happened in the time it'd taken him to drive Olivia home, swing by his place to change into slacks and a dress shirt, and return to the school.

Students, dressed in black pants or skirts and white shirts, stood just inside the main entrance and handed out programs.

Artwork lined the hall and students and parents milled around each piece. A couple of adults with clipboards jotted notes as they looked at each piece.

He made his way to the atrium, which was also lined with artwork. An X-shaped partition divided the space into quarters.

Abby had changed into a deep blue dress that accentuated the dip of her waist and showed off her shapely legs to their full effect.

Once more he had the thought: he was fucked.

She was talking to a couple of people looking at a large sculpture on a tall square pedestal. She must have felt his stare, because she looked up, caught sight of him, and smiled. Excusing herself, she walked over to him.

"You look nice," she said.

He took the opportunity to lean down and kiss her cheek. It wasn't nearly enough but would have to do for where they were. "Thanks. I clean up good. You look really nice as well."

She smiled. "Thank you. And thank you for taking Olivia home as well. I thought about calling a rideshare for her but wasn't comfortable with it."

"It's no problem." He dropped his voice. "Don't suppose you have time to sneak off to the eraser room?"

She laughed. "No, sorry."

"Damn. It was worth a shot."

A trio of people with clipboards stood in front of one of the paintings. "Who are they?" he asked.

"Art college scouts," she said.

"Really?"

"Yeah. It's a big deal for the seniors." She pointed to a small group of older students along the wall of the atrium, wringing their hands, and craning their necks to try to see what the scouts were writing.

"One of them the artist?" he asked.

"The girl with the long hair in the polka-dot dress. She's very talented. One of the scouts is from the Rhode Island School of Design. There's another one here from the Royal College of Art in London, but I haven't told any of the kids that—they'd freak out too much."

"Wow. And these are your students?"

"Yeah. They are." She said it softly, the pride evident in her voice.

"Where did you go to art school?" he asked.

"I went to NYU Institute of Fine Arts," she said. "But for art history and restoration, not art itself."

"Why not art itself?"

"I'm not that good."

He raised an eyebrow. "I find that hard to believe."

"Oh, believe it. Don't get me wrong, I can draw and paint and sculpt. I'm *technically* very good. But artistically, I suck."

"I don't understand."

She pulled him off to the side, allowing people access to the pictures they'd been standing in front of. "Okay. You said you make custom motorcycles."

"Yeah, but that's not the same as...this." He gestured to the artwork around him.

"Do you design each motorcycle?" she asked.

"Yeah."

"Do you create the motorcycle, or do you use mass-produced parts?"

"Depends on the bike. Parts of the frame I'll make myself. The engine, I usually get factory made. I'm not looking to make a fuel injection system from scratch," he said.

"But each frame is unique?"

"They all have the same basic parts, but design wise, each one is different in some way."

She lifted a shoulder and smiled. "Then you're creating art. Except your medium is metal."

"Huh. I never thought of it that way. I just like making bikes that look cool."

Abby gestured back to the students. "And they just want to create paintings or drawings that are cool."

"But why do you say you suck artistically?"

"I don't have a good imagination. I can't imagine something and create it from nothing. I need a reference." She grinned. "One of my art teachers told me I'd make a great forger if I ever wanted to pursue a life of crime."

"Did they mean it as a compliment?" he asked.

"Yes and no. She meant it as I'm a good artist, but I'll never be great." She shrugged. "She wasn't wrong."

"And now you teach."

Abby smiled. "Now I teach. I can teach the kids the technical aspects of creating art and give them the freedom and encouragement to be artistic."

He could see her passion as she spoke and hear it in her voice. He remembered their first conversation when she asked him what he was passionate about. He saw the same spark he saw then, and it intrigued him just as much now.

"You glow, you know. When you talk about your art and your students."

She blushed.

"I need to walk around and check on some of my students," she said. "Are you sticking around for the theater showcase?"

"Uh…"

Abby laughed. "You don't have to. I'm only staying because some of my kids designed the costumes, and I promised I'd help them backstage."

"I'm going to look at some more of the art, but wander in the direction of the door," he said.

"Okay. I'll talk to you tomorrow?"

"Probably before then." He'd tell her good night, just as he had for the last few weeks.

She smiled and left, looking back over her shoulder once before disappearing down a hall.

Tinker shoved his hands into his pockets and settled back on his heels. Yeah...he was fucked. And weirdly, he was okay with it.

LOSING HER SHIT

Holy hell, Abby was exhausted. It pressed on her more and more the closer she got to home. She hoped her mom had put Will to bed, because that's where she wanted to be. No shower. No taking off her makeup. Hell, she might just sleep in her clothes. Plop facedown on her bed and not get up until well past noon.

She'd been going nonstop for almost sixteen hours. Even before students had arrived for the day, panicked and anxious about their exhibits, she'd gotten two hours of work in. Then Rebecca, the elementary art teacher, had a last-minute appointment and she'd asked Abby to cover her classes. As frustrated as Abby had been at losing that hour, Rebecca had covered for her on more than one occasion when Abby had needed to take a sick day for Will. It hadn't set her back too much, but a few students had started to spiral when she hadn't been readily available to help them.

Abby pulled into her drive and frowned at Tinker's car, parked behind her mom's sedan. Had he left it for some reason? She clearly remembered saying she'd talk to him tomorrow.

Please god, let him have a dead battery. She didn't have the energy tonight. This was the sucky part of dating.

That and when she'd seen him talking to Melanie's mom. He'd been in the main hall where the elementary and middle school art was displayed. Melanie had two pieces up and Abby had caught sight of Tinker talking to her and her mom. There was nothing outwardly unusual about it—Tinker had a close relationship with them. Abby knew that.

But she'd had a *feeling*, and she didn't know if she was *allowed* to have a *feeling*.

She wasn't even sure what she and Tinker were doing. What was their status? Were they dating? Were they fooling around? Why had she ever thought this was a good idea?

She dragged herself from the car and got her bag, lunch box, and shoes from the back seat.

Will's shriek of excitement was audible through the front door.

"Ugh." She rested her head against the door and seriously contemplated getting back in her car and driving away. It was hours past his bedtime, which meant he was wound up and would throw a tantrum when she tried to get him to bed.

She sighed and opened the door. Setting her bags and shoes down inside the door, she stepped into the living room. Tinker, Olivia, Will, and her mom were gathered around the coffee table playing cards. Will slapped a card on the table and shouted, "uno!"

He laughed like a maniacal miniature supervillain, falling back onto the floor and rolling around.

"What's going on?" Abby hoped her voice was calm. She was going for calm. She wanted to be calm. She was not calm. She was about three steps away from "in today's top breaking news story" and "orange is no one's color."

"Hey, honey. Will was too hyper for bed, so we've been playing Uno," her mom said.

"For two hours?" Abby asked.

Sue had the grace to blanche when she looked at the clock. "Oh, shoot. I'm sorry, honey. I didn't realize it was that late."

"It's my fault," Tinker said. "He was excited I was here."

"Mm-hmm." Her throat actually hurt from the strain of not saying what she wanted to say. *So why didn't you leave?*

But she didn't. She could see Olivia tensing up. As happy as Abby was to see her interacting and having fun, she wished it had been at ten in the morning instead of almost ten at night.

"Will, say goodnight. It's past your bedtime."

"Mama, no."

Abby rounded the couch. "Yes. Come on. You can play cards again tomorrow."

Will ran to the other side of the couch. "No," he cried.

"William Liam Day. If you make me chase you, you will lose TV privileges tomorrow."

"Abby, a few more minutes isn't going to hurt," Tinker said.

"Do not." She cut her eyes to him. "Tell me how to parent my child."

His face went blank. She watched the mask fall back into place. This was the guy she'd seen that first night at the party.

She hadn't even realized anything had changed until she watched it happen in real time.

The words couldn't be taken back. She couldn't explain right then that she didn't mean it the way it sounded. That she needed to get her kid to bed, and she didn't need anyone arguing.

She'd apologize later. After Will was in bed.

Will still tried to avoid her grasp when she picked him up, but he didn't try to run again. He squirmed and kicked and arched his back. She held him tightly.

It'd be his own fault if she dropped him because he was thrashing around, but then he'd be hurt, and she'd feel like an even shittier mother than she did in that moment.

Will pleaded for more time. Tried to bargain for a story. Claimed he didn't like the stuffy she'd picked out. And through it all, insisted he wasn't tired.

It took less than two minutes for him to fall asleep.

Her mom padded softly into his room and knelt next to the bed, looking over his sleeping form at Abby. "Olivia went to bed," she whispered.

Abby nodded.

"Tinker left," her mom said.

"Okay."

"We're sorry, honey. We really lost track of time."

"I know."

"I'll call you tomorrow, okay?"

Abby nodded. Her mom left and the backs of her eyes began to sting. She inhaled deeply and let it out slowly, counting an additional one hundred and twenty seconds to make sure Will was fully asleep, then slid off his bed and walked softly out of his room. She closed the door, leaving it cracked like she did any other night.

Back in the living room, everything was clean. There was no evidence that only twenty minutes earlier there had been bowls of popcorn and cups scattered around.

Her chin trembled and she pressed her lips together. Back in her room, she managed to take off her dress and change into a ratty T-shirt and shorts before the first tear fell to her cheek.

Deep sobs shook her body. She didn't even know why she was crying.

She slid to the floor of her closet, tucked into the corner next to the door. It was her pity corner. That's what she called it anyway. The one she curled into when she wanted to hide from the world. The first time had been when Will was one and teething. He'd cried for what seemed like days. She'd gotten him to nap and then her neighbor had laid on his horn for some reason and startled Will awake. It was the only time she'd let Will cry it out because she'd been too busy crying herself out.

The last time she'd crawled into it, Will had been three and had thrown a massive tantrum. They'd battled for hours before she'd finally gotten him to sleep. That's when she'd figured out the bear hugging.

"Abby?" Olivia called from Abby's bedroom.

Shit. She hadn't closed her door all the way.

"Are you okay?"

Abby wiped her cheeks. "Yeah, sweetie. I'm just changing."

"Okay. Are you sure?"

Abby tried to make her voice as normal as possible. "Yeah. It's late. You should go to bed."

"Okay. Goodnight."

"Goodnight."

Abby gave her a few seconds to leave, then crawled forward and pulled the closet door closed.

Olivia was too perceptive to believe everything was all right, but she didn't need Abby's emotional burdens laid at her feet.

Abby grabbed a workout shirt from the laundry basket and used it to muffle her sobs. It didn't smell the greatest, but it was already dirty, and she didn't care about getting snot on it.

She'd just started to get her breathing under control when the closet door clicked open. Her head shot up. "Olivia—"

Except it wasn't Olivia.

BREAKING DOWN

Tinker pulled the door shut as he stepped into the closet.

Abby had always appreciated how big her closet was. Except with Tinker filling it and displacing all the air, it seemed very, very small.

He knelt next to her, scooped her up in his arms, and turned so he was in the corner, and she was cocooned in his lap.

She didn't even have time to protest. "Tinker—"

He pressed a kiss to her forehead. "You get it all out?"

Well...she'd been getting there until he asked. Now, tears filled the corners of her eyes again, and she shook her head.

"Yeah." He kissed her head again and pressed her face against his neck, tucking her head under his chin.

He held her while she cried like a baby. He was far gentler with her than she'd been with Will.

Tinker didn't say anything, just kept his arms firmly around her.

She remembered telling him the night of the barbecue, *sometimes you have to bear hug him and let him cry it out.*

An involuntary laugh escaped. "Sorry," she whispered.

"You want to talk about it?" he asked.

"I think I just needed to cry," she said. "Why are you here?"

"Olivia called me. Said you were upset, and she didn't know what to do. Thought you were crying because of her."

"No," she said.

"Me?" he asked.

"No. At least…not entirely."

"But partly."

"A little bit, but not the main reason," she said honestly.

"Let's start there. 'Cause I don't like that I'm any part of a reason you're crying. What'd I do?"

"It's not—"

"You've been honest with me up 'til now. Don't start lying."

Abby opened her mouth to ask about Melanie's mom but wasn't even sure how to bring it up without sounding like a jealous psycho, especially if she had no right to be jealous. Instead, she asked, "What are we? What are we doing?"

"How do you mean?" he asked.

"Are we dating? Are you my boyfriend?" She dropped her hands to her lap and picked at her cuticles, too embarrassed to raise her head and look at him.

"I'm too old to be anyone's boyfriend," he said.

Abby stiffened.

"*But.*" He lifted her chin, forcing her to meet his gaze. "I told you I wanted to see where this goes, so if you need to put a label on it, then yeah. I'm your boyfriend."

A smile pulled at the corners of her mouth, and she melted back into his embrace.

"But if you gotta introduce me to people, tell them I'm your man. Boyfriend makes me sound like a teeny bopper boy band member."

Her man. A warm gooey feeling ran through her.

"Okay," she whispered.

"What else?" He kissed her quickly, then tucked her head

back under his chin, maybe knowing it'd be easier for her to talk if she didn't have to look at him. "About me. Something must have prompted that question."

She contemplated lying, but at this point she was in for a penny. "I saw you talking to Melanie's mom."

"At the showcase?"

She nodded.

He grunted. "Melanie saw me and wanted to show me her artwork. Becky came up while she was showing me." He moved under her. "Were you jealous?"

She couldn't tell if his tone was disbelieving or pleased. Maybe both? "Did you date her?"

"Becky? No. Why would you ask that?"

"I saw you arguing with her," she admitted.

"What? When?"

"The night we met. Earlier in the night before we…met. It looked like a lover's spat."

"Ah." He shifted from side to side. "You know Melanie is a VACA case, right?"

"Yeah."

He sighed. "Becky's doing the best she can, but she's the kind of woman who needs a man to take care of her, and she's not exactly selective about who that man is."

"She wanted you to be that man," Abby said.

"Yeah."

"But you didn't want to be."

"No," he said simply.

"Why not?"

"To put it bluntly, she's a hot mess and needs to figure her own shit out before she drags another man into Melanie's life."

Yeah. That was blunt.

She thought about their current position, tucked into the corner of her closet. "Am I the kind of woman who needs to be taken care of?"

"No."

No. That was it? Just, no? She frowned. "What kind of woman am I?"

He tilted her chin up again. "The kind of woman who can take care of herself and everyone around her. The kind of woman who saves her breakdown for the closet so no one else will see. The kind of woman that makes a guy like me want to take care of you. Because I see the burdens you carry, and I want to lighten the load."

Well, fuck. Her vision blurred as tears immediately filled her eyes. That was the nicest thing a man, hell anyone, had ever said to her.

"You wanna unload some?" he asked. "You've had a hell of a lot going on the last few weeks."

Abby hiccuped and tucked her head back down. "I think I really did just need to cry. I was exhausted and looking forward to going to bed. Instead, I had to be mean mom, which always makes me feel like shit. I could tell Olivia was upset because I was upset."

She paused and continued in a whisper, "Then I jumped on you, and you shut down and left."

"I left because your mom said I should. I figured she knew better than I did. What do you mean I shut down?"

"It was the look on your face," she said. "It was just... blank."

"I don't know what the look was, but I'm sorry it upset you," Tinker said.

"It scared me."

Tinker stiffened under her. "How?"

"I thought you were going to ghost me again."

She felt the tension ease out of him. "Because of a look?"

"Because of a look and because you left."

"I'm not going to ghost you again, Abby. You had every right to be angry with me. I shouldn't have tried to step in. I was going to call in the morning and apologize for making the night harder on you. We really didn't mean to keep Will up."

"I know," she said.

"Have you talked to anyone about what's going on? A therapist?"

She sighed. "Not yet. It's one of those things I keep meaning to do, and it keeps falling down on the list of priorities."

"You need to make an appointment," he said firmly. "It's not healthy to pretend everything is okay when it's not."

Abby looked at him again. "Do you go to therapy?"

He gave her a half smile. "We're required to at TLC. Monthly check-ins. More if we had an especially difficult job."

"Really?"

"Yeah. Paige is big on mental health. She had a couple of friends who struggled hard with PTSD."

"Huh." They lapsed into silence. Her eyelids grew heavy and the lengths between blinks grew longer each time.

"Abby." Tinker's voice rumbled softly in his chest.

"Hmm?"

"You asleep?"

"Almost," she admitted.

"Why don't we get you in bed?"

That didn't sound like fun at all. She was comfy. But it was late, and Tinker probably was not comfy. She inhaled deeply and exhaled slowly. "Okay."

She blinked and sat up, letting out a jaw-cracking yawn.

"Yeah. Let's get you to bed." He patted her thigh.

Abby realized how short her shorts were when she stood. Tinker ran his hands up the outside of her legs until he reached her hips and applied pressure to move her back.

"I need some room to get up," he said.

Oh. Yeah.

He stood and gathered her into a hug, cocooning her again. They stood like that for several seconds. Abby breathed him in.

The faint traces of his aftershave or cologne lingered. Something deep and woodsy.

Tinker kissed the top of her head. "Come on. Bed."

She nodded and led the way out of the closet. Padding over to the bed, she tossed the sham pillow to the other side, pulled back the covers, and got in.

Tinker leaned over her, bracing his hands on either side of her body. "Goodnight, Abigail."

It was the first time he'd called her by her full name. She took in his steady gaze. "Goodnight, Christian."

He bent his elbows, lowered himself slowly, and kissed her.

It was sweet. Gentle. Quick.

He stood and turned to leave.

Abby grabbed his hand. "Tinker?"

He raised an eyebrow.

"Thank you for coming back."

He smiled softly. "You're welcome. Get some sleep. I'll check on you tomorrow."

Abby nodded and let go of his hand. Her eyes fell closed as he slipped through the doorway.

DATE NIGHT

$\mathcal{A}$bby took a deep breath and smoothed a hand down the skirt of her red dress. Releasing the breath quickly, she grabbed her clutch from the dresser and left her room before she could second-guess her choice.

"Mommy, you look beautiful," Will said from his spot on the couch.

Abby smiled. "Thank you, sweetie." She leaned down and kissed the top of his head. "You're going to be good for Maw Maw tonight, right?"

"Yes, Mama."

"And you're going to listen and go to bed without a fight?"

"Yes, Mama."

"I love you."

He rose on his knees to plant a wet kiss on her cheek and hug her. "Love you too." He flopped back down and pulled his fuzzy blanket over him, already focused back on the Disney Channel.

Abby found her mom in the kitchen. "Hey. Olivia's in her room. She's video chatting with Sierra on my tablet."

"Okay." Her mom turned from the sink, and she looked Abby

up and down, eyebrows raised. "Wow. Are you going to be home tonight?"

"Yes. Just maybe…don't wait up."

Her mom turned back to the sink. "Mm-hmm. Text me if you plan on spending the night."

"That's not the plan," Abby said firmly.

Her mom shut off the water and turned while drying her hands on a dish towel. "Are you wearing matching underwear?"

Abby opened and closed her mouth. "Yes."

A sly grin spread across her mother's face. "I'll just assume you're spending the night."

"Mother."

Her phone dinged and she pulled it from the clutch.

Tink: Hey. I'm running late from the job I was working. Can you meet me at my place?

Abby: Sure. No problem.

A text bubble popped up with an address in North Charleston.

Tink: Park in the back. There're stairs up to the apartment.

"Tinker is running late, so I'm going to meet him at his place."

"Okay. You should take a change of clothes, just in case," her mom said.

Abby rolled her eyes. "Mom, just because you got some recently doesn't mean the rest of us need to jump in bed with a man."

Sue waved her hand and left the kitchen. "Oh, don't be so judgmental. And you're right. You don't need to jump into bed with a man."

"Thank you."

"Can I suggest a catapult?" her mom asked.

"Mother! I'm leaving." She grabbed her keys from beside the door and left.

She and Tinker would get there eventually and, yes, she was

wearing *the* dress, but that didn't mean she was going to fall into bed with him on their second official date, much less spend the night. She tried to ignore the little voice in her head calling her a hypocritical prude. At least her mother had the decency to find a room with a lock and didn't get fingered in the middle of a game of hide-and-seek.

Really, what did it matter at that point? Having actual sex with him was semantics. Part of him had been *in* her. They'd done a sexual act. Arguing with herself that it didn't count was ridiculous. She needed to get over her internal hang-ups and admit she wanted to have sex with Tinker. Damn what anyone else thought.

Although everyone she knew thought she *should* be hopping into bed with him. Even her own mother.

And after last night… He'd held her, let her cry, and hadn't pushed to make her share everything or even make it better. And he'd apologized and admitted he'd been wrong. And done it again that morning when he'd called and asked her to dinner that night. That was honestly sexier than seeing him in the tight black T-shirts he liked to wear.

Her GPS announced she'd arrived at her destination. She glanced at the two-story garage with Charleston Choppers painted across the front and drove around to the back of the building. It was technically in downtown Charleston, but on the north edge of the area, not in the bougie section of town.

Picking her way across the gravel to the stairs, she climbed up to the surprisingly large landing and knocked on the door. And waited. She glanced around at the surrounding darkness. If there were any buildings behind them, they were completely dark. She knocked again and, after counting to ten, pulled her phone from her purse and called Tinker.

He answered on the fifth ring. "Hey. You close?"

"I'm here. I just knocked."

"Shit. Okay. Hang on a sec." The line went dead.

The lock clicked as it turned and the door opened, but she couldn't see Tinker. She stepped into an open, loft-style living room, dining room, and kitchen. The door closed behind her, revealing Tinker in nothing but a towel wrapped around his waist.

Her breath hitched at the sight of him, and warmth flashed through her as his gaze dragged up and down her body.

"Damn." He locked the door and crowded her against it. His mouth on hers was as demanding as always, and they were both panting when he finally pulled back. "Damn. I need to jump in the shower. Make yourself comfortable—I just need fifteen minutes."

He spun and headed across the space to a door on the opposite side. Abby watched the muscles of his back bunch and move as he ran a hand through his hair. She stared at the door he'd disappeared through and thought about what her mother had said.

Why couldn't she jump into bed with him? Her internal judgment? Societal pressure to be a good girl? Screw that. What had being a good girl done for her? An ex-husband and single motherhood. She tossed her purse onto the dark leather couch and followed him.

A large bed took up most of the room. Simple bedside lamps lit the room. The shower shut off and kicked her heart into marathon speeds. If she was going to do this, she couldn't be subtle. Go big or go home.

She slipped off her shoes and took the dress off, laying it over a chair in the corner. She sat at the edge of the bed facing the door to the bathroom and waited. It took only a few moments for her anxiety to kick in. What was she doing? The door opened and she froze.

So did Tinker, a towel wrapped around his waist. Water dripped from his head and trailed down his chest, following the sparse hair on his chest and center of his stomach.

He ran a hand over his mouth. "Abby." His voice was guttural. "What are you doing?"

"I thought we could stay in instead of going out."

"You need to be really sure about this."

She didn't know where she found the courage, but she held his fiery gaze. "I'm sure."

He ate up the space between them in two steps and knelt beside the bed, grabbing her hips and pulling her to the edge of the bed. The sudden movement caused her to fall back. Her eyes widened as he put his hot mouth over her pussy and rubbed his tongue against her through her underwear.

"Christian!" She grabbed his head.

He pulled back but stayed between her legs. "I'm sorry. I should have worked up to that, but I've thought of you in my bed like this and it seemed too good to be true."

"It's okay. It's just...I haven't had a lot of...um..." She gestured vaguely. She shouldn't talk about having sex with other guys while she was getting ready to have sex with this guy. Right?

"You haven't had a lot of oral sex?"

She cleared her throat. "No."

"Your ex didn't...?"

Abby stared at the blades of the ceiling fan over her head. "He wasn't a fan. It always felt like he was doing it as a chore—reluctantly and under duress."

She sucked in a breath when his tongue pressed and wriggled against her folds, finding her clit through the thin fabric of her underwear.

"Believe me, this isn't a chore and I'm definitely not under duress. I want you to come all over my face. I want you begging me to stop because you don't think you can take any more right until you come all over me again."

"Holy shit," she whispered.

"Sound like a plan?" he asked.

"Yes," she said with a gasp. "Yes, that sounds like a really good plan."

"Good."

Damn, his tongue was magic. He rubbed and sucked and pushed through her underwear and quickly drove her to an orgasm. She didn't even have time to think about it—it was just there, pulling her into its powerful wave. He finally pulled her soaked panties down her legs.

"Beautiful," he murmured.

Abby shifted to move up the bed, to give him room to join her, but he put a hand on her belly and pressed her back down.

"Not yet." He pushed her thighs apart, spreading her wide.

She was fully exposed to him and wasn't sure how she felt. Definitely uncomfortable and out of her element. "Christian?"

He glanced up at her. "Shhh." He held her gaze as he spread her even more with his thumbs and slowly lowered his mouth to her again. His thick tongue languidly traced around her opening, then stroked up one side and down the other.

She dropped her head back to the bed and tried to remember how to breathe. It was a struggle. All her brain function had diverted to concentrating on the path of his tongue, on where it would go next. Would he lick, trace, suck, flick? There didn't seem to be a pattern.

She didn't know if it was the remnants of the first orgasm or another one, but the throbbing, electric feeling started to build again. Slower this time, potentially more powerful, all at the mercy of his tongue. She grabbed his wrists, still holding her thighs wide—she needed something to hold on to. Something to anchor her to the here and now. If she didn't, she might burst into tiny atoms.

The second orgasm crashed into her with the force of a freight train. Her back arched and her legs strained against Tinker's strong grasp. Operating on primal instinct, she rolled her hips with the waves coursing through her until they dissipated enough to let her slowly, slowly begin releasing her muscles.

Tinker kissed his way up her stomach to her neck. He slid an arm under the small of her back and lifted her up the bed. She tried to help, but she had no strength in her arms—not even enough to hold herself upright. He unhooked her bra and pulled the straps down her arms.

He plumped one breast and sucked hard on the nipple. Sizzles shot out from his hot mouth, and Abby tried to concentrate on that instead of worrying about how her other breast sagged to the side. She used her arm to press against the side of her breast and lift it up under the pretense of running her hand over his head. Not that she didn't want to touch him. Two birds, one stone, and all of that.

"Stop that, Abby," he said against her skin.

"Stop what?"

"You're getting into your head."

"What? I'm not," she protested.

"You've been trying to shield your body from me since I got you fully naked."

She licked her lips. "I'm feeling very exposed."

Tinker stared at her, his expression enigmatic. "Will you trust me?"

"I— With what?"

"With you. With your body." He ran one hand softly down her body from shoulder to hip and back up again, never breaking eye contact.

She was there, wasn't she? "Yes," she whispered.

ONE HAND READ

*A*bby followed Tinker's movements as he reached over to the bedside table and pulled out a black cotton eye mask.

"You blindfold a lot of women?" She wasn't sure how she felt about that. Was this something he did a lot?

Tinker grinned. "It's for me. I work nights sometimes and it's hard to sleep during the day."

"Oh." That made sense. Probably more sense than thinking Tinker had a drawer full of blindfolds and straps.

"But I have been blindfolded," he said.

"Really?"

"Yup. Tied up too." He lifted an eyebrow.

So much for her earlier thought. His admission sent a zing of something through her. He glanced down and ran a thumb around her stiff nipple.

"You like the idea of that, don't you?" he asked.

"I'm—" She licked her lips. "I'm not sure."

"Your body's sure." He trailed his fingers down her body and through her slick folds. "I think you're wetter from the idea of being tied up than you were when I was sucking on your clit."

He rubbed a circle at the top of her clit, causing her to gasp. "Tinker."

He slipped the eye mask over her eyes. "I don't want you to think about anything except what my mouth and hands are doing to you, understand?"

"Yes," she whispered.

"Good. Put your hands above your head."

She did as he asked and heard Velcro ripping right before a thick canvas strap wrapped around her wrist.

"Wait. Wait!" She pulled against his grasp and tried to lift the eye mask.

"Shhh. If you're not comfortable, I'll undo them," he assured her.

"I'm nervous. I've never been tied up before."

"You have full control, Abby. If you say stop or any variation of stop, I'll stop. The straps are Velcro, and you can undo them at any time. Feel with your hands."

He guided her fingers to the straps. She felt the edge of the strap and lifted it a little, hearing the distinctive ripping sound. Okay. Okay. She could get out any time she wanted. Did she want to be tied up? He was right—she was excited by this.

"If you want to switch positions, you can tie me up and blindfold me. I'll let you do anything you want to me…within reason."

She smiled at his addendum. "I'm okay."

"Good girl."

Oh god. She'd just decided to not be a good girl. But those words…from his mouth. She'd read those words. Imagined them said in that tone, but to actually hear them. She might combust right then and there.

"Focus on my hands," he said. "On my mouth."

He started slow, kissing along her jawline, right beneath her ear, tracing down her neck and along her collarbone. She had no choice but to focus on the soft touch of his mouth and tongue. The soft, yet scratchy texture of his beard as it tickled her skin added yet another sensation to the mix. He seemed in no hurry, content to explore every inch of her. The smooth, gentle glide of his lips against her skin lulled her into a tranquil, meditative state.

The bed shifted under her as he changed positions, and she felt something long and warm against her thigh. She moved her leg, but he stopped her.

"Uh-uh. Be still," he said.

"Please, Christian."

"Mmm, Abby. I'm just getting started." He pushed her breasts together and licked one of her nipples. "I've been imagining the taste of you for days. If I'd planned better, I'd have bought chocolate syrup to drizzle all over your body. I'd spend hours licking it from your skin."

She inhaled sharply at the image, but the practical side of her brain kicked in. "That seems very messy."

He sucked her other nipple into his mouth and chuckled, before releasing it with a soft pop. "Sex is always messy, if you're doing it right. But that's okay, you taste delicious without the syrup. Sweet and tangy." He slid a hand through her folds again. "Juicy."

A warm blush stole across her whole body. On her body. In her body. His words were sexy by themselves. But together with his mouth and hands... The wave was rising in her again, no longer content to build slowly. He moved from one breast to the other. Sometimes sucking, sometimes rubbing, sometimes licking and blowing cool air to make her nipple pucker, some-times scraping his teeth across the sensitive flesh. And some-times...sometimes he did nothing, but she imagined the weight of his stare as if he was assessing the best way to torture her next.

The desire flowing through her centered around an empti-ness. She hovered on the edge of an abyss knowing, if she could only go over, the feeling of falling would be ecstasy. But she needed a push. Needed something to fill the emptiness growing increasingly each second.

"Christian," she whispered. "Please."

"Please, what?" he asked.

"Please fuck me," she begged. He wasn't the only one with a dirty mouth.

She heard the crinkle of a wrapper and then felt the blunt tip of his cock, pushing at her entrance. He pushed forward, then eased back to push forward again. It had been so long since she'd had anything other than a vibrator. The feeling was different. Thicker. She tilted her hips and he finally slid in fully. She sucked in a lungful of air as she adjusted to the stretch.

He nipped at the side of her neck. "Feels like I've been waiting forever to be here."

She whimpered and rolled her hips, but he didn't move.

"Christian. Move."

"In a minute. Fuck, Abby. I can feel you around me." He took her mouth, his tongue thrusting the way she wanted his cock to thrust.

Finally, he shifted. Slowly at first with shallow thrusts, then he picked up speed, lengthening his thrust but keeping an even, steady speed.

She imagined the wave of her orgasm like the waves at a beach. She could feel the friction of his cock dragging against the walls of her sheath, building the force needed for the wave to crest. Tinker hooked an arm under her leg, and she wrapped the other one around his waist.

The change of angle was exactly what she needed. Her orgasm crested and exploded through her. She arched her back and neck with a shout. The eye mask slipped from her head, and she blinked to focus her eyes.

God, he looked feral. Teeth clenched and bared, the cords of his neck straining, and his biceps bulged as he held himself up.

He caught her gaze. "I need to let go, Abby."

"Yes," she gasped.

"Fuck." He pulled out and ripped the straps from her hand before flipping her over like she was weightless. He pulled her hips up and slid back in with one smooth stroke.

A hand slid from the base of her spine to her neck and gently pushed her head down before gripping her hips tight. "Hold on."

He withdrew slowly, then slammed back in with enough force to drive her forward. She didn't need to hold on—she needed to brace.

She set her hands against the headboard and did her best to push back against him. Her face was buried in the pillows, effectively blindfolding her again. All she heard was the slap of their skin and his deep grunts. All she could feel was the slide of his cock in and out and the slap of his balls against her with each hard thrust.

"Again, Abby."

She shook her head against the pillows. "I can't."

His hand glided around her hip and rubbed her clit. "Try. Reach for it. One more time. Come for me, baby. Squeeze my dick like before."

Abby sobbed. She concentrated on the pull against her sensitive muscles. He pinched her clit, and she shouted as another orgasm rushed through her.

"Ah! Fuck!" Tinker shouted and buried himself deep, rubbing in circles as he hunched over her back. He stilled, then took them to their sides. Pulling her close to his front, he curled around her. They were still connected, but she could feel him softening.

"Give me a minute and I'll get a cloth to clean you up," he said against the back of her neck.

"Okay." Her voice was hoarse from screaming.

"You okay?" he asked.

"I think I died."

He chuckled. "I'm pretty sure you killed me, so it makes sense."

"You were right, though," she said.

"About what?"

"You are good with your hands."

She felt his smile against her skin when he kissed her shoulder. "I'll be right back."

"Okay."

She was drifting off when something wet and warm rubbed between her legs. She cracked open her eyes. "You're really cleaning me up?"

A self-satisfied smile spread across his face. "I'm taking it as a compliment you haven't moved in the last few minutes, so yeah, I'm cleaning you up."

Abby smiled and her eyes slid shut.

PILLOW TALK

Tinker trailed his fingertips gently up and down Abby's hip. God, she was beautiful. And she was there —in his bed. He wasn't sure what had made her decide to hop into it with him, and he wasn't stupid enough to press the issue. She was there and he was going to do everything he could to keep her there.

She stirred, inhaling deeply before turning to look over her shoulder.

"What time is it?" she asked.

"'Bout one," he said.

She bolted up, pulling the sheet around her breasts. "Shit. I need to text my mom."

"Your purse in the living room?" he asked.

"Yes."

"Hang tight."

He threw back the covers and walked naked out of the room. He grinned as he imagined the blush staining her skin. In the living room, he grabbed her purse from beside the couch. When he returned to his room, it was hard to tell for sure in the dim light of his room if she was blushing, but the way she lowered her gaze suggested she was.

He smiled as he handed Abby her purse, then slid a hand behind her head and kissed her. "You can look your fill anytime you want. Text your mom." He released her, went into the bathroom, and closed the door.

After relieving himself, he washed his hands and slid into a pair of flannel pants hanging on the towel rack. He guzzled two glasses of water, refilled the glass, and took it to Abby.

She drank half of it before she set it on the table next to the bed. "Thank you. I didn't realize how thirsty I was."

He lay back on the bed and adjusted the pillows behind him. "You're welcome. I drank two glasses, so I figured you were thirsty."

She rested on her side, facing him. "Where did you grow up? Before you said your family moved here for Dani."

He chuckled. "Until I was fifteen, we lived in a place called No Nuts."

"What?" She laughed. "You're lying."

He held up his right hand. "Swear on my bike. It's a little town in Ohio, about an hour from Cincinnati."

"Why is it called No Nuts?"

"Well, the story goes there was a nut farmer—"

"A nut farmer?" she asked.

"I don't know what else to call him," he said. "Anyway, there was a guy who grew nuts—walnuts and pecans. One day, he called the local police to report a crime."

"Someone stole his nuts?"

He mock-glared at her. "Can I tell the story?"

"Sorry. Please go on."

"As I was saying, he called the local police to report someone had broken in and ruined all his nuts. Turns out a family of squirrels had nested in his nut cellar and had been eating his nuts all winter. When the police told him there wasn't anything they could do, he shouted, 'But I ain't got no nuts!' And that's how the town got its name."

Abby laughed. "That story can't be true."

Tinker shrugged. "I don't know if it is or not, but that's the local folklore. I've heard stranger things."

"How long were you in the Marines?" she asked.

"About six years, give or take," he said.

"That must have been tough."

"It was, but it was what I needed to do at the time."

"You must have been young when you went in," she said.

"I enlisted as soon as I could."

Her brows furrowed. "What about Dani? Did she go with you?"

They were getting into uncomfortable territory. He wasn't ready to share that information yet. "She lived with a family friend until I was out of the Marines."

Abby got quiet. He didn't mean to shut her down, but he couldn't talk about what'd happened. Not there, naked in his bed after some of the best sex of his life. It was an ugly story, and he didn't want to dirty their time together. Telling her would lead to more questions.

Thankfully, she moved on. "Um…so…the straps."

He grinned. "I was wondering if you'd get around to asking."

"Is that something you do a lot?"

Shifting onto his side to face her, he propped his head on his hand. "Do you mean am I in the BDSM lifestyle?"

She shrugged, toying with the edge of the sheet. "I guess."

"We had a job a while ago that introduced me to BDSM. I was curious so I did some research, went to a couple of munches, kind of like introductions to BDSM, and got invited to some private parties. I tried both sides—dominating and being dominated. I figured out pretty quick I wasn't fully into it. I like to get kinky but tied and up blindfolded is about as far as I like it."

"You've never done any hardcore BDSM?"

"No. I like to watch, but I can't give up full control, and I don't want to take it." He brushed a strand of hair over her shoulder and trailed his fingers down her arm. "What about you? Are you into it?"

She hunched her shoulders. "I'm not sure. I've read about it in romance books, but I've never tried it. I'd never even been tied up before now."

"But you enjoyed it?" Had he gone too far too fast? Should he have just stuck to the blindfold and left the straps out of it?

"Mm-hmm."

"I can't tell if that's a 'let's do it again mm-hmm' or 'I'm calling the cops as soon as I get my clothes on mm-hmm.'"

She dropped her head onto the pillow. All he caught were some mumbled words.

"What?"

Her chest expanded as she drew in breath. She lifted her face away from the pillow. "Let'sdoitagainandmaybesomeotherstuff." She dropped her face back into the pillow.

He grinned because she couldn't see him. "What kind of other stuff?"

She mumbled into the pillow again.

"Abby, you have to turn over—I can't understand you."

She rolled onto her back but covered her face with her hands. "Maybe some anal play?"

Immediate erection. Well, hot damn. He leaned across her and clicked on the lamp next to the bed.

"Why did you turn the light on?" she asked.

"I want to see how red your skin is getting," he admitted.

"Oh god." She pulled the sheet up over her head and tried to burrow beneath the covers.

He tried to pull the sheet from her head, but she had a death grip on it. "Oh, no, you don't. We're going to talk about doing butt stuff."

"Don't say it like that!"

He changed tactics and pulled the sheet over his head, so he was under the covers with her. "How should I say it? Just come right out and say you want me to fuck you in the ass?"

Her gasp about sucked all the air out of the room. "Not right now!"

He couldn't hold it in anymore and rolled onto his back, laughing.

"Stop laughing!" She sat up, pulled the covers off his head, and smacked him in the face with a pillow.

That made him laugh harder. He grabbed the pillow and rolled over on top of her with it smooshed between them. One more chuckle escaped.

"I will gladly fuck you in the ass anytime you want me to, but I get the feeling you've never done that before." He pulled the pillow from between them, not giving her a chance to roll away.

She shook her head. "Everything I've done has been very vanilla." Her fingers glided softly over his arm, and he knew she was tracing the tattoos.

Moving his hips so his cock was nestled right in the center of her, he rubbed back and forth. God, he loved that hitch in her breath. Her lips parted and he took advantage, sliding his tongue in deep and slow.

Abby wrapped her arms around his shoulders and raised her legs to bracket his hips. She moaned deep in her throat, and his cock pulsed. He circled his hips just enough to shift back and forth. She was wet again and the temptation to slide into her was almost overwhelming.

Almost, but he didn't. They needed to be safe, and he'd glove up until they discussed what she was comfortable with.

He grabbed another condom from the drawer next to his bed, quickly sheathed his dick, and settled back between her legs. He wanted to work her up even more. Abby had been so responsive during foreplay the last time, he knew she'd come quickly if he could get her close enough.

"What else are you interested in? Nipple clamps?" He pinched one nipple between his fingers and sucked hard on the other.

Her sharp intake of breath told him that was definitely a yes.

"What about spanking you with my hand while I'm fucking you in the ass? How about a butt plug while I fuck you?"

She grunted deep in her throat and squeezed his ass while rubbing against his cock. His Abby was a dirty, dirty girl.

"Role play?" He thumbed her clit softly. "I can be the naughty student in detention."

Abby reached between them and palmed his sac, rolling it gently like a set of chime balls. It was his turn to groan.

"Christian. I need you to fuck me now." She grasped his shaft firmly and guided the tip to her core.

He grinned against her mouth. "Yes, ma'am."

He slid into her in one smooth motion and immediately withdrew halfway.

She grabbed the back of his head and pulled his mouth to hers. Their kiss involved a lot of tongue and sucking, mimicking the motion below. He kept a steady pace, in and out, pressing hard and as deep as he could with each thrust. Her muscles clenched around him, grasping at him, unwilling to let him go each time he pulled back.

"God, Abby. You feel so fucking good." He shortened his strokes, almost there. His orgasm was building, the tension taking hold at the base of his cock. Sliding his hand between them, he coated his fingers in their juices and slid his arm under her to finger her ass. Not deep. Just pressing.

And she shouted as she came, clamping down on him so hard he could barely move. So he buried deep and rotated his hips while he shouted his own release into her hot, open mouth.

They weren't even kissing at that point. Just panting into each other's mouths.

Damn. He'd never been so close to a woman before. Physically or...like this. As he became aware of things around him again, other than Abby, he felt her fingers tracing up and down his back.

"Yes, to the butt plug," Abby said. "Especially if it vibrates."

Fucking hell. It was a long time before they got back to sleep.

DOUBTS

"**Y**ou know, if you don't stop grinning like that, someone's going to figure out you got laid."

Abby smiled even harder as Lindsey and Naomi joined her at the small table in the teacher's lounge. "I don't know what you're talking about."

"Sure you don't," Lindsey said. "Let's see. Can't stop smiling. Good mood. One might even say chipper."

"Blushes every time her phone buzzes," Naomi added.

"All the hallmarks of a well-fucked woman," Lindsey finished.

Abby gasped. "Lindsey!"

"What? Am I wrong?"

"That's not the point," Abby said.

"Is it because I said 'well-fucked'? I don't know how else to describe it, 'cause 'laid' doesn't cover all of this." She used a carrot stick to gesture at Abby.

"Spill," Naomi said. "We left you alone yesterday. That's plenty of time. Give us the deets."

Abby grinned and let out a squeak. That's the only way she could describe it. As if all the excitement rushed up out of her and got caught in her throat, escaping through a tiny hole in her vocal cords. She felt like a teenager wanting to gush over her new boyfriend, not a woman trudging along the uphill slope toward forty.

She leaned forward and whispered, "I have never had sex like that. Ever. I thought 'came so hard she blacked out' was just an expression. I didn't know it actually happened."

Naomi stared, slack-jawed.

"You actually passed out?" Lindsey asked.

Abby nodded. "I think so. At least for a couple of seconds."

"How many times?" Lindsey asked.

"Five."

"You had five orgasms?" Naomi asked.

Abby's eyes widened and she glanced around. Naomi hadn't yelled, but she hadn't whispered either. Abby didn't need Mr. McGaw, the history teacher, knowing her business. Thankfully, he was doing his sudoku in the corner and not paying them any attention.

"Could you not yell? We had sex five times. I came more than that."

They both gaped at her. "What?" Lindsey asked.

"I know! Right? I'm still sore."

"Now you're just bragging and being mean," Naomi said.

Abby's phone rang and she checked the screen before answering. "Hey, Mom."

"Hey, sweetie. I wanted to let you know I picked Will up early. The daycare called and said he was running a low temperature."

"Do you need me to come home?"

"No, I've got it covered."

She felt a tap on her arm and glanced up at Naomi, who mouthed *is everything okay?* She moved her phone away from her mouth. "Will has a fever."

"What, honey?" Her mom asked.

"Nothing, I was just telling Naomi and Lindsey that Will has a fever."

"Oh, say hi for me. I'll see you when you get home. Around four, right?"

"Probably a little earlier than that. Olivia and I don't have any after-school activities, so we should be able to leave as soon as last period is over. I can review assignments at home."

"Okay, I'll see you then. Love you."

"Love you too." Abby ended the call and set her phone face down on the table.

"Is Will okay?" Lindsey asked.

"Oh, yeah. His daycare is a little militant on temperature. Anything over 99.1 and one of us gets called," Abby said.

"Why'd they call your mom?" Naomi asked.

"She's listed as the first contact for emergencies. It makes more sense since I'm going to call her to pick him up anyway."

"Cool. Can we go back to you bragging about your sexcapades?" Lindsey set her elbow on the table and rested her chin in her hand.

"Oh my god. No." Abby felt the heat rising up her neck.

"Why not?" Lindsey all but whined.

"For one, this is not the place or time," she said in a harsh whisper. "For another…it's private. Just accept that it was the best sex I've ever had and that's all you're getting."

"Was it as good as you imagine the sex in your favorite MC book to be?" Naomi teased.

Her face was on fire.

Lindsey gaped at her. "Oh my god. As good or better?"

Abby cleared her throat and made a show of packing her empty containers into her lunch bag. "Better."

She stood and walked out of the lounge to the sound of Lindsey and Naomi cackling behind her.

⁓

WILL WAS CURLED on the couch watching TV when she and Olivia arrived home.

"Hey, Bubs."

"Hi, Mama."

Abby brushed his hair back from his face and pressed a kiss to his forehead. He was warm. There was a small trash can in front of the couch, but it was empty.

Her mom was in the kitchen, washing a glass. "Hey, honey."

"Hey." She kissed her mom on the cheek and set her lunch bag next to the sink. "Has he thrown up?"

Her mom unzipped the bag and took the empty containers out. "No, but he said his tummy was hurting, so better safe than sorry. I gave him some watered-down apple juice to sip on. He didn't seem too interested. I don't know if that's because of his tummy or because it's watered down."

"Mom, you don't have to wash my dishes."

She waved a sudsy hand. "Pssh. I'm here and I'm almost done anyway."

Abby shook her head and rolled her eyes. "Thank you."

"You're welcome." She shut off the water and grabbed a dishtowel to dry her hands. "See? All done."

"Thank you, Mom."

She gave her a saintly smile. "I gave Will some Tylenol about an hour ago. You might want to get some Motrin as well. I noticed you didn't have any."

"I forgot to get some after the last time he was sick. I'll run by the pharmacy later."

"Okay. Well, I'm off. Call if you need anything." Her mom gave her a quick hug and peck on the cheek.

"I will."

"Is Olivia in her room?" she asked.

"She headed that way when we got home."

"I'll pop in and say hi on my way out. Oh, there's some mail for you on the table."

"Thanks." Abby took some ground beef from the freezer and set it in the sink. Looked like it was spaghetti bolognese for dinner for her and Olivia. Will could have some plain noodles since his stomach was upset.

She grabbed the mail from the dining room table and headed back into the living room. She sat at the end of the couch and patted Will on the leg. "You hungry, Bubs?"

He shook his head, eyes glued to the TV.

Most of the mail was bills, account statements, and the postal equivalent of spam, except for the large manila envelope. There was a return address from Kentucky, but no name.

A sliver of unease slithered through her. She didn't know anyone in Kentucky—except for Olivia's aunt. She glanced down the hall toward the bedrooms.

A sense of dread settled over her. She was tempted to ignore it and give it to her lawyer to open. But that wouldn't change the contents.

She patted Will on his leg. "I'll be right back. Okay?"

He nodded and she went into her office that doubled as her art studio. Grabbing the letter opener from the desk drawer, she slid it along the flap fold. She tossed the letter opener back in the drawer and peeked inside the envelope. There were only a few pages of paper, and she pulled them out.

Tinker's photo stared up at her from the corner of the top page. More specifically, Tinker's mug shot photo. He was much younger in the photo. Jeez. He must have been in his late teens when this was taken.

Someone had done her the favor of highlighting certain parts of the report.

Felony Assault and Battery of a High and Aggravated Nature

Assault, 2nd Degree

According to the dates on the report, Tinker was only twenty when he was charged.

The arrest record was attached, along with a short, typed message.

This isn't going to look good when we go to court. Send Olivia back and this stays buried.

Abby's lip curled and she snarled at the page in her hand. That bitch. At the same time, she couldn't stop looking at Tinker's mugshot. Her initial reaction was to dismiss it as fake. There was so much you could do with Photoshop or AI these days.

But the vague memory from the night she'd met Tinker rose to the surface. Julia had called him a convicted criminal. Dani's reaction had been anger and defensiveness. That meant there was some truth to it, right?

Abby scanned the police report as she walked back to the kitchen. The report looked like a copy of a copy and was difficult to read. Olivia's aunt hadn't taken the time to highlight anything in the actual narrative, but a few words jumped out at her. Tinker's full name. Bloody. Multiple. Mangled. Who the hell wrote "mangled" in a police report?

"Mama?" Will called weakly from the living room.

Abby walked into the hall. "Yeah, Bubs?"

"I don't feel good."

"Okay, why don't you—"

Blurgh.

Abby dropped the papers and envelope on the counter and rushed to the couch. She grabbed the trash can and held it closer to Will's head, now hanging over the side of the couch. Crap. At least he'd managed to aim well.

Looked like she was calling out of work tomorrow.

TRUST

inker ended the call without leaving a voicemail. He tried texting Abby again but the warning under the message said she had do-not-disturb on. She was avoiding him, and he didn't know why.

They'd talked Sunday after she'd gone home and again Monday night like they had almost every night for the past few weeks. But he hadn't heard from her since their good morning texts on Tuesday.

He slumped in his chair. Fuck. Was this payback from when he'd ghosted her? He immediately dismissed the thought. Abby wasn't that kind of woman. She'd have told him to get fucked if she didn't want anything to do with him. He thought about calling the school, but that felt kind of stalkerish.

Maybe Angie could track her phone. He shook his head and scrubbed a hand through his hair. Fucking hell. What was wrong with him?

Graham appeared at his desk and leaned against the edge. "You good?"

Tinker sat up in his chair. "Yeah. Why?"

"You look a little stressed. Everything good for the party on Saturday?"

Tinker tossed his phone onto the pile of papers next to his keyboard. "Yeah, we're set. I've sent everyone their assignments. We're doing a walk-through Friday after lunch when the event coordinator is setting up and again on Saturday before the party starts."

"Sounds good. I'll drop in at some point on Saturday and do a check-in. I'm meeting with another potential client in that area," Graham said.

Tinker cocked an eyebrow. "Checking up on me?"

Graham smirked. "I check up on everyone. Even Paige. Besides, I want to see what a hundred and fifty grand birthday party looks like."

"Holy shit, are you serious?"

"Half of that is our fee. Fucking kid's birthday party." Graham shook his head. "Paige quoted him the price thinking he'd balk. Guy didn't even blink."

Tinker frowned. "We sure this guy's legit?"

"Yeah. Paige had Angie run him. He married old Charleston money. It's not his, but he likes to throw it around like it is. He's not doing anything illegal. Immoral is another story, but the wife's prenup covers that."

"Damn," Tinker said.

"That's not our problem. Unless she wants to hire us to get proof of his infidelity." Graham clapped him on the shoulder. "Let me or Paige know if you need anything."

Tinker nodded once. "Will do."

He looked at his phone again, but it was as blank and silent as it had been five minutes ago. Fuuuccckkk. He should head down to the gym or the garage. But he knew neither working out nor tinkering on the vehicles would distract him.

Maybe Angie could hack her phone and see if Abby blocked him. He glanced across the room toward Angie's corner. Jayne, their armorer, was leaning back in a chair in her large workspace, feet kicked up on the edge of her desk. Angie was making a show of ignoring him. If there were ever two people who needed to get over themselves and bang, it was those two.

Fuck it. He needed to pull up his Underoos and confront her in person. If she was blowing him off, and not in the good way, he wanted to know. He deserved to know.

Yeah, he was a fucking hypocrite. He grabbed his keys and headed for the hall. He didn't care.

TINKER KNOCKED HARDER and glanced at Abby's car in the driveway. Unless they'd decided to go for a walk around the block, they were home. He braced against the door frame and waited. He'd wait all night if he had to.

He straightened when the door opened.

Abby stared, bleary-eyed, from the half-open door. "Tinker? What are you doing here?"

She looked like crap. Wrapped in a blanket with her hair piled on top of her head, her face was pale with dark circles under her eyes. Hell, she looked like she'd lost weight in the last few days. Tinker hesitated, maybe now wasn't a good time. On the other hand, if he let it fester, he'd get more pissed and then say something that would make him a dick.

Fuck it. If she was done with him, timing wasn't going to matter. He pushed in and closed the door behind him.

"What the hell, Tinker?" She pulled the blanket tighter around her.

"Why are you ignoring my calls?"

Abby stared at him like he'd grown two additional heads. "Are you serious right now?"

"Yeah, Abby, I'm serious. We fucked and a day later you

ghost me. I'd like to know why." He shrugged out of his jacket and threw it on the bench by the door.

She stared at the jacket, stared at him, and walked away mumbling something that sounded suspiciously like for fuck's sake.

He followed her into the kitchen and watched her fill up an electric kettle and set it on its base. She turned and adjusted the blanket again. "I've been taking care of two sick kids since Tuesday afternoon. I didn't think I needed to take care of a third."

Well, fuck. That stung. He didn't think he was being childish by asking what the hell was going on. Wasn't everyone always telling him he needed to communicate more? Damn it, he was communicating.

"You couldn't have sent me a text letting me know that?"

Abby wiped her forehead with the edge of the blanket. "Tinker, I have been thrown up on twice. I have one clingy kid that would barely let me pee by myself without throwing a fit and another kid pretending like they didn't need me at all. So no, my first thought between tag-teaming bouts of vomiting and diarrhea was not to let you know I couldn't talk."

Now he felt like an ass. But it didn't explain her complete lack of silence. She could have texted him at least once to let him know the kids were sick.

"So it has nothing to do with me ghosting you before?"

She looked at him like he'd sprouted a third head. Hell, maybe he had. He was so far out of his depth he might as well have been in the middle of the ocean.

"No, it has nothing to do with you ghosting me before. I've been knee-deep in sick kids for the last... I don't even know what day it is."

"Thursday," he said.

"That's it? It feels longer than that."

The kettle clicked off, and she turned back to it.

Well, he was a dumbass. "Do you need anything? Food? Meds?"

She shook her head as she opened the cabinet.

He looked at the opposite counter and saw a few papers. But what caught his eye was the picture. His booking photo. There was no mistaking that it was him.

He picked up the papers. It was his arrest record.

"Where did you get this?"

Abby glanced over her shoulder and froze, the cabinet door half open. She slowly closed it. "It was sent to me."

"By who?" And how the fuck had that person gotten a copy. His record was expunged.

"If I had to guess from the note that came with it, Olivia's aunt." She wouldn't look at him, her gaze fixed on the mug and tea bag she was dunking.

Tinker shuffled through the sheets, seeing the short note on the last page. "Is this why you weren't answering my calls?"

She frowned. "I just told you the kids have been sick for the last two days."

"So this has nothing to do with it?" He gestured with the pages.

She grabbed the edges of the blanket and crossed her arms. "Honestly? I haven't had time to think about it."

He tossed the papers on the counter, crossed his arms, and leaned against the opposite counter. "What's there to think about? Whether I'm a threat? Whether you want to keep seeing me?"

She wiped her forehead with the blanket. "How to approach you about it, for one, Tinker. What was I supposed to do? Call you and say, 'hey, tell me about that time you went to jail for aggravated assault'?"

Abby gestured with the blanket. "And again, when was I supposed to do that in the last two days? Sorry, I've been so busy getting thrown up on. And let's be honest here—this is something *you* should have told me way before now."

She was judging him without knowing the full story, just like he knew she would. Like everyone before her had. He shouldn't blame her, but he did. She should know him. Know this one thing wasn't who he was.

Maybe she had a point, he should have told her before now, but it was hard to see it through the hurt. Anger. He needed— wanted—to be angry at her, because being angry was easier than being whatever the hell this was.

He shrugged, going for nonchalant. "Well, now you know. What else is there?"

"Why?" she asked softly.

That gave him pause. "What?"

"Why did you do it?"

He opened his mouth and closed it again. There was no short answer to that question. It'd be better if she just told him to fuck off. Easier.

"Does it matter?" he asked.

"Yes, it does." She wiped her forehead with the blanket again. "Why?"

"Why does it matter?" she asked.

"Yeah, why does it matter why I did it? I put a guy in a wheelchair for the rest of his life. What does it matter why?"

"Because I'm not a person who thinks in black or white, Tinker. Because I have to believe there's a reason you beat a guy so severely he's in a wheelchair because otherwise, I don't know what to do."

"Do you trust me?" It really all came down to that one question.

"I want to," she said.

"That's not an answer," he said.

"It's not a yes or no question. It'd be really fucking stupid to blindly trust a guy I've only known for six weeks, especially when there are two young kids in the mix."

He tried to interrupt, but she talked over him.

"Trust is earned, Tinker, not given out like alms in front of a church. And it's a two-way street. You want it? You need to give it, and you obviously don't trust me fully, otherwise you'd have started this conversation explaining instead of 'what the fucking?'"

She spun and vomited into the sink.

What the fuck were alms?

SICK

$\mathcal{A}$bby's glorious tirade was ruined when she emptied her guts into the sink. She'd felt nauseated all day but had been staving it off with lukewarm tea and fleeting hopes it would pass. No such luck. She knew it was a long shot—no way she could avoid getting sick after being thrown up on twice and having to hose down a crying kid after a bout of diarrhea.

Abby braced her arm on the edge of the sink and rested her head on it. Behind her, a cabinet opened and closed, then the fridge. Tinker placed a gentle hand on the middle of her back. She tilted her head and took the small glass of water he held, swished, spit, then took a small sip.

"How long have you been sick?" His voice was soft as he took the glass back.

"A few hours. Started feeling nauseous a bit ago."

"Why didn't you say anything?"

She let the blanket fall. Now she was hot. "Would it have mattered?"

"Probably not."

His voice was gentle. She liked it and hated it at the same time. Hated him seeing her in this state. Liked that he was trying to be nice, even when he was angry with her. She might need an intervention.

"Let's get you to bed." He slid an arm under her knees and another around her back, lifting her into his arms.

Her stomach rolled and she groaned.

"You gonna be sick again?"

She closed her eyes and shook her head. She refused. "I hate throwing up."

"I don't know anyone who likes it."

She kept her eyes closed and her head pressed against his shoulder. "I didn't mean to ghost you. I really didn't have time to process it. Will threw up almost as soon as I opened the envelope. I haven't even read all of it."

She didn't know if she was making things better or worse. She should probably shut up and concentrate on not throwing up on him.

"We don't have to talk about it right now."

Abby raised her head and glared at him. "You seemed pretty insistent a few minutes ago."

"That was before you blew chunks." He managed to get her to her room without any more jostling and laid her down in her bed. "I'll get you a glass of water."

He left her room and returned a few minutes later with the promised water, setting it on the bedside table.

"You want me to move him into his room?" He nodded at Will on the other side of the bed.

"No, it's easier to get a bucket under him if he's here." She pulled the coverlet over her shoulder, suddenly cold.

He nodded. "I moved the papers to the top shelf of your bookcase. I didn't want Olivia to see them until you're ready to explain everything to her."

His voice was flat. Matter of fact. Hardly any intonation. It bothered her. She'd take him yelling at her again over this... nothing.

"Tinker—"

"I'll give you your space, Abby. Read the full report, then let me know if you still want to know why." He turned and strode out of her room.

She wanted to call out to him, but what would she say? *Let me read it now and we can discuss it afterward?* It wasn't that easy. God, none of this was easy. She needed to talk to someone about it. She needed her mom.

She grabbed her phone from the bedside table. Her mom answered on the second ring.

"Hey, honey. How are the kids?"

"Hey. I think they're over the worst of it, but now I'm infected."

"Oh, no. Do you want me to come over?"

Tears welled up and she felt her throat constrict. "Can you?" Her voice sounded thick.

"Abby? What's wrong? Is this more than just being sick?"

She nodded, then realized her mom couldn't see her. "I got in a fight with Tinker."

"What kind of fight?" her mom asked slowly.

Damn it. She heard the hesitation in her mom's voice and understood Tinker's reaction better. "Just an argument, but I need someone to talk to. Do you have time?"

"Of course. I'll be over in about thirty minutes. I need to finish checking out and drop the groceries off at home. How's your vegetable situation? I think a hearty chicken and vegetable soup would do wonders. I'll grab a few more things."

Abby chuckled softly. Her mom was the original *Chicken Soup for the Soul* mom. She believed it fixed everything. Cold? Chicken soup. Broken leg? Chicken soup. Broken heart? Chicken soup.

"Thank you." Abby paused. "There are some papers on the top shelf of the bookcase. Can you read them when you get here?"

"Of course. Is that what you and Tinker were arguing over?"

Her mom was also incredibly perceptive. "Yes."

"Is it bad?" her mom asked.

"It's not great," Abby said.

"Okay. Whatever it is, we'll work through it. I'll be there soon."

"Thank you, Mom."

"I love you, sweetie. Try to get some rest."

"Love you too." Abby ended the call and set her phone down.

Sighing, she rolled to her side and placed the back of her hand on Will's forehead. He was warm, but not hot like he was before, and he hadn't woken up since earlier that morning. He was probably over the worst of it and would sleep the rest of it away.

Tucking her hand under the pillow, she closed her eyes, her mind drifting to Tinker. There had to be a reason for what he did. She couldn't believe he could be violent for no reason. Didn't want to believe it. There was no way a man as protective and caring as him would do something like that to another person and not have a motive. He'd been so good with Will and Olivia.

Melanie.

Her eyes flew open. Oh. God.

Another wave of nausea hit her, but not from whatever bug she had. Abby thought about their past conversations, how he'd always steered away from talking about Dani and her switch from dancing to fighting. Whoever Tinker had attacked had hurt Dani.

Her stomach gurgled and spasmed as a wave of real nausea hit her. She threw back the covers and bolted for her bathroom, shutting the door behind her. By the time she returned to her bed, she was wrung out.

Burrowing under the covers, she stared at Will with his brown hair sticking out in every direction. She could only imagine the violence she would be capable of if someone hurt him. She settled her hand gently on his arm, needing the small physical connection with him as her eyes drifted shut.

ABBY WOKE SLOWLY with a heavy weight pressing on the right side of her neck. Fuzzbutt's fur tickled the corner of her mouth, and she rubbed the spot, before petting the cat. She blinked several times before moving the cat off her neck. He let out a squeak of protest. "I know, buddy."

The display on the bedside clock showed 11:03. She glanced at her windows and noted it was dark. God, she hoped that was eleven o'clock that night and she hadn't slept for more than twenty-four hours. The space beside her was empty.

She flipped on the bedside lamp and got up, shuffling across the hall to Olivia's room. She opened the door and peeked in. The dim lamp on the opposite side of the room highlighted Olivia's form under the covers. Abby padded in next to the bed and placed her hand on Olivia's forehead. She was no longer warm.

Olivia's eyes blinked open and she jolted away from Abby's hand.

"I'm sorry. I was just checking on you. Go back to sleep."

Olivia nodded, but the fear still lingered in her eyes.

Abby backed away before turning to leave the room. Damn it. She hadn't even thought about Olivia's reaction when she touched her. It didn't matter that she hadn't meant to wake her or frighten her.

She thought about the note Olivia's aunt had sent. Fuck. That. Bitch.

Will was tucked into his bed. He didn't wake when she touched his forehead. His fever had broken as well. He was wearing new pajamas, so he'd gotten up at some point. Her mom must have convinced him to go back to sleep in his own bed, which was a miracle in and of itself.

Abby tiptoed back out of the room and down the hall, finding her mom asleep on the couch. In the kitchen, she found a container of chicken soup and her tea from earlier.

Staring at the microwave, she briefly considered warming up one or both but didn't want to take the risk of waking her mom. She shrugged and sipped the cold tea.

Back in the living room, she found Tinker's record on the top shelf of the bookcase. She didn't know if her mom had returned them or even had a chance to look at them.

Abby took her mug and the papers back to her room. Back in bed, she read the full police report.

By itself, out of any kind of context, it was damning. Tinker had beaten a man named Dimitrii Popov. One sentence in the report caught her attention and confirmed her fears.

She closed her eyes as the words she'd read played through her head.

During initial questioning, the suspect admitted to assaulting the victim, stating that the victim had previously sexually assaulted the suspect's minor sibling.

THROWING THINGS

"**F**uck!"

Tinker turned the steel bar over to look at the hole he'd punched in the underside, the side that wasn't supposed to have a hole. It was the second bar he'd done that to.

He threw it against the far wall of the garage, where it smashed against the metal sheeting with a satisfying bang. Running a hand over his head, he admitted defeat. There was no way he could focus on the bike he was building, not with his head all over the place.

"Got your text. Rough day?" Dani joined him at the worktable in the center of the garage and hopped up to sit on the workbench across from him.

"You could say that."

"Wanna talk about it?"

"Yeah. You in the abstaining from drinking part of your training yet?"

Dani stared at him assessingly. "Depends. Is this a beer or whiskey conversation?"

"We can start with beer. May need to switch to whiskey, depending on how it goes," he said.

She hopped off the bench. "All right. Office?"

"Yeah." He led the way into the office at the back of the garage. Grabbing two bottles of beer from the small fridge, he popped the tops and held one out to Dani. She took it and sat cross-legged in the overstuffed chair.

Tinker sat on the small couch and took a long drink from his beer before setting it on the table next to him. He leaned forward and rested his forearms on his knees.

"Jesus, Christian. Do you have cancer?"

He could hear the worry in her voice. "No," he assured her.

"Then what? You're freaking me out."

"Abby knows about my arrest."

"Oh."

He looked up at her, trying to judge her reaction.

"You hadn't told her before?" Dani asked.

Tinker shook his head.

"How did she find out?"

"Olivia's aunt." He took a sip of beer. "Got a copy of my arrest record somehow. Sent it to Abby with a note threatening to do something with it if Abby doesn't send Olivia back to her."

"What the fuck?" Dani said.

"Yeah."

"What does Abby have to do with something you did twenty years ago? Something that shouldn't even be in your record anymore, I might add."

"Who the fuck knows? My guess is she's going to use it against Abby because I'm a violent criminal, and if Abby's with me, she's unfit to be Olivia's guardian."

"Well, that's bullshit," Dani said. "On several fronts."

"Yeah, well, that's where we are."

Dani took a deep breath. "How did Abby take it?"

"I'm not really sure yet." He took another sip of his beer.

"How are you not sure? Have you talked to her?"

Tinker nodded. "I hadn't heard from her in a couple of days. I thought she'd ghosted me after we...ya know." He shrugged. It was more than 'ya know,' but he wasn't going to get into details with his kid sister. Hell, he wouldn't get into details with anyone, but especially his kid sister. He sipped his beer.

"Went to her house to make her tell me to my face she didn't want anything to do with me," he added.

"And?" she asked.

"And she vomited in her kitchen sink."

Dani's look of outrage was almost comical. "Because of what you did? Did you explain why you did it?"

Tinker chuckled. "I didn't get that far. She threw up because her kids got her sick—she'd been taking care of them the last couple of days."

"Oh." Dani's entire body relaxed into the chair. "So you haven't told her the details yet."

Tinker shook his head. "She has the report. I told her to read it, then decide if she still wanted to be associated with me."

"Christian." Dani's voice was heavy with admonishment.

"I wanted you to know she found out."

"I'm okay if she knows. You don't need to hide what happened from people."

They sat in silence for several minutes until he decided to ask the question that had been burning a hole inside him for almost two decades.

"Do you hate me?"

Dani unfolded from the chair and sat next to him on the couch, resting her head on his shoulder. "Truthfully? I did."

Tinker winced. Fuck, that hurt. He knew it was coming and he didn't blame her. He could almost guarantee he hated himself more.

"For a long time. It took me a hell of a lot of therapy to understand you were just a kid yourself and had no idea what the fuck you were doing." Dani paused. "I think the worst part was you never talked to me."

"I talked to you," he protested. "I called you all the time."

"You talked *at* me. You told me Mom and Dad died. You told me you were going to join the Marines. You told me I was going to live with Dimitrii. You told me everything would be fine.

"You never *asked* me how I was doing or how I felt or what I wanted. Even after everything that happened, you never asked. And we didn't ever talk about it, not really. We talked about the aftermath—what came next. You going to jail, me going into the system. We were so busy trying to survive it all, we never stopped to talk about how we got there."

Tinker laid his head against the top of hers. "I'm sorry."

"I know," she said quietly. "I forgave you a long time ago. But Christian...you have to forgive yourself. What happened isn't your fault."

"Isn't it? You said it yourself. I made decisions without really thinking about the consequences. If I hadn't joined the Marines, you wouldn't have had to live with Dimitrii, and—"

"I didn't want to leave Charleston, Christian. I didn't want to give up dancing or lose training time or find a new teacher or give up my shot at getting my pro card. Back then, neither of us had any reason to think something like that would happen."

Tinker lifted his head to shake it. "I could have—"

"What? Shipped me off to great aunt what's-her-face that we don't actually have? Taken me with you? Put me into foster care?"

"You ended up there anyway," he said dryly.

"Not the point." She raised her head and shifted so she was facing him on the couch. "You were seventeen. Your parents had been killed, and you were suddenly responsible for a thirteen-year-old sister. You made the best decision you could at the time."

Fuck. He needed another beer. Or whiskey.

"Look at me," Dani demanded.

He turned his head. Apparently not enough, because she grabbed both sides of his face and turned his head fully to face her.

"I wanted him dead. More than you. I've done a lot of therapy and a lot of healing, and I still wouldn't piss on him if he were on fire. Our lives went sideways, but I'm happy now. I love my life. I love fighting. I love Angie and everyone at Leonidas. I love you. And I forgive you."

There was a tight, stuttering feeling in his chest. Dani was right—they'd never talked about it. He threw an arm around her shoulders and pulled her into a headlock like he used to do when they were kids.

She ended up half across him, but not fighting his hold.

"Too much emotion for you?" she asked.

"Yeah," he admitted.

He took a shuddering breath and let her go. "I love you too, Squirt."

She smiled. "I'm not done yet. You have to forgive yourself, Christian. It's the only way you're going to be able to move on from this. I know why you volunteer for VACA. It doesn't matter how many kids you help protect if you can't forgive yourself."

He gave her a long, steady look. Dani was touching on things he'd never admitted to himself. Not really. He knew why he did what he did, but he'd never given voice to it. "You moonlighting as a therapist?"

She stood up from the couch and brushed her hair back from her face. "Years and years of therapy. I know all the tricks."

A thought struck him. "Do you miss it? Dancing?"

"Oh. I still dance." She grabbed the beer bottle from the table and tossed it in the trash.

"Not like you used to," he said softly.

She was quiet for several moments and he wasn't sure she would answer.

"I still love to dance," she said finally. "I still love it more than fighting. But I can't dance like I did before. He ruined that for me. Timmy asks me to fill in for his classes when one of his other instructors is sick, and I'll help him out, but I can't ever do it professionally again."

"You like teaching the kids, though, right?" He nodded at the long glass window that separated her gym from the garage.

She grinned. "Oh, yeah. Even the kids who act like it's torture secretly enjoy it." She looked at her watch. "Speaking of, the after-school class will be here soon, and I need to set up. We're working on kicks, so I'm going to make them do barre work. Nothing like holding a plié for an entire minute to build those quads."

"You're still lead for the event Saturday, right?"

"Yeah, why?"

"You need any help?"

He shrugged. "Sure. Another person will help. I didn't schedule you since I thought you'd be training. Your fight's in three weeks, right?"

"Yeah, but I won't start working out twice a day until Monday, so I can help out."

"Cool. I'll forward you the schedule. I'm on site all day tomorrow, starting around noon. The dad wants us to go through the guest list. Apparently, he has a photo book with headshots of all the people attending."

Dani frowned. "This is just a sixteenth birthday party, right?"

"That's what they keep saying."

"Rich people are so weird."

"Got that right," he said.

She paused at the office door. "You should tell Abby the truth, not just what's in the arrest record."

"Maybe I should end things." He put his elbows on his knees

and grabbed the back of his head with both hands. "It'll be easier in the long run."

The couch dipped as Dani sat back down. "Easier for who?"

He dropped one hand and turned to face her. "Everyone. Abby won't have to worry about my past affecting her custody case, and I won't have to worry about—"

"Getting your heart broken?"

He didn't say anything.

"Tinker, this is the first time I can remember you ever being with someone for more than a couple of days."

"I dated Lisa Montgomery for an entire year," he protested.

"High school doesn't count," Dani said dryly. "Look, I like Abby. She's funny and smart. And I like how you've been since you met her. She's a mom. I think she'll understand."

He nodded, hoping she was right. "I don't want her to look at me differently."

Dani cocked her head. "Christian, you're a sexy, tatted, bike riding, former Marine, security guy. How do you think she looks at you now?"

That was...disturbing. "As my sister, could you refrain from using the word sexy to describe me?"

She stood and walked back to the door. "You're deflecting, but I'm going to let you do it because it's been an emotional day for you. And how do you think I feel hearing all my friends talk about you? If I hear them say you belong on the cover of a book one more time, *I'm* going to puke."

"What book?" he asked, frustrated.

"What do you mean, what book?"

"You're like the third person who's said something about me and a book. What book are you talking about?"

"Who else said something about a book?"

"Abby, the first night we met. Then her friend Lindsey."

Dani let out a small chuckle and said through a shit-eating grin, "You should ask her to show you which book. After you talk about why you were arrested. It'll help ease any lingering tension."

"That makes absolutely no sense," he said.

"Oh, it will," she said in a singsong voice as she left.

What book? That reminded him. He pulled his phone out of his pocket and typed *alms* into the search bar.

APOLOGIES

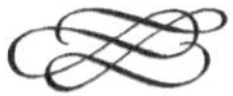

$\mathscr{A}$bby raised her fist but paused with it a hairsbreadth away from the door. Closing her eyes, she took a deep breath and exhaled. The tight ball of anxiety under her breastbone was shiver inducing. She could get through this. She just needed to knock.

Three sharp raps on the door later, she wanted to bolt down the stairs and to her car, drive away, and disappear.

But nothing happened. She cocked her head and listened. Did she work herself up into almost vomiting only for Tinker to not be home? She knocked again and waited. Nothing.

She threw up her hands. All that anxiety for nothing. He wasn't even home. She'd practiced their entire conversation on the drive to his house. Reworded it probably ten times. Emphasized different words, different consonants, modulated her tone. Was it too sharp? Too pleading? Too desperate?

Her plan to show up and launch into her speech without giving him any time to prep was out the window.

"Damn it," she muttered. Shaking her head, she pulled her phone from her back pocket and unlocked it.

"Are...you...busy?" she said to herself as she typed.

Dots appeared immediately and she almost dropped her phone.

In the garage.

Why?

Abby stared down at the wood slats under her feet. Unfortunately, she didn't magically develop X-ray vision to see what Tinker was doing.

She shoved her phone into her back pocket as goose bumps flowed across her skin. "You can do this," she whispered. "You need to do this."

Concentrating on each step, she descended the stairs and walked around the corner of the building to the door of the garage. She raised her fist, but hesitated, then tried the doorknob. It turned easily under her hand and the door swung open silently.

Tinker stood at a metal bench toward the back of the garage, half turned away from her, his head lowered toward something in his hand. He raised it to his ear, and she realized it was his phone at the exact moment hers rang in her back pocket.

Tinker turned at the sound and ended the call before Abby could get the phone out of her pocket.

He stared at her. Waiting.

Right, this was her move. She crossed the floor until she was a few feet from him.

"Hi," she said lamely.

"Hi."

Abby opened her mouth and closed it. Everything she had rehearsed flew out of her head. The gentle, but clear opening? Gone. Her unemotional explanation about how she felt about finding out his past? *Au revoir.*

"Are you here to tell me you don't trust me?" Tinker asked.

That snapped Abby out of her fugue. "What? No."

He took a step closer. "Are you here to tell me to fuck off?"

She shook her head. "No."

Tinker nodded shortly and closed the distance between them. One hand slid behind her head and the other around her waist, jerking her to him. His mouth closed over hers and every single thought flew from her mind.

He was the one with the presence of mind to end the kiss. He pressed his forehead to hers, breathing heavily.

Reality intruded. "We do need to talk."

He nodded, not lifting his head from hers. "I honestly didn't expect to see you again."

"Why?"

Tinker raised his head. "Because very few people ask why—they just take off." He dropped his hands and stepped back. "I get it. It's a huge fucking red flag."

What would she have done if she'd found out on their first date? "I can't say what I would have done if you had told me right from the start. But here? Now? I don't want to go anywhere. But—"

He tensed and crossed his arms.

"I want to hear what happened from you. I know what the arrest report said happened, but I would like you to tell me."

"Yeah." Tinker nodded and took a couple of steps away. Maybe putting distance between them would make the telling easier. All he knew was he wouldn't be able to get through it if she was close to him.

"I told you pieces of this, so you know our parents died when I was seventeen." He glanced sideways at her, catching her nod.

"Dani's MMA nickname is 'The Dancer.' She got it because from the age of five until she was sixteen years old, she was a ballroom dancer. She was a ranked junior world champion and had more titles than I can even remember. We had moved to Charleston the year before so Dani could train with this dance coach, Dimitrii Popov, who had coached five or six international world champions. This guy was good, and he offered Dani a spot."

Fuck, this was hard. He rubbed the ridge of his orbital bone with the heel of his hand.

"How did you feel about moving to Charleston?" Abby asked softly.

"Me?" He tried to remember how he felt back then. "I didn't mind it. It sucked changing schools and leaving all my friends, but Dani and I have always been close. I was really proud of her, and I knew it was a great opportunity. We went to every single one of her competitions."

He chuckled as a memory surfaced. "We'd been here a few months, and some dumb ass tried giving me shit one time because my picture ended up in the local news from one of Dani's competitions. My mom used to make us wear matching Team Knight T-shirts. They were black and the letters were in bright pink sequins. He thought it'd be cool to call me a fag and try to make fun of me for wearing it. The next day I wore a neon pink T-shirt that had 'real men wear sparkles' written on it in iron-on glitter letters. Shoved him into the lockers so hard it left a dent. Then I made out with his girlfriend."

"Of course you did."

He shot her a grin and shrugged. "I was sixteen."

"Mm-hmm. Continue, maybe without the commentary on your teenage escapades."

"Just saying, I rocked those shirts." Still grinning, he grabbed a wrench from the workbench next to him. Having it in his hands gave him something to focus on. "We were good.

"And then...we weren't. It was late August and one of those big storms we get rolled in. My parents were on their way home from date night. Visibility was bad. Some drunk fuck who thought he didn't have to obey the laws of physics hydroplaned through a stoplight and plowed into my parents. They died at the scene."

He turned the wrench over in his hands. The sharp pain of that night had long since eased to a dull ache, but it still hurt. "I had just started my senior year. Dani was in ninth. And it was just us."

"There was no one else? No other family?"

Tinker shook his head. "My mom's parents died when we were still kids, and my dad was no contact with his family. I never got the full story, but I'd overheard enough over the years to know they weren't an option. Neither of them had brothers or sisters. We were it."

"What did you do?" Abby asked.

Tinker inhaled deeply and let it out slowly. "We had some money from my parents' life insurance and the insurance payout from the accident, and we ended up being eligible for their social security benefits, so it wasn't like I had to drop out of school to find a job to support us. But I needed a way to support us both long term and prove to the courts I could continue to support Dani.

"I was a few months shy of eighteen, so I took the GED, and as soon as I got the results, I enlisted in the Marines."

"Why the Marines?"

He gave a half-hearted smile. "They got to me first. The recruiting office had all the services. I was going to talk to the Army recruiter, but the Marine recruiter grabbed me as soon as I walked in the door."

"Why not the Air Force or Navy?"

"Back then the Air Force didn't take people with GEDs—I don't know about now. And I get seasick, so the Navy was out."

He glanced at her, trying to gauge her reaction so far. She

leaned against the half wall that separated the reception desk from the rest of the garage, her arms crossed.

"What about Dani?"

Tinker stared over her shoulder, unseeing. This was when things got hard. "She couldn't come with me, obviously. I had boot camp, then infantry school, then MOS school. Hell, it was almost nine months before I was able to go home."

"Did she stay with friends?"

He shook his head slowly. "She moved in with Dimitrii and his wife."

Tinker didn't want to continue. He wanted to stop telling the story. Maybe if he didn't say it out loud, Abby would never need to know.

"Tinker," she said softly.

He licked his lips and nodded. "They offered to take Dani in. She'd been training with them for almost two years at that point and already spent most of the time with them anyway; she'd basically just be sleeping there instead of at home. It seemed like a good plan. His wife, Ksenia, was a dancer too. She was a lot younger than he was—had been one of his students. That should have tipped me off.

"When I came home the first time, Dani was quieter. Withdrawn. I thought it was because of everything that had happened, you know? Our parents died. I left. I told myself she felt abandoned and that was why she was distant." He put the wrench down and fiddled with a screwdriver. It was easier than looking at Abby.

"I got lucky and was able to get stationed at Beaufort, so only an hour and a half, two hours from here. At first, I was coming back every weekend, but I was fucking nineteen years old. I wanted to party and get shit-faced with my buddies, so the weekends back to Charleston got further and further apart. When I did make it, she was withdrawn. Moody. I thought it was typical teenager stuff, you know. Being mad at me because I wasn't here every weekend. I'd feel guilty and come back more often, but her attitude didn't get better, and I thought, well, if she's going to be pissy whether I'm here or not, I may as well stay at Beaufort. We texted and I still called her all the time, but she was either training or with her friends or just didn't want to talk. Then I got deployed to Iraq.

"Ten months of absolute hell. I tried to call as often as I could, but back then, comms sucked. If you could even get a phone when it was normal hours here, it wasn't always a good connection. Half the time there was a comms blackout because of having to notify all the next of kin of the casualties."

He tossed the screwdriver onto the bench and turned, leaning against it and crossing his arms.

"I got a Red Cross notification Dani was in the hospital. She'd collapsed at school and was taken to the ER and then admitted. It took me three days to get home. Seventy-four hours of airports and planes and feeling caged. When I finally saw her—she was…" He rubbed the back of his head, remembering the first time he'd seen Dani. "My first thought was *what the fuck*? It's hard to describe. She was *gaunt*. Not just gaunt, but almost hollow, inside and out. I knew it was more than depression or teenage angst. Something was really wrong.

"Then she told me she wanted to leave Charleston and didn't want to dance anymore. That's when I knew it was more than just teenage bullshit."

SOUL BARED

bby knew what was coming. God, she knew. And she didn't want to know. Maybe if he didn't say the words, they could both pretend none of this ever happened and go back to the way things were before. But that wasn't fair. Not to her, not to him…not to Dani.

She waited, heart pounding in her chest, and let the silence stretch, giving Tinker the time he needed to say what he needed to say.

"I finally got her to tell me what was going on." His chest expanded as he inhaled deeply. "She was pregnant. I knew. I knew and I still hoped she'd tell me it was some fuckwit boy from school."

Abby held on to her emotions by a thread when all she wanted to do was throw her head back and scream. But this was Tinker's story, and she needed to let him get it out. He hadn't looked at her in several minutes. He stared vacantly at the far wall, and she wasn't even sure if he was still talking to her or just talking to get it out.

"He started grooming her almost as soon as she went to live with them. She said it started with touches that lasted a little too long. Playing with her hair. Accidentally walking in on her changing or touching her chest when he was demonstrating a dance move. All things she could initially write off as accidental or innocent. He slowly ratcheted it up until there was no mistaking things. He started—"

Tinker licked his lips. "He started raping her a week after I left for Iraq."

Abby couldn't stop the sharp inhale of breath. "Did she ever tell anyone?"

He glanced at her quickly, then back at his feet. "She tried to tell his wife at the beginning. That bitch—" He snarled the word. "Told her that's just the way he was. That Dani wasn't the first and he'd get tired of her soon enough.

"That's what sent me over the edge. The fact that she'd tried to ask for help and was told 'he'd get tired of her eventually.'" He pushed away from the bench and began pacing. "I took her to Planned Parenthood."

Tinker stopped, faced her, and shoved his hands into the front pockets of his jeans. "When I got her safe, I went and found him at his dance studio and beat him until his face was nothing but a bloody pulp. I stomped on his legs so hard his kneecaps shattered. He can walk, technically. He's not paralyzed, but he needs crutches or a wheelchair."

His voice was monotonous, as if he were reading from a menu. "I would have killed him, Abby. That was my intention. I wanted him dead."

"What stopped you?" she asked softly.

"His wife walked in. Saw the blood and me wailing on him and screamed. It snapped me out of it. I realized if I went to jail for murder, Dani would always be alone."

"What happened?"

Tinker looked down at his feet and shifted his weight back on his heels. "I waited for the cops. Sat in one of the chairs along the wall and just waited. I sat there listening to him groaning, thinking it wasn't enough. I knew I was fucked. Knew I should have thought about Dani and what was going to happen to her, but all I could think was that he should've been dead."

"What did happen to her?"

"She went into the system. Too old and too much trauma to be taken in by a family so she went to a halfway house. That's where she met Angie."

Abby tilted her head. "Angie was a foster kid?"

Tinker nodded. "Yeah."

"What happened after you were arrested?"

"I didn't have money for bail, and the Marines wouldn't accept responsibility for me initially, so I sat in jail until I found a lawyer that got me released on the condition I would be confined to base except for any court appointments. I was put in hold status and assigned to the civil engineer detachment."

He walked over to the bench, sorting and arranging the tools on top. "They couldn't redeploy me. I found out a buddy of mine was killed while on patrol. While I was emptying trash cans around the barracks."

She could have wrapped herself in his guilt and stayed warm through the winter. It oozed from him like an invisible sludge ready to surround and suffocate him and anyone around him. How long had he been carrying it all? Had he ever talked to anyone? Had anyone ever told him he didn't have to carry it?

He turned and leaned against the bench again, crossed his arms, and went back into what she was beginning to think of as his defense pose.

"I lucked out with my lawyer. The lady was vicious. She played up the fact that I'd been called home from Iraq to find my sister in the hospital. That I'd stepped off one battlefield and found myself in another one I shouldn't have had to deal with. That I was trying to support my kid sister after the death of our parents, and I'd trusted Dimitrii with Dani's wellbeing, and he'd done the worst thing humanly possible.

"Then she went after Dimitrii. She found six former students who he'd molested and raped. Two of them were willing to testify. That was enough. The jury found me not guilty of the most serious charges that could have sent me to jail for twenty years. Found me guilty of assault in the second degree and recommended probation. The judge signed off on it."

Abby frowned. "I don't understand. How did you end up spending eighteen months in jail if you were given probation?"

Tinker smiled sardonically. "Because after my civilian trial, the Marines took their turn."

"How? Isn't that double jeopardy?"

"Not under the Uniform Code of Military Justice. The military is federal, so they were able to charge me separately. Technically different charges, but for the same reason. The lawyer who handled my civilian case advised, but the military defense council had the lead since it was a military court. He recommended a judge-only trial. He knew the assigned judge had a soft spot for violence against kids. I got eighteen months, busted down to E-1—the lowest rank—and forfeiture of fifty percent of my pay for one year."

He tucked his hands into his pockets again. "So, that's what I did and why I did it."

Abby assessed the man standing there. She looked past the baggy faded jeans and the black T-shirt and the tattoos. And she saw the boy he had probably been. Seventeen with the responsibility of a sister thrust on him and no idea how to navigate a world he should have been guided through.

"I have some questions, if you don't mind answering them," she said softly.

"I'd be surprised if you didn't," he said.

"When did you start working for Graham?"

Tinker straightened and frowned. He looked confused, like he hadn't expected that to be her question.

"Twelve years ago, I think. Maybe more. I'm not sure. I've

been with Graham and Paige since the beginning, before they were even Leonidas."

Abby nodded. "How did you meet them?"

"In Iraq, actually."

"Before all of this happened?" she asked.

He shook his head. "After. I couldn't get a job anywhere with my record and my discharge. I guess the good thing about war is companies are willing to overlook things. I worked for a security contractor. Well…a subcontractor, of a subcontractor, of a contractor. I was assigned to the FOB Graham was deployed to. We got to talking one day."

"What's a FOB?"

"Forward Operating Base. A smaller base away from the bigger bases."

"How can you work with VACA with a conviction?"

He nodded and took a few steps closer to her. "Graham and Paige got my record expunged and my discharge upgraded to general. I'm honestly still not sure how they managed to pull it off—I would have been happy with other than honorable."

Abby shook her head. "I don't know what the difference is."

"It's basically the difference between really bad and not so bad, but not great. It only shows up in my military record, not any kind of background check. Since my record was expunged, it doesn't show up on a basic background check, which is all VACA requires. I told Kat and Pothole about it anyway, but I don't think they really care. Pothole told me I'm exactly the kind of guy they want protecting kids."

Abby nodded again. "But, if your record was expunged, how did Olivia's aunt get a copy of it?"

Tinker moved next to her and leaned against the wall, close enough she could feel the heat from his body.

"That's the kicker. My record is only expunged at the state level, not the federal level. If I had to go through a full security clearance, I'd be denied because it never goes away. There are certain jobs Leonidas contracts for that I can't do." He shrugged. "But mostly it's not an issue."

"What—" Abby hesitated. "What happened to the guy? Dani's dance teacher."

Beside her, Tinker went rigid for several seconds. "He was charged, got three years, but ended up serving them in a state rehabilitation center. Last I heard, he'd moved back to Europe somewhere."

That was disappointing. She'd hoped he was still in jail. Her mind wandered, not really focusing on anything in particular. Dani—she'd like to see her fight. The countless kids Tinker had helped. To what she would do if something happened to Will or Olivia.

She liked to imagine she'd go all vigilante justice and gladly spend the rest of her life in jail. Then some hotshot femme boss producer would buy the rights to her memoir and make it into an Oscar-winning movie.

"I know it's a lot to take in, Abby," Tinker said. "It's a lot to deal with. I'll understand if you need to end things between us."

Abby took a breath and stepped in front of Tinker. "Shut up."

He frowned and stood to his full height.

"I understand why you didn't tell me in the beginning. I wish you had chosen to tell me yourself instead of finding out the way I did, but it is what it is."

Tinker rested his hands on her hips. "I would have, eventually. But it's not like I had a plan to tell you or not tell you."

She nodded and licked her lips. She'd had a long debate with herself over the next part, but if they were going to be honest, they needed to be honest about everything.

"What I'm most upset about is the way you treated me after you realized I knew. You didn't let me process. You shut down. You can't throw a stink bomb into a room and then get mad when someone says it stinks."

His mouth twitched. "I know. I just..." He looked over her

head, took a deep breath, and blew it out. "The first time I thought about getting serious with someone, I told her up front. Her revulsion was immediate. She called me a monster. Told me she wanted nothing to do with me. Dani and Angie told me it was a her problem, except it happened the next time and the next. So, I quit telling women."

Abby's brows pinched together. "How did that work when you got into a relationship?"

Tinker looked at her. "I haven't been in a relationship."

"*E*ver?"

Abby's look of incredulity was almost comical. Tinker knew better than to laugh out loud though.

"Dani says high school doesn't count." He shrugged.

Her jaw dropped. "What's the longest you've dated a woman?"

"What do you define as dating?"

She shrugged. "I don't know. Dinner? Texting? Talking frequently."

"We met, what? Two? Two and a half months ago?" he asked.

She nodded and pressed her lips tightly together. She looked like she was bracing for bad news.

"About two months or so."

"So this is the longest relationship you've ever had?"

"Abby, you are the *only* adult relationship I've ever had."

"I don't— But you— You've been with other women, right?"

His lips twitched. "I didn't take a vow of celibacy—I just swore off relationships."

"How does that even work? You find some random woman whenever and then never see her again?"

"I wasn't hiring sex workers, if that's what you're asking." He couldn't stop the chuckle that escaped.

Abby smacked him on the chest. "Stop laughing. I'm serious."

He cleared his throat and tried for a serious face. "Sorry."

"I'm trying to understand how it worked."

How *had* it worked? His last hookup had been a good six months before he met Abby. It felt like a lifetime ago.

"I don't know. There wasn't ever any plan," he said. "I'd meet a woman, we'd hook up with the mutual understanding that it was just sex. The longest…arrangement I had was around three months."

"What happened?" she asked.

Tinker shrugged. "She started trying to make plans and hinting she wanted more than just sex. I told her it wasn't working anymore."

The little line between her brows appeared. "Were you in an arrangement when you asked me out?"

He shook his head. "No. Hadn't been for a while."

"Why did you ask me out if that's not what you normally do?"

"I honestly have no idea."

He said it before thinking, but with the look of hurt that flashed across her face, he realized how it sounded. Tilting her chin up, he kissed her softly.

"I didn't mean that the way it sounded, but I really don't know what made me ask you out. Your friend Lindsey made that joke about carrying your books home, and I couldn't get the image out of my head. I showed back up at the school and told myself I'd give it fifteen minutes. If you came out, I'd ask you out. If you didn't…" He shrugged.

"What?"

He smiled, finally admitting the truth to himself. "I'd have waited another fifteen minutes."

Her smile was worth the admission. "That's really sweet."

"I will deny everything if you ever mention it to anyone I work with. I have a reputation to protect."

"What reputation is that?"

"Stoic loner."

The corner of her eyebrow went up.

"Reformed stoic loner," he corrected.

Lowering his head slowly, he pressed his lips to hers. She opened her mouth, and he followed her lead, letting her deepen the kiss. Before long, they were both breathing heavily.

He dragged his mouth away and pressed his forehead to hers. "I'm guessing you're okay with my history since you didn't kick me in the junk and run for the door, but I need to know for sure." He lifted his head and looked down at her.

"Have you ever read your arrest report?" she asked.

He shook his head.

"You told the officers you beat him up because he molested Dani."

"I did?"

She nodded. "I knew why you did it before I came, but I needed you to trust me enough to tell me yourself." She laid her hand along the side of his face. "I'm okay with your history, Christian. And if I'm honest, it made me fall for you even more."

A warm feeling spread through his chest the way a good whiskey did. God, this woman would break him. "You fell for me?"

A blush spread across her cheeks. "Yeah," she whispered.

Tinker grasped the sides of Abby's face, his thumbs brushing against her temples. "I fell for you too."

Her smile was blinding for a moment, then she became serious. "But if you ever shut down on me again, I *will* kick you in the junk."

He grinned. "I can't make any promises. I'm new to this whole relationship thing, but I promise I'll try."

"Okay."

"Okay." Still grinning, he pressed his lips to hers again.

Abby wrapped her arms around his neck as their mouths meshed, and their tongues tangled together. Bending at the knees, he wrapped his arms around her waist and picked her up, holding her close. She wrapped her legs around his hips, and he moved a hand down to her ass to support her weight.

She whimpered and clenched her legs tighter around him as she pulled at his T-shirt. They broke apart long enough to get it over his head. Her arms roamed across his shoulders and arms.

Fuck. He wanted inside her. Stumbling to the nearest work-bench, he set her on it and pulled her shirt over her head. She kept her legs hooked behind his thighs as she fumbled with his belt.

Pulling down the cup of her bra, he ran a thumb over her hard nipple before sucking on it.

Abby's head fell back and she moaned. God, he loved that sound. He sucked harder and rubbed her nipple with the flat of his tongue.

She pushed against his shoulders, and he reluctantly released her breast. Abby pushed again and he stepped back. She hopped down from the bench and pushed his jeans down his hips.

"What—?"

Abby knelt in front of him and he swayed. "Abby, you don't—"

"Shut up, Tinker." She grasped his cock and freed it from his boxers, sliding her mouth down the head without any hesitation.

"Yes, ma'am." He braced one hand against the bench and brushed her hair away from her face.

She gazed up at him, slowly easing her mouth down his shaft. Her tongue rubbed back and forth on the underside, warm and wet. *Fuck.* Abby on her knees with his dick down her throat was the hottest fucking thing he'd ever seen. She pulled back, then eased back down again. With one hand, she grasped the base of his shaft and ran it up and down in time with her mouth. She dug the fingers of her other hand into his ass as if she was afraid he'd try to back up.

Un-fucking-likely. He clenched his fingers in her hair at the base of her neck, not pulling or pushing. Just holding, making her pull against his grip to suck his cock.

She grunted as she strained against his hold, and he almost blew his wad then and there. He held on to it, wanting it to last longer. Wanted to give her more. Wanted to give her what *she* wanted.

"Do you want it dirty, Abby?" he asked in a harsh voice.

Her gaze flew to his and he could see the excitement in her eyes. Yeah, she wanted dirty.

"You want me to tell you to take my cock?"

She hummed her assent.

"Take it so deep you reach my balls? So deep you gag?"

Her breath brushed across his skin as she breathed heavily through her nose, and she groaned again.

How dirty would she let him go? He tightened his grip and held her still, only the tip still in her mouth. "You tap my ass if you want me to stop. Understand?"

She nodded and pressed her tongue to the slit along his head. *Fuuuck.*

"Let go with your hand. Undo your pants and push them down your hips."

She followed his orders.

"Play with your clit. Make yourself come while I fuck your face."

Her eyes almost rolled back in her head, but she slid one hand into her light blue underwear and began rubbing.

"Underwear too. I want to watch."

She moaned deeply and pushed her underwear down, exposing the sparse thatch of hair.

"That's it. Now do what you were doing."

Fuck. He'd been wrong. *This* was the hottest thing he'd ever seen.

"Yeah, that's it." He breathed heavily as he slowly fed his cock into her mouth. Pulling back, he kept his pace slow, keeping in mind how much she'd taken before. He gradually increased his pace, watching her fingers rub her clit. Picking up his pace to match hers, he shortened his strokes.

He wasn't going to last much longer. Her fingers dug deeper into his ass, and he knew she was close too.

"You want me to come down your throat or on your tits?"

She sucked him long and hard, then swallowed, pulling him deeper into her throat.

"Fuck. Mouth it is." He picked up his pace, cautiously watching to see if it became too much.

He could feel her exhale along the sensitive skin of his dick each time he withdrew. The tingle started deep, coiling at the base of his shaft.

"Can you come with me, Abby? I want you to swallow me down while you come."

She whimpered against him and that was it. He pressed hard into her mouth as his orgasm exploded out of him. Her throat convulsed around him and he eased back, afraid he was suffocating her.

Her nails dug into his ass and he hissed. It recharged his orgasm and he froze, afraid if he gave into the urge, he'd shove hard and choke her. A shudder ran through his body and then his strength failed. He braced both hands against the edge of the table and pulled gently from her mouth.

Abby rested her forehead against his thigh. They stayed like that for several minutes, catching their breath before he helped her up. He pulled his jeans up before helping Abby with hers.

Her shirt was on the bench and he grabbed it. "Do you need to be home soon?"

She shook her head. "My mom's with the kids."

"Good." He pulled her shirt over her head and didn't care that he'd put it on her backwards and inside out. Not bothering to do more than zip his pants enough to keep them up, he grabbed her hand and led her toward the door.

"Where are we going?" she asked.

"Upstairs. I'm not done with you yet."

"Oh. Okay."

He glanced over his shoulder and found her grinning.

"Can I tie you up this time?"

His hand spasmed around hers. *Fuck*.

ROUTINE

"Is Tinker coming over for dinner again?" Olivia asked from the high counter where she was working on her homework.

Abby glanced up from the pork chops she was breading. "He's planning to. Is that okay?"

Olivia nodded. "Yeah."

Grabbing a paper towel, Abby wiped her hands. "Is everything okay? I can tell him there's a change of plans if you don't want him here. This is your house too, and I want you to feel comfortable."

"I like Tinker," Olivia said. "You know…he doesn't have to leave at night."

Spit went down the wrong pipe and Abby went into a coughing fit.

"What?" she choked out.

Olivia shrugged. "I mean, he's been here almost every night since we all got sick. I know he doesn't leave till late." She shrugged again. "I'm just saying if you guys are at that stage, it'd be okay if he stayed."

Abby did her best impression of a goldfish. "I...I...uh, we'll talk about it."

"Cool."

This was not a conversation she'd ever expected to have with Olivia. To be honest, it wasn't a conversation she'd expected to have at all since she'd never anticipated being in this situation before Will left for college.

Abby slid some cutlets in the hot oil as the doorbell rang.

"I get it!" Will yelled from the living room.

"Shoot, can you grab him?" Abby asked.

"On it." Olivia hopped down from the stool. "Willy Nilly, you're not allowed to answer the door."

Abby smiled at Olivia's nickname for Will.

"But it's Tinker," Will said.

"You don't know that. It could be a door-to-door salesman, and you don't have any money."

"You're not the boss of me, Olly Bolly!"

"Am too."

"Am not!"

Abby chuckled as she put the last cutlets in the pan. She heard the door open and close and Will say, "See! Told you!" A few seconds later, Tinker rounded the corner, holding a giggling Will upside down. Olivia trailed behind them, shaking her head as only a too-cool preteen could.

Tinker flipped Will right side up and set him on his feet, holding him steady until he wasn't dizzy.

"Hey." He leaned down and kissed her quickly.

Abby smiled up at him. "Hey."

"Yuck." Upon that proclamation, Will ran back to the living room.

It'd been almost two weeks since they'd had their heart to heart, and this was the fifth night Tinker had been over for dinner. They'd settled into a nice routine of dinner, dishes, bedtime routine, and heavy make-out sessions on the couch before he left. He'd even joined them at the aquarium last Sunday. It was nice and normal and maybe Olivia was right. Maybe he could stay over a couple nights instead of leaving them both in a state of need. 'Cause the phone sex wasn't going to cut it for much longer.

"Smells good," Tinker said. "You need any help?"

Abby shook her head. "No, everything should be ready in about fifteen minutes."

Tinker nodded and stole a green bean waiting to be cooked. "I know it's short notice, but is there any chance you can slip away for a while tonight?"

"I'm not sure. What's going on?"

"The weather's perfect for a ride."

Abby flipped the cutlets. "Like on your motorcycle?"

"Yeah. I haven't taken you yet." Tinker crossed his arms and leaned a hip against the counter next to the stove.

A spark of excitement burst in her before quickly dissipating. "I think my mom's got something going on tonight."

"I can watch Will, if that's what you're worried about," Olivia said.

Abby took a step back to look around Tinker as he looked over his shoulder. "Eavesdropping?"

Olivia rolled her eyes. "I've been sitting here the entire time, it's hardly eavesdropping."

Tinker's mouth tilted up at the corners. "She's got you there."

Abby narrowed her eyes. Just what she needed—Tinker and Olivia ganging up on her.

"What's your rate?" Tinker asked.

"Huh?" Olivia's look of confusion probably matched her own.

"For babysitting," he clarified. "How much do you charge per hour?"

Olivia looked between Abby and Tinker. "I wasn't going to ask for money."

"If you're doing a job, you should get paid for the work," Tinker said.

Olivia's eyes were wide, and she fidgeted with the pencil on her notebook. "I was just offering to do a favor for Abby."

Tinker opened his mouth, and Abby smacked him in the stomach with the back of her hand. "Quit. You're freaking her out. Take these, watch the cutlets." She handed him the tongs and moved around him to stand across the counter from Olivia.

"Thank you for offering to watch Will. It's a lot of responsibility. Are you ready for that?" Abby asked.

Olivia nodded. "I used to watch our neighbor's son after school until his mom came home. Plus…" She shrugged.

"Plus, what?" Abby asked.

"I mean, I kind of owe you."

Abby leaned her arms on the counter. "What do you mean? Owe me for what?"

"For taking me in." Her voice was small and soft.

"Olivia." Abby took Olivia's hands in hers. "You don't owe me anything. There is no score. If you want to watch Will to be nice, I will accept your offer, but if you're offering to watch him because you feel like you *have* to, I'm not going to accept."

Olivia nodded quietly, refusing to look at Abby.

"Hey. Where is this coming from? Did something happen?"

Olivia shook her head.

"Are you worried about the hearing?"

Olivia shrugged. That was the issue. The initial custody hearing was scheduled for next week. Abby had been talking to their lawyer—with and without Olivia—for the last few days. She could kick herself for not realizing how stressed Olivia would be.

"Are you worried your aunt is going to win?"

"A little," she admitted.

Abby heard movement behind her. Tinker pressed a kiss to

her forehead. "I'm going to go sit with Will. I took the pan off the counter."

She watched him walk away, momentarily distracted by his insight and kindness to give her and Olivia the moment alone.

"It'd be easier for you and Tinker if I wasn't here."

Abby's head snapped back to Olivia. "What? Why would you say that? Is that why you said he should sleep over and why you offered to watch Will?"

Olivia shrugged her shoulders.

Letting out a long sigh, Abby lifted Olivia's chin, forcing her to meet her gaze. "My life is better because you're here, not harder. I don't ever want you to think you're not wanted here, or things would be better if you weren't here. *Ever.*"

"But you'd be able to see Tinker more if I wasn't here."

Abby shook her head. "No, I wouldn't. We both still have work, and I still have Will. And honestly, he's a bigger consideration than you are. Not because he's my biological child, but because he's little and he's never had an adult male in his life. You at least understand Tinker and I are in a romantic relationship. Will just thinks Tinker is a big jungle gym to climb on."

"He does climb on him a lot."

Abby smiled. "Yes, and Tinker is very tolerant."

"It probably helps he's a big kid too."

"Probably." She rubbed her thumb across the back of Olivia's hand and noticed the paint stains. "Are you good? I don't want you stressing about any of this. We'll figure it out."

Olivia nodded. "I can still watch Will if you want to go for a ride with Tinker."

"Let's see how Will is after dinner." Abby patted her hand and stood up. "If he has his grumpy pants on, we can go another time. No reason your first-time babysitting should be when he's being difficult."

~

IT WAS TOO late by the time dinner was over and Will had his bath. He'd been too excited about climbing on Tinker to settle for his usual bedtime routine, so they'd postponed the ride until the weekend. Instead, they took their glasses out to the back patio, lit the citronella candles, and sat in the bench swing to watch the sun set over the tops of the trees.

Abby leaned against Tinker's side, one leg tucked under her.

"What are you thinking about?" he asked.

"How would you feel about staying overnight?"

The swing stopped and Tinker shifted to look at her. Abby sat up and faced him across the bench.

"Really?"

"Yeah. Not tonight, but maybe Friday?"

Tinker played with the end of her ponytail. "You ready for that?"

"Honestly? I'm not sure. I've been sleeping in the middle of my bed for so long, I'm not sure how good I'm going to be about sharing it."

Tinker grinned. "What about the kids?"

Abby took a deep breath. "Olivia actually suggested it."

His gaze flew to hers. "Really?"

"Yup. She thinks she's cramping our style." Abby chuckled. "But it made me think that it's going to happen at some point. At least, I'd like it to happen at some point."

"I'd like it to happen too," Tinker said. "How do you think Will is going to handle it?"

Abby shifted to lean against him again. "I honestly have no idea. I guess we'll see."

Tinker put the swing back in motion. "Can I ask you something?"

"Sure," she said.

"What books?"

Abby frowned and turned to face him again. "What?"

"The first night we met, you said something about it never

working out like it does in books, and you mentioned you'd read about BDSM stuff in books. Then Dani said something about book covers? Something like that. So, I'm wondering what books."

Abby dropped her leg and held her glass out to Tinker. "Hold this." She stood and walked into the house before she could change her mind, not daring to look back at Tinker. She couldn't believe she was going to do this. Flipping the light on in her office, where she'd moved her racier books, she ran a finger along the spine and chose a Joanna Wylde. Between her, Lindsey, and Naomi, it was well read.

Abby bit the corner of her lip and stared down at the cover depicting the torso of a well-muscled, shirtless man wearing only a leather vest, and wondered if she should pick something less...explicit. But it wasn't even one of the more explicit books she owned. She definitely wasn't going to start with her E.M. Gayle or L.K. Knight books. She scanned the titles again.

"Is that it?"

She jumped at Tinker's voice behind her and put a hand to her chest. Her cheeks grew warm as he took the book from her hand and read the description on the back.

He cocked an eyebrow and gave her an assessing look. "Is this the book you were talking about?"

Abby clasped her forearms behind her back. "Not that book specifically, but in general, yes."

"This says book two. How many books are there?"

"In that series? Five or six."

"How many series are there?" He stepped closer to her book-case and read some of the titles. "You have very eclectic tastes. You've got romance next to art history books and biographies next to Lord of the Rings."

"Sometimes I don't want to think about what I'm reading." She looked down as she shrugged.

Tinker stepped closer and wrapped an arm around her. "I'm

not giving you grief. But I am going to borrow this." He held up the book. "And take notes."

Abby couldn't stop her smile. "Seriously?"

"Oh yeah. For when we sleep over." He lowered his mouth to hers.

MELANIE

*A*bby was setting up her room for the senior class, which mainly involved making sure enough materials were available. It was her favorite class since she didn't really instruct the students so much as guide them in the genre they favored. Most of them were working on end-of-year projects or building their art portfolios for submission to college admissions boards.

"Abby?" Principal Newton stood in the doorway of her classroom. "Do you have a minute?"

She dropped the brushes into the old coffee can. "Of course."

He stepped into the classroom and closed the door.

Her stomach dropped; he had on his bad news face. It was the face he'd used to tell them a teacher had died last year. Was it Will? Olivia? Her mom? "What's wrong? What happened?"

"I know you have a connection to the Veterans Against Child Abuse group, so I wanted to tell you in person instead of hearing it from somewhere else. Melanie Driscoll is in the hospital," he said gently.

Abby brought a hand to her mouth. "Oh, god. What happened?"

"She was beaten pretty severely. Her social worker called to let us know she wouldn't be in school. I know she's a favorite of yours and you have a relationship with some of the people at VACA. I thought you'd want to know."

Tinker. Oh, god. "I— I need to go." She untied the smock and slipped it over her head, throwing it on her desk. "I need to— Shit. My class."

"It's okay. I'll get someone to cover it. I'll cover it myself if I need to. Go do what you need to do."

Abby grabbed her purse from the table behind the door. She stopped in the doorway. "Thank you, Isaac."

He nodded and she ran for the entrance, ignoring the call of one snarky student who told her no running in the halls.

Her phone rang through the car speakers as she pulled out of the teacher's parking lot.

"Hello?"

"Abby, it's Katherine. Have you spoken to Tinker in the last hour?"

"No, but I heard what happened. The school got a call," Abby said.

"Have you tried calling him? He's not answering his cell phone or his work phone," Katherine said.

"I'm on my way there now."

"Abby…Tinker is going to lose his shit when he finds out. He was really close to Melanie."

"I know." Abby came to a stop at the red light and tapped her thumb against the steering wheel. "How did this even happen?"

"The mom's boyfriend was released on probation."

Abby placed her hand on her forehead and closed her eyes. "Jesus." She could only imagine how Tinker was going to react when he heard. She jumped when a horn sounded behind her and raised her hand in apology.

"I'll be at his office soon. I'll call as soon as I can," she promised.

"Okay," Katherine said. "We're here when you need us."

Abby didn't remember the rest of the drive to TLC, only the frantic urgency to get there as quickly as she could. Shoving through the exterior and interior glass doors of TLC's entry, she found Graham Senior at the reception desk, magazine in hand and coffee cup in the other. So normal. Maybe Tinker hadn't heard.

"Hey, pretty lady," Graham Senior said. "Here to see Tinker?"

"He's here?" she confirmed.

"Far as I know. Haven't seen him pass through here since he came in this morning." He must have sensed her panic because he set his mug and magazine down and straightened in his chair. "What's wrong?"

A roar came from the hallway on her right that led to the offices. And Tinker.

"Abby wait—"

But she couldn't—she needed to get to Tinker. She raced down the short hallway. He was off to the side of the room, close to his desk. Paige, Graham, Angie, and a couple of guys whose names she couldn't recall at the moment stood around him. They looked like game wardens trying to calm down a cornered animal. With his fists clenched, every muscle in his body clenched, neck tendons straining, that's what he looked like—a cornered animal.

He roared again. Putting his whole body into releasing his anger.

Through the rage and anger she saw what was really driving him though. Pain. So much pain. The pain of someone who tried to take on the hurt of others and had failed.

"Christian," she said softly.

His head jerked in her direction.

Graham saw where he looked and stepped toward him. "Tinker, calm down."

Tinker shoved past him. If she didn't know him, didn't know

how gentle and tender he could be, how caring he was down to his very core, she'd be afraid of the raging beast bearing down on her.

"Abby." His voice was guttural, as if the strain of his rage made it hard to talk.

"I know," she said.

He grabbed her and crumpled. It was the only way to describe how quickly he fell to the ground, taking her with him and holding her like the last lifeline available to him. His arms banded tightly around her ribs, and he buried his head in her neck, folding in on himself and engulfing her. She did the only thing she could—wrapped her body around him and held on. The force of his sobs shook his whole body.

Her heart broke for him. All he wanted to do was protect kids from the monsters in the world. She petted his head, running one hand down the close-cropped hair at the back of his neck. "Shhhh. Shhhh." She tried to gentle him the same way she would Will when he had a bad dream.

She looked behind him at his friends and coworkers. Many of them had their mouths open, staring at her in shock. Her brows pinched. What had they expected him to do?

Paige gathered herself first and started shooing people away. They didn't go far. Angie's workstation was in the far corner and she positioned her chair to face them. She sat cross-legged, elbows on knees, hands folded prayer-like. Everyone else did pretty much the same—positioned chairs so they could keep an eye on them. Or maybe just Tinker.

Abby saw worry etched on their faces. She knew they cared and maybe were a little scared that this big, strong man had finally reached his limit.

Paige came close and said, "Call us, when you need us."

Abby nodded, then tucked her head down close to Tinker's. She didn't know how long they sat like that. Every now and then, he would grip her tighter, his fingers digging into her ribs. A sob would escape, then he'd slowly ease off. One leg was asleep and her hip was cramping, but she'd stay like that until he was ready. Finally, he slowly lifted his head as if the weight of it was almost too much.

She framed his face with her hands and searched his blood-shot eyes.

"This is my fault," he said hoarsely.

She frowned. "What?"

"She asked me out."

"Who?"

"Becky, her mom," he said. "Told me point blank Melanie needed a dad and she wanted it to be me."

"Christian, no. Don't do that to yourself. You can't control the choices other people make in their lives," she said.

"If I'd said yes, if I had agreed to even a date—"

"We wouldn't have met," she said. "I wouldn't know you. I wouldn't know the strong and caring man in front of me. Choices have consequences, bad *and* good. Becky made her own choices. For all you know, she would have done the exact same thing even if you had agreed to go out with her. Her taking her ex-boyfriend back was not something you could control."

"I—"

"No," she said firmly. "I'm not letting you do this to yourself. You can't save everyone, Christian. As much as you want to and as much as you try, you can't. And if you try to take on the guilt of every fucked-up person in this world, you will destroy yourself."

"She's just a little girl." The pain in his voice broke her heart all over again.

"I know." She ran a hand down the side of his face. "We'll help her."

He buried his face back in her neck and let out a shuddering breath.

She felt another presence close and looked up. Dani stood over them, tears tracking down her face. Abby didn't know if she was crying for Melanie or her brother. Either way, she sat down behind Tinker and wrapped legs and arms around him, pressing against his back. A few seconds later, Angie sat on Tinker's left, facing Abby, and rested her head on his shoulder.

CONSEQUENCES

They'd tried to convince Tinker to go home, but what good would that have done? Let him stew by himself? He finally compromised on moving to one of the bunk rooms, getting out of the way, while they promised to let him know when they had news.

Abby stayed by his side the entire time. He owed her an apology. Fuck, he owed everyone an apology. His computer was probably busted. Throwing it against the wall would do that.

There was no telling how much more damage he would've done or who he would've hurt if Abby hadn't shown up. He'd needed an outlet for his rage, or it would have overwhelmed him. And it had all transformed into crippling helplessness at the sight of Abby. He'd needed her the way a drowning man needed a life raft.

She was his rescue. His lifeline. As soon as they'd gotten into the room, he'd all but collapsed onto the bed, pulling Abby with him. He'd wrapped himself around her, refusing to let her go. It was selfish, he knew. She was probably uncomfortable.

He loosened his hold and put a few inches of space between them.

"I'm sorry." His voice was rough, thick with mucus and strained from yelling.

"Don't. You have nothing to apologize for."

"I hurt you."

Her palm rested on the side of his face. She pulled against the arm banded around her upper back, and he attempted to relax his hold.

"I'm not hurt," she said softly. "I was a little uncomfortable when my hip cramped, but it's fine. It's cramped worse during sex."

He appreciated she was trying to joke, but he still didn't like causing her any discomfort.

"I'm sorry you had to see me like that."

"Like what? A human with emotions? Christian, look at me."

He slowly raised his gaze to hers.

"This is not your fault. You could not have prevented it. Say it."

She didn't get it. "If I had—"

"No. I understand you're upset and you feel responsible, but you are not. You're not Melanie's dad and you're not responsible for her mom's decisions. You can't keep taking the weight of the world on your shoulders—it will crush you."

Intellectually, he knew she was right. Emotionally? Not so much.

"I don't know what to do," he admitted.

"Neither do I, but we'll figure it out. Together."

He swallowed hard and cupped her face. He didn't deserve her. She'd seen him at his worst, and she was still there, still letting him hold her. And in that moment, he wouldn't have let her go if the building was on fire.

"I love you."

Her smile was soft and built slowly. "I love you too."

Their kiss was gentle, sweet. There was no heat behind it, just a silent promise. The promise he was making to her.

They broke apart at the knock on the door.

"Come in," Abby called.

Dani stuck her head around the door. "Hey. Katherine called. They're heading to the hospital. They asked if you were up to going—I said I'd ask."

"Can you?" Tinker asked. He didn't know if he could handle it right then without Abby.

"Yes," Abby said. "Let's go see Melanie."

THE WAITING room was full of his VACA brothers and sisters, most of them wearing their vests. Katherine was talking to a woman wearing scrubs when they arrived, and Pothole hovered close by.

The nurse walked down the hall and Katherine approached them. "Hey."

Katherine pulled Tinker into a tight hug, and he tucked his head into her neck. She slowly eased back and assessed him closely. "Melanie is still out of it, but they're going to let us go back a few at a time to sit with her."

"How bad is it?" Tinker asked.

Abby slipped her hand back into his and squeezed. He squeezed back. He'd barely let go of her hand to get in and out of the car. She'd had to sit in the middle between him and Dani because he refused to let go of her. She grounded him and as long as she was close, he kept his shit in check.

"Her arm is broken." Katherine drew his attention back. "Two of her ribs are cracked. Her face looks bad, but nothing is broken."

Tinker clenched his free hand and gritted his teeth.

"Tinker." Abby brushed her free hand over his, and he realized he was gripping her hand too tight.

"Sorry." He relaxed her grip and tried to let go of her hand.

She clasped both her hands around his, brushing her thumb over his knuckles. "It's okay."

"You good?" Katherine asked. "You guys can go back first, or you can wait a bit."

Tinker shook his head. "I'd rather go now."

Katherine nodded. "She's in room 412."

Tinker nodded and took a deep breath. Abby remained close to his side as they made their way down the hall. It seemed to stretch on forever, expanding further with every step he took. They reached Melanie's room, directly in front of the nurse's station, sooner than he expected.

It was bad. Holy fuck, it was bad. The entire side of her face was one huge purple bruise. Her arm rested on the covers, wrapped in a beige cast.

He swallowed hard and stepped across the threshold. She was so small in the bed. A tube ran under her nose and around her ears. More tubes ran from her good arm and wires poked out of the top of her surgical gown.

Fighting to breathe, he concentrated on the low, steady beeping of the machine beside her bed and the strong squeeze of Abby's hand in his.

Had it been this bad last time? He'd met Melanie after charges had already been brought against her mom's boyfriend.

As if the thought conjured her, Becky stood from the chair on the far side of the room. "Tinker! You're here."

She rounded the bed and tried to throw herself against him, wrapping her arms around his waist and pressing the side of her face against his chest.

Tinker stood frozen, revulsion crawling through him. He wanted to push her away. Hard. But he'd never hurt a woman in his life and he wasn't going to start now, no matter how much he didn't want her touching him.

"You need to back up."

The force of Abby's voice surprised him. It apparently

surprised Becky as well because she did exactly what she was told.

"What—?" Becky looked between him and Abby. "What is she doing here?"

"I'm his woman."

Despite all the shit he'd been dealing with for the last couple hours, those three words brought a smile to his lips. *His* woman. Fuck yeah, she was.

"Tinker." Becky lowered her voice. "Can I speak to you privately?"

He shook his head. "No."

"Tinker, please. You don't understand, if you had just—"

"Don't you fucking dare." Abby dropped his hand and stepped in front of him. "This has nothing to do with Tinker. This happened because of you and your shitty decisions."

Becky took a step back. "You don't know what you're talking about. You don't understand what it's like. I needed someone to take care of us. To take care of Melanie."

Abby took a step forward. "Are you fucking kidding me? I know exactly what it's like. It is not anyone's job to take care of you or Melanie. That is *your* job."

Tears streamed down Becky's face. Maybe he should step in.

"If Tinker had just given me a chance, I wouldn't have had to go back to John. This wouldn't have happened," Becky said angrily.

The way Abby moved, he thought she was going to punch Becky. Instead, she jabbed her finger at Melanie, making her step back as she advanced.

"*You* are her mother. It is *your* job to protect your child. The only thing you ever have to do in life is love her and protect her. Do not blame this on anyone except yourself and your own selfish decisions."

Becky hit the end of Melanie's bed, and she sat on the edge of the mattress.

Abby's shoulders rose and fell with her angry breaths.

"Is everything okay in here?" a voice asked from the doorway.

Tinker turned. The woman who'd been speaking to Katherine earlier stood in the doorway, looking between Becky and Abby.

"No, it's not. I want her out of here." Becky pointed angrily at Abby.

The woman turned and gestured to the door. "It might be best if you folks let Melanie rest. She's going to be really groggy when she wakes up, and all this commotion might be too much for her."

Becky glared at them as they left the room. The woman, Liza according to her name tag, slid the large glass door closed behind them.

"I'm sorry," Abby told her. "I lost my temper. I shouldn't have shouted."

"To be honest, I'm glad someone did," Liza said. "That poor girl." She shook her head and walked over to the nurses' station.

Katherine was still in the waiting room when they reached it, although the number of VACA members had decreased. "How is she?"

"She was still out," Tinker said.

"Thank god," Abby added.

Katherine looked between them. "Why thank god?"

"I yelled at Becky." Abby covered her face with both hands before dropping them.

"Why?" Katherine asked. "What happened?"

"Abby defended my honor," Tinker said.

"Don't make fun." Abby glared at him briefly before turning back to Katherine. "I got angry because she was trying to blame Tinker for what happened. Trying to say if he'd gone out with her she wouldn't have had to go back to her ex. It was complete bullshit. I almost slapped her. I wanted to so badly."

Abby took a deep breath and shook her head. "But I'm always telling Will and my students that violence isn't the answer."

"Sometimes it is," Katherine said. "I'm not going to lie and say I didn't want to slap her myself. Maybe it will knock some sense into her. Especially since she's losing custody of Melanie as it is."

"What?" Abby gasped.

Katherine nodded. "The social worker was here earlier before you arrived. Becky knew the danger her ex posed and knowingly put Melanie in harm's way. CPS is taking it very seriously."

"Does she have family, or will she go into foster care?" Abby asked.

Katherine grimaced. "Foster care is the most likely scenario."

"Shit," Abby said.

"I'll work with her social worker to see if we can get her into one of the families we work with," Katherine said.

"It's not that. It's just— I..." Abby stumbled over her words.

"What is it?" Tinker asked.

She looked up at him, her gaze uncertain. "I'm a certified foster parent. I had to go through the process so Olivia could stay with me. Could Melanie...?" Abby shook her head. "They probably won't let me take her."

"You know what, let me talk to some people," Katherine said. "I'll see what I can do."

COURT

*A*bby sat with Olivia on the hard wooden bench in the hall outside courtroom two as they waited for their lawyer, Magda. Worried about parking and being there on time, Abby had made sure they were there early. Watching Olivia's leg tap up and down, she wondered if she should have timed it better.

She stared at a seam in the carpet where two pieces didn't quite meet. It bothered her more than it should have. How effective could this court be if they couldn't even get carpet tiles laid properly?

"Abby," Olivia said.

"Yeah, sweetie?"

"Look." Olivia pointed to her right.

Abby glanced over and her lips parted. Marching toward her like an avenging army was almost every woman she knew. Along with Tinker and an older man she'd never met.

She and Olivia stood as they drew near. Abby hugged her mom first, then Lindsey, Naomi, Angie, Dani, and Katherine. Even Paige gave her a quick hug. Tinker leaned down and gave her a quick kiss before wrapping his arm around her waist. He looked a lot better than he had a few days ago. The lines around his eyes weren't so intense, and the furrow between his brows had relaxed. Was he less worried now or pretending for her sake?

Abby asked, "What are you guys doing here?"

"You didn't think we'd let you do this alone, did you?" Naomi asked.

"Don't you have class? And work?" Abby asked.

"We took PTO," Lindsey said.

"And this is our work for the day." Paige gestured to the older man. "Abby, this is Stuart Bakas. He's the lawyer who handled Tinker's expungement. He's here for support and to answer any questions if issues come up."

Abby blinked several times. If she started tearing up now, she wouldn't stop crying. At the moment, her emotions were being held together with dental floss and chewing gum. Her hold was fragile at best.

"Thank you, everyone. It means more than you can imagine."

Her mom pulled Olivia close. "We're going to fight for our girl."

Looking for something to distract her, Abby told Tinker, "You look nice."

He smirked and ran a hand down the forest green tie.

"Don't let the suit fool you," Dani said. "There's a grease spot on his ass."

Tinker twisted. "Shit. Seriously?"

Angie and Dani laughed. Tinker glared, which made Olivia break out into giggles.

"Abby? Olivia?"

The group parted to reveal Magda.

"Hi, Magda," Abby said. "This is—"

"We're her family," Angie said.

Dani rolled her eyes. "You have got to stop adopting strays."

Tinker glanced down at Abby with a soft look. "I'm pretty sure we're the strays in this situation."

There was that prickle again. "These are my friends and family."

"It's wonderful that you're all here," Magda said. "Stuart, it's lovely to see you again. Thank you for the information you sent over."

The two lawyers shook hands. "Maggie. Glad to be of service."

"You know each other?" Sue asked.

"Oh, yes," Magda said. "You can't swing a cat in this neighborhood without hitting someone you've worked with or against."

"Why would you swing a cat?" Olivia's expression was almost comical in its disgust.

"It's an expression, dear." Abby's mom squeezed Olivia's shoulder before rubbing it.

Olivia wrinkled her nose. "Eww."

Magda chuckled and glanced at her watch. "Our case should be called in a few minutes. Shall we go in?"

A lead weight settled in Abby's stomach. "If I wanted to take Olivia and run, would you come with us?" she asked Tinker in a low voice.

He kissed the top of her head. "In a heartbeat."

"Okay. Good."

"Hey. You've got this," he whispered. "And we've got you."

Abby smiled. "Thank you. Just in case, can you wait out front with the engine running so we can make a fast getaway?"

He grinned and kissed the top of her head.

She was only half joking.

The courtroom was smaller than she'd expected—only five rows of seats behind the two tables facing the judge's bench. She, Olivia, and her mom sat in the front row with Magda on the left side of the room. Olivia's guardian ad litem sat on the right side of the room, along with a few other people. A man in a dark blue suit seemed agitated as he talked on his phone.

"Do you see your aunt?" Abby whispered.

Olivia shook her head.

Abby leaned toward Magda. "What happens if her aunt doesn't show?"

"If she doesn't have a good reason, she may lose any claim to custody," Magda said.

"Really?"

Magda nodded.

"Fingers crossed," Abby said.

"What's Angie doing?" Olivia whispered.

Abby looked behind them and saw Angie had pulled out a laptop and was typing furiously. "She might have work to do."

A bailiff and two other women entered and strode down the aisle to the front of the court. One woman sat at a small table to the left of the bench, and the other went to the small table parallel to the other wall. The bailiff knocked on a door behind the small table. It opened and she spoke briefly to the person inside. Stepping to the front of the bench she called, "All rise. The Honorable Eleanore Atwal presiding."

Everyone stood and waited for the judge to enter and take her seat. "Be seated. Please call the first case."

The woman at the long table stood with a large manila folder in her hand and approached the bench. "Case 25FA2716, Edith Holder vs Abigail Day—child custody case."

Magda patted Abby's knee. "That's us."

Abby stood and smoothed down her skirt. She ran a hand over Olivia's hair and smiled, then followed Magda to a table facing the judge. The man who'd been talking on the phone walked to the other table.

"Good morning, everyone. Counsel, please state your appearance for the record."

"Good morning, Your Honor. Magda Barber, counsel for the petitioner, Abigail Day and Olivia Holder."

"Ronald Fritz for the defendant, Edith Holder, Your Honor," the man at the other table said.

The judge looked up. "One of the petitioners and the defendant have the same last name? Explain that to me."

"My client is the child's aunt, Your Honor," Ronald said.

"Half-aunt, your honor. The child's mother and the defendant were only half-sisters," Magda said.

"Where *is* your client, Mr. Fritz?"

Ronald's face became pinched. "She is unable to attend today, Your Honor."

Judge Atwal leaned back in her chair. "Was your client aware they needed to be here in person?"

"Yes, Your Honor."

"Did you request dispensation?" Judge Atwal asked.

Abby licked her lips and her breathing became shallow. The judge's tone was *not* friendly. Was this...was this going to end today because Olivia's aunt didn't show?

"Are you asking for a continuance?"

The muscle in Ronald's jaw jumped and Abby could almost hear his teeth grinding. "No, Your Honor."

"Then why exactly are we here?" the judge asked.

"Your Honor, my client wishes to withdraw her claim of custody for the child," Ronald gritted out.

Abby grabbed the arm of her chair and several gasps sounded behind her. She turned and looked at her mom and Olivia, sitting directly behind her. Their shocked expressions must have mirrored her own.

"Your Honor, given that Ms. Holder has failed to show and has withdrawn her counter petition, we ask the court to grant full custody to Ms. Day," Magda said.

"Just a moment, Ms. Barber—I have a few more questions for Mr. Fritz." Judge Atwel turned her attention back to the other lawyer. "Mr. Fritz, when did you become aware that your client wished to withdraw her petition?"

Fritz tapped the table with his fingers. "Only ten minutes ago, Your Honor."

The judge raised her eyebrows. "Is your client aware that by failing to appear and withdrawing her petition, she cannot revisit this issue in the future and abandons all claims of custody of the child?"

"I have made her aware, Your Honor."

Judge Atwel shrugged and leaned forward. "All right. Let the record show the defendant, Edith Holder, has withdrawn her petition for custody. Her petition is dismissed by the court."

She jotted a note and looked up. "You're free to go, Mr. Fritz."

He nodded, picked up his briefcase, and left the courtroom without looking back.

"Now what?" Abby whispered.

"Now, Ms. Day, I hear your petition for custody," Judge Atwel said.

Heat bloomed across her cheeks. "Sorry, Your Honor."

"Completely understandable." The judge leaned her arms on her desk. "Can you please explain your relationship with the child?"

Abby stood and told their story. Haltingly at first, trying to put everything into context. It was a strange situation, and she needed to make sure the judge understood.

"And that's why we're here today," Abby finished.

"That is…one of the most unusual situations I've ever heard in my court," Judge Atwel said.

"Yes, Your Honor."

"Does the child, Olivia, have a guardian ad litem?"

"I'm here, Your Honor," a voice said behind them.

Judge Atwel nodded. "Good to see you again."

"You too, Your Honor."

"Is Olivia here?" Judge Atwel asked.

Abby glanced behind her at Olivia, who stood. "Yes, Your Honor."

"All right. Here's what I'm going to do. I'm going to speak with Olivia in my chambers. Then I'm going to speak with her guardian ad litem, and I will render my decision afterward." She stepped down from her bench and gestured for Olivia to follow her.

Olivia looked at Abby and Abby nodded encouragingly. The chamber doors shut behind Olivia and the judge with a sharp click. A sense of dread, of finality, washed through Abby. She couldn't sit. There was too much nervous energy. She paced back and forth, watching the door nervously. Fifteen minutes later, it opened a crack and the bailiff stepped toward it, leaned in, then called for the guardian ad litem to go into chambers.

Olivia didn't come out.

Oh, god. They'd whisked her out another door. They'd already decided Abby wasn't fit to be Olivia's guardian. They were going to take her away and she'd never see her again.

"Hey." Tinker wrapped his arms around her.

So focused on the door, she'd completely blocked out everyone else. Tucking her face into the pocket of his shoulder, she wrapped his arms around his waist. "She's going to say no."

"She's not. It's not a bad thing that the judge is talking to Olivia and her ad litem. It means she's listening to what they're saying and factoring it into her decision," he assured her.

Katherine joined them. "He's right. Judge Atwel is one of the fairest judges in the family court. You honestly couldn't have gotten assigned a better judge."

Abby nodded. A little worry and fear dissipated, but she wouldn't feel good until Olivia was back in the courtroom.

As if her thoughts had manifested, the door opened, and Olivia exited followed by her ad litem and the judge. Tinker kissed the top of Abby's head, and he and Katherine returned to their seats. Abby remained standing. Olivia, beaming, bounced to a stop next to Abby.

Finally...*finally*, a glimmer of hope shot through Abby.

Judge Atwel took her seat. "All right. Ms. Day, under normal circumstances Olivia would need to be in your physical custody for at least six months to make that custody permanent."

There went that glimmer.

"However, after speaking with Olivia and her guardian ad litem, and given the unusual circumstances of this case, let the record reflect that full custody of the minor, Olivia Holder, is given to Abigail Day." She banged her gavel.

Abby struggled for words. "That's— That's it?"

Judge Atwel gave her an amused look. "Do you want more? I'm sure we can schedule more hearings, but that would be a waste of time and money."

"No! No, I just wasn't expecting a decision today. Thank you. Thank you so much."

Abby hugged Olivia tightly. Everyone joined them, hugging and laughing.

Judge Atwel banged her gavel several times. "Okay, folks. I know this is a happy occasion, but please go be happy out in the hall—I have other cases to hear."

"Yes, Your Honor. Thank you," Magda said. She ushered and shooed them out of the courtroom.

Abby glanced back before leaving to see both the judge and the clerk grab tissues.

AFTER PARTY

The celebration continued in the hall.

"I don't understand," Abby said. "Do you know why she withdrew her petition? Not that I'm complaining, but I'm surprised."

Magda shook her head. "I don't. But that's not my job to worry about."

Dani raised her hand. "That would be me and Angie."

Everyone looked at her.

"What did you do?" Tinker asked.

"I told my bestie about the threatening letter Abby received in the mail," Dani said.

"What threatening letter?" Magda asked.

"The one telling Abby about Tinker's arrest and threatening to out him if Abby didn't turn over custody of Olivia."

There was a chorus of *what* from almost everyone, including Olivia.

"You know what? I don't want to know," Magda said. "My part of this is done. We were successful. I don't need to know more. Abby, Olivia, congratulations. Please call if you need me."

She hugged each of them and waved her goodbyes as she left their group.

"I do need to know more," Paige said. "What did you do?"

Tinker wrapped an arm low around Abby's hips and pulled her close as he explained the letter and coming clean with Abby.

"I wasn't going to let that stand," Angie said. "So I did some digging. Nothing fully illegal. Just some research into Olivia's aunt and her husband."

Paige shook her head. "I'm going to ignore the part of whether it was legal. What did you find?"

"Some not great stuff about the aunt and some really not great stuff about the husband. I shared that info with Stuart." She shrugged. "That's all."

For some reason, Abby did not think that was all.

"I shared the information with Mr. Fritz, who I'm assuming shared the information with his client, who felt it was better to drop her petition than have said information brought to light," Stuart said.

"You did that for me?" Abby leaned against Tinker.

"Technically, I did it for Tinker." Angie pointed at him, then shifted her hand to Abby. "But you're part of Tinker, which makes you family. Like I said. So, yeah. I did it for you."

Paige shook her head. "I'm glad you work for us."

Angie scrunched up her shoulders and grinned. "Me too."

Me three. At that point, Abby felt it went without saying, but she said it anyway. "Thank you, all, for everything. For supporting us and helping us. I don't know what we would have done without you."

Tinker kissed the side of her head, and she closed her eyes, finally letting go of the tension she'd been holding all day.

"This is getting really sappy," Lindsey said. "How about we all meet up at Abby's and celebrate?"

"That sounds like a great plan," her mom said.

NAOMI AND LINDSEY stopped on the way to grab food and drinks. They even took the time to buy a sheet cake with *Happy Family Day* written on it.

Abby's mom picked Will up early from daycare, and several of Olivia's friends came once school let out. The rest of Leonidas showed and before long the house was bursting with people.

Abby went to her room to change from her skirt to jeans and a T-shirt. As she was hanging her blouse, it all hit her and she grabbed the bar, resting her head on her hand.

"Do you always come to your closet when you need to cry?"

She smiled and turned her head without lifting it. "I'm not crying—I just need a minute to process."

Tinker stepped into the closet and pulled the door closed behind him. He pulled her into his arms and hugged her gently, softly rocking from side to side.

"I talked to your mom," he said.

"Yeah?"

"I asked her if she would mind if I took you on a bike ride."

Abby leaned her head back. "You did?"

He met her gaze and nodded.

"What did she say?"

"She said sure."

"She did, huh?"

"Yup. Graham Senior came with Graham. Apparently, they shut the whole office down."

Abby froze. "They better not have sex on my couch."

Tinker threw his head back and laughed. "I think they can control themselves for a few hours."

"Humph."

"Grab a jacket, the ride can get a bit chilly." Tinker kissed her and patted her ass before leaving the closet.

She shook her head but grabbed her jacket off the hanger and followed him out to the living room.

"You're good with us ducking out for a while?" she asked her mom.

"Of course. Go have fun," she said.

Abby kissed her mom's cheek. "We'll be back soon."

Her mom shooed her off. Abby took Tinker's hand and followed him outside. He settled a helmet on her head and showed her where to put her feet. They pulled out of her subdivision and were soon on their way.

Abby rested her chin on Tinker's shoulder and stared at the road ahead of them. Tinker rested his left hand on her outer thigh and patted her leg. She smiled and tucked her head against his back, wrapping her arms tighter around his waist.

His bike hummed under her ass and the wind tugged at her ponytail under the helmet. He hadn't said where he was taking her, but they'd headed south toward Folly Beach. They passed the salt marshes, then crossed the bridge to Folly Island. Tinker turned left a block short of the beach access road and continued east, passing houses ranging from large summer rentals to ordinary family homes. The bike rumbled down the rough paved road until the houses grew farther apart, and then there was nothing but sand and the sound of the surf.

He pulled off to the left and stopped the bike close to a small SUV. Tinker cut the engine and steadied the bike while she swung a leg over the back of it to dismount. Hopefully, it looked more graceful than it felt.

Abby unbuckled the helmet strap as Tinker pushed out the kickstand and settled the bike.

Tinker pulled a blanket and a bottle of water from one of the saddlebags. "Come on." He took her hand in his and led them toward the beach.

"Where're we going?"

"To hopefully catch the sunset."

The pavement ended and they hit sand. He took them to the right, around the rocks, toward the small breaker. She couldn't see other people on the beach, not even the owner of the other car.

He spread the blanket down at the edge of the high tide line where the sand was flat and compact and sat in the middle of it, patting the space next to him.

Abby sat, trying not to get her sandy boots on the blanket. The sky was clear, and pink and blue streaks outlining the light-house hinted at sunset. "You know, I've never been down this far."

"Never?

"Nope. We've been to Folly a couple of times, but not down here. We usually go to Isle of Palms. We go early, before the crowds and the worst of the heat, get lunch at Coconut Joe's, and then head home."

"Hmm." Tinker hooked his arms over his upraised knees and stared out at the ocean. "I usually ride down to Edisto, but this is my favorite spot close to town."

The setting sun lit up his profile. "Why Edisto?"

"The ride, mostly. I take the rural routes instead of Highway 17. Slower route, fewer people. Most people go there to get away from the crowds. I.O.P.? Sullivan? They're too…"

"Developed? Touristy?" Abby finished.

"Yeah. Actually." He cocked his head and looked at her. "I was heading out to ride to Edisto the night I met you."

"Really?"

"Really. But you were looking at Ned like he'd insulted your family tree, so I stopped to ask if you were okay," he said.

"I still maintain Ned is a silly name, even if it is alliterative. Kind of."

Tinker chuckled. "What would you have named him?"

"I don't know. Charles? Richard?"

"Charles the Knight?" Tinker shook his head. "Nah. Ned fits."

Abby smiled and shook her head, looking out at the last rays settling on the horizon.

Tinker reclined, one head behind his head, and tugged on the back of her hoodie. Abby lay back, resting her head in the pocket of his shoulder.

"Thank you for bringing me out here." She sighed and relaxed against his warmth, listening to the crash of waves. It was so easy to imagine they were in a bubble, where nothing could touch them.

"I have something serious I want to discuss with you," he said.

Abby froze.

"It's not bad." Tinker shifted and rose on one elbow. "At least, I hope it's not bad."

"What is it?" Abby whispered.

"It's too soon right now, but at some point in the future, I'm going to ask you to marry me."

Something she hadn't felt in a long time started unfurling in her belly and spread through her. A smile spread across her face. "Really?"

"I meant it, when I said I love you. I didn't say it because I was under duress."

"Duress?" Her eyebrows went up.

"Emotional duress," he said.

"I didn't say I love you because you were under duress either," she said.

He smiled. "Good. I meant it when I said I was in it for the long haul. This is the long haul."

"Okay," she said.

"Okay." He lowered his head and their mouths met.

It began sweet and quickly turned scorching. Abby pulled back at the same time she had the urge to pull him closer and wrap her legs around his waist. Public be damned. "We're going to miss the sunset."

"Yeah." His sigh was heavy with disappointment as he lay back on the blanket, one arm bent under his head, the other holding her close. "There is something else I want to talk about."

Abby craned her neck to look at him. "What's that?"

"That book you gave me."

Christian "Tinker" Knight stood in the courtroom, feet braced apart, waiting for the judge to continue.

"I now pronounce you man and wife," Judge Atwel said.

Tinker grinned as Sue and Graham Senior kissed to the cheers around them. Graham slapped his dad on the back, jarring him and earning him a glare.

Tinker didn't miss the tear Abby wiped away. She might have griped that it was ridiculous for her mom to get remarried so quickly after meeting Senior, but she couldn't hide how happy she was for her.

Sue and Graham Senior had elected for a courthouse wedding and had reached out to ask Judge Atwel to officiate since she'd been responsible for keeping their family intact. At least, that's what Sue told him.

Will spun on his heel, bored with all the adults. Olivia shushed him and he stuck his tongue out at her. They'd settled into a typical sibling relationship. There'd been a lot of adjustment in the last six months.

Tinker had moved in a month after Abby was officially

granted custody of Olivia. Abby had not lied—she was a bed hog. But that worked out fine for him.

She'd also received approval to foster Melanie. That transition hadn't been easy, but they'd settled into a routine quickly. The hardest part had been Melanie's supervised visits with her mom. Becky had been required to go through three months of parenting classes before the visits began. By that time, Tinker had been living with Abby. Awkward was an understatement.

"I believe there's one more order of business before we call it a day," Judge Atwel said.

There was another reason they'd asked Judge Atwel to officiate the wedding.

"Olivia, Abby and Will have a very important question to ask you," Judge Atwel said.

Olivia's eyes widened as everyone's attention turned to her. Will covered his mouth with his hands and giggled.

"Will?" Abby prompted.

"Livie, will you be my big sister?" Will looked at his mom and sagged as only a little kid could. "Really forever?"

"Yes, really forever," Abby said.

"Ugh. Will you be my sister forever?" Will asked, begrudgingly.

Olivia burst into tears and covered her face with her small bouquet.

"Ah, shit," Tinker said.

"Oh, sweetie, I'm sorry," Abby rushed forward to hug Olivia. "We don't have to." Her voice was low and reassuring.

Olivia shook her head and mumbled something into her hands.

"What did she say?" Sue asked.

Abby smiled. "She said yes. She just wasn't expecting it and is very happy."

They gave Olivia time to dry her eyes before they signed the adoption paperwork. Judge Atwel's clerk circumvented a major

Will melt down when he found out there was nowhere for him to sign by quickly drawing up "sibling" adoption papers.

They'd adjourned to a small anteroom for cake, champagne, and apple juice when Will threw a grenade into the middle of the group.

During a lull in conversation he all but shouted, "How come Tinker's not my dad?"

All eyes turned to Abby and Tinker.

Abby stared at him wide-eyed, silently begging him to say something.

Tinker placed his head on Will's head. "You know, buddy. That's a good question."

Reaching into his pocket, he pulled out the small box he'd been carrying around for the past month, waiting for the perfect moment. He couldn't think of a more perfect moment than right then.

"Wanna help me?" he asked Will. Will nodded eagerly and joined Tinker as he sank to one knee in front of Abby.

He opened the box, revealing a circle-cut ruby set in a simple platinum band. "Abigail Day, will you marry me?"

Tears fell as she nodded. Will jumped up and knocked the box from Tinker's hand, sending the ring flying. Everyone except Senior searched on their hands and knees before Olivia found the ring next to the leg of a chair.

"You sure you're ready for all this chaos?" Abby asked as he slid the ring on her finger.

He'd never been more sure of anything in his life.

"Absolutely."

AFTERWORD

STORY INSPIRATION

Several years ago, well before Roe v. Wade was overturned, I read a blog post about a woman who became pregnant and whose husband told her to get an abortion or get a divorce. She chose an abortion, but it didn't save her marriage and they ended up divorcing a couple of years later.

That led me to wonder about the woman who chose divorce as the first option. And that led to Abby.

A NOTE ABOUT ABORTION

I am prochoice. Abortion is health care.

It is also a deeply personal decision that should be made by a woman with her partner, medical provider, and/or spiritual or religious advisor.

What a woman does with her body is *her* choice - it is not mine and it is not yours. If you are anti-abortion, don't get one. Do not force your personal beliefs on others.

ABOUT THE AUTHOR

Tarina is an award-winning and bestselling author of military and contemporary romance. She has spent her entire life in and around the military - first as a dependent and then as an enlisted Air Force member.

The military gave her plenty of material to work with and she strives to create characters who authentically represent all facets of the military life - the good and the not so great, while ~~torturing~~ guiding her characters to their HEA.

Subscribe to Tarina's newsletter

Follow Tarina on Social Media.

ALSO BY TARINA DEATON

The Combat Hearts Series

Stitched Up Heart

Half-Broke Heart

Locked-Down Heart

Rescued Heart

Imperfect Heart

Holiday Heart (only available to newsletter subscribers)

The Jilted Duet

Make Me Believe

Believe In Me (Coming Soon)

The Leonidas Corporation

Found in the Lost

Truth in the Lie

Flaw in the Defense